To women; without whom there'd be no life such as we now know it.

WOMEN,

AND

TOM

GERVASI

By Way of Introduction, Disclaimer, Release of All Rights and Coming Clean.

Over the happy moment of this work's first introduction to the public, a legal issue lingers like a dark cloud. I've been asked many times *why* I allowed the author to use my real name, thus subjecting me to endless rumor and slander. My answer is: *that's* why.

If only our courts would draw the distinction I believe exists between malevolent and benevolent slander, needless litigation might then end, and slander bloom. The current work is surely of the benevolent kind. The situation it depicts is so far from the humdrum truth of my own life that I can only be grateful for it. Its public proliferation in print, as dramatic performance, computer program, microfiche or *je m'en fiche,* in no way hinders me from finding gainful employment in my chosen field—which happens to be other than that of seducing women.

As for women, my hope of course was that the use of my name might create for me at least a notoriety where otherwise no reputation of any kind, sad to say, exists. This hope seems dim. In fact, most women ignore the suggestion of verisimilitude in this work as effectively as they continue to ignore me.

The author has exercised exemplary care. To be on the safe side, he craftily approached me for permission to use my name before he had finished the manuscript. Delighted with the prospect of immortality, I made my pact with the devil.

One must add, however, that the author consulted me only *just* before he had finished the manuscript. He had written all but the last few pages of it. At that point he was faced with the prospect of having to go back through all of his neatly typed pages to make 4,361 changes of name. Was this necessary? The shrewd fellow appealed to me for mercy. He knew he had his man.

Since his inspiration cannot have been me, one sees that it was the sheer accident of my name. I see him now as he was, in the throes of creation, poised before his typewriter, about to write Don Giovanni, writing Tom Gervasi instead, and having a chuckle each time. Could I deny him all those chuckles? How was I to deny them retroactively? Could I willfully, knowingly dash my own vainglorious hopes? These were the key issues at stake in the case. You see before you their solution.

—Tom Gervasi

I. THE UNEXPECTED GUEST. BUT A PLACE IS LAID FOR HIM, NEVERTHELESS, AT THE EVENING TABLE. TOM GERVASI *MIGHT* SHOW UP. DREAMS *DO* TURN OUT, AT TIMES. NIGHT IS THE SEAT OF DREAMS. COULD TOM GERVASI SIT THERE? THERE, AS HIMSELF, REAL? THE POTENTIAL HOSTESS HOPES SO. SHE'S GONE THROUGH TROUBLE, TO PREPARE. JUST IN CASE. IF HE *SHOULD* SHOW UP. TOM GERVASI.

All over this big city of ours, the light is waning, as it should be, for it's scheduled soon to be evening; and the light isn't about to rudely disappoint the eager dinner society crowd by hanging about and delaying proceedings. The light has already received a pat-on-the-back for its nice day-display; but it wouldn't want to outstay its welcome, especially with dinner preparations clanking away in kitchens, mixed occasionally with amorous expectations for the ritual festivities ahead. So the light has stolen away. It won't be missed. Appetites dream of the huge evening feast, throats of evening drunkenness, hearts and loins of an erotic evening romance, topped off with the chocolate whip cream of immortal love, by whose grand scale lesser values take on their truly trivial aspects. Love is solemn. The sky is black. Artificial light warms interior rooms. The sexes are about to mingle.

All around the city, women are setting places at table. For dinner parties, or just for one hoped-for guest. Some of these women are placing plate, eating utensils, napkin, for a guest who'll never arrive; and this is a mathematical certainty in most of their cases, to the point of the eventual sigh of despair. The reason being, that these particular women are all hoping (in a subdued sort of "would-like" wish) for the same guest, whom they've laid a place for, at tables where there'll be other guests or none. This particular presumed-upon guest can't be ubiquitous this evening, or ever. So in most cases, he'll disappoint, to degrees of varying severity. He's semi-expected. Usually, he doesn't arrive. Nor phone to apologise. He's in the hearts of these patient, would-be hostesses. Tom Gervasi is his name. The man-about-town, who usually doesn't arrive. There's only one of him, for so many women-fussed-over dinners. He's coveted, but he's rare. He's rare, so more coveted. Mainly, he doesn't materialize. He's the stuff of dreams. Feminine fantasies have woven him in. He's a godly myth, the prince who *may* arrive. He *has* arrived—once or twice. And may, magically, again. He's wished for. He's waited upon. In vain, to sighs. His "turning up" is really *not* expected. It's a rare bonus, heaven's enchantment dropped down. The miracles that nuns wait for. Signs of heaven, a comet or a burning star, a relic left over from a supernatural age, wonderful signs of some deity. Thus, a lower aristocratic Victorian household may "hope" that the Prince of Wales may drop by, one evening. A place is in readiness, at table, for that unlikely eventuality: "just in case." "What if he *did*—we wouldn't be caught unprepared. How would it look, were he to walk in, and we had nothing to give him? It *might* happen, that he comes by. We owe it to that possibility. Not to be caught short. On the off-chance, of course."

It's not "we," waiting for Tom Gervasi. It's isolated female "I"s, though there may be other guests at the time, accounted for, palpable, "there": but not held so dearly, as the one who probably won't turn up. *Yet*, he *might*. Thus come fairy elves from the rainbow, unicorns from a celestial pasture, manna from heaven, the windfall in the night, the surprise sweepstake announcement. Heavenly chance. Buddha's visit. The student Prince, doffing his disguise. The King who roams Baghdad as a beggar. All come to light, at one enchanted stroke. "It *is* Tom Gervasi! Why Tom, can that be you! Oh, what a delightful surprise! This is *most* unexpected! *Do* drop in, make yourself at home. What can I get you to drink, Tom? Are you hungry? By luck, there *are* a few leftovers. Would you like to try Potluck? And now that you're here, you mustn't go rushing off again. Take off your shoes, it's more comfortable. Would you like a bath?— there's *plenty* of hot water. Won't you stay the night? It wouldn't put me out the *least*, I can assure you. Yes, *do* stay! Oh, what fun! The bed is already made. Yes, do stay. Now that you're here. Stay, Tom. Do."

If there are other guests, they've gotten the message and scattered. If not, it's just as well. "What a lovely surprise! Why, Tom Gervasi, of all people! What are you doing, around these parts? Haven't seen you in *ages*! Well, you're not going *anywhere* tonight, Tom. It's too late. You're staying right here! Can I refill your drink? Oh, you naughty boy! You caught me unawares. If only I had known! But let's make the most of it. You look tired. Take off your shirt. Oh, don't wait on ceremony. You know me. Just be comfortable. Just us two. We'll shut the world out, won't we? Just us, all night long. Just us. What a pleasant surprise! Why, as I live and breathe—Tom Gervasi! I hadn't expected you! Well, now that you're here, I'm *certainly* not put out. I *assure* you: it's no inconvenience at all. Not the least. Why, it's delightful! It's an unexpected pleasure, I assure you. Take off your clothes. I'm only thinking of your comfort. Let's be casual. Let's not *us* be formal, Tom Gervasi! Why, I wouldn't *think* of it, not with you! But I *do* regret, as I hadn't expected you, that I'm not looking my best tonight. Here, let me sit next to you. I must look after you,

you look so tired. Dinner's cooking, it's not long to wait. Refresh your drink with more ice? Oh Tom, I just wasn't prepared! *Look* at me. Am I *that* ugly?. Am I turning fat? Here, feel me, here. Too fat? Feel here. Am I *still* good-looking, Tom? Can you *still* be attracted to me? Here, feel up here: are my legs turning too soft? Feel me all over, Tom. Am I still attractive, Tom? Can you still like me, just a little bit? Why Tom!—you're such a naughty boy! Take your hands off me! The dinner is almost ready. You've already eaten? Oh, but you can eat a little more. It won't hurt you. Tom! Stop undressing me! You're a beast! You're fresh, you take liberties! Oh, Tom! I'm so excited: It's you! It's you!"

Thus, the seduction scene goes on. Further explicitness is not required here. In *this* case, Tom Gervasi *did* arrive. Ah, but all over the city, women sigh. He never did arrive. He just never turned up. The women now turn their hopes off. It's too late now. The social evening is done. Dark hours will intervene. Then, slowly, morning. With its wealth of light. Too bright, too commonplace, for the private hope. The secret dream. Of Tom Gervasi, as himself. Playing his one role. Turning up, in real life.

II. THE SOLILOQUY OF TOM GERVASI. A MEDITATION ON WOMEN AND LIFE. FROM MOTHER, THROUGH BERTHA, AND OTHER WOMEN. EVOLVED FROM THE SEA, HE'S BOUND THROUGH A TIME WORLD, WITHIN A WELL-WOMENED LIFE.

"Were it not for life, there'd be no women," Tom Gervasi reasoned. "Thus, it's plain that I owe a great debt of gratitude to being, existence—life. Then, the women follow, in natural order.

"But the reverse can be true, as well. Where would *life* be, without women?

"A person has to get born. Women excel, in getting them born, and in keeping them alive in their early helpless state, till youngsters develop to the point of fending for themselves and going out on their own. That's life. But women brought it about, and must be given top credit.

"Which came first, life or women? That's so far back, there's no record of it.

"My mother gave me life, with my father's help. I was only allowed one mother, for a woman. What for mother was singular, for girlfriends are now plural. This shows in what way I've developed. Women don't mean 'mother' to me any more. This difference is crucial. I'm now an adult. I have powerful relations with women, as a man. I'm held in women's esteem; and in their soft arms. As a living man, I know what I am. Life is a person, living it. In my case, that includes women.

"Well, I'm off to see Bertha. I'll ring the bell, she'll let me in. She'll give me a drink and a dinner. Then we'll fool around, and off will go our clothes. We'll tumble into bed, with excitement.

"And I used to be an infant, in my *mother's* arms! Well, a person changes. Take me, for example.

"I'm getting tired of Bertha. We've gotten into a routine, a predictable rut. She wants to break it, and go away with me. But my job is demanding, I must stay here. But she suggests going away weekends. That's fine, the *place* might change, but it's still Bertha the same, me the same. All over again, us two, us two. I'm dragging on. It's a bore.

"I want a change of women. I'm allowed that with girlfriends, but I was stuck with the same mother.

"I'm *free* now, I'm grown up. Free to change women. Free, to do what I want. I'm a man, with power. I'm not helpless. I don't need my mother, any more.

"I need a change of women. I'll have to tell Bertha. She won't take well to it.

"But that won't stop me. I'm my own, now. *I* boss *women* about.

"I don't take orders, from any mother. I *give* orders—to girlfriends.

"I'm a bold man. I'll unBertha me, and make a nice new discovery.

"More women ahead. More life. Life and women, within the time of earth. United, as I change.

"I bear the life and women, the earth, the time, and my own changes.

"I flow, from my mother. Now Bertha's discarded. I face unknown women ahead. All within this life. Bound to an earth time. Within a sea of women, from Mother Fish on.

"The women left behind; now Bertha. I bulge with *her* no more. I'm light, for what's ahead.

"Within a life of time. A world of women. From my Mother Fish. Inland from the ocean. On shore. Up to the hills. This is *civilised* evolution. It's a social development. The ages of me. A man timed by women. On the watered land. Within one soul's life. Within a womened world."

III. SHIRLEY'S CAMPAIGN TO SNARE TOM GERVASI
FOR HER OWN, DESPITE HIS BEING HER WORLD'S
IDOL AND SHE BEING A HUMBLE FLOCK MEMBER.
SHE'LL CUT THROUGH THIS RANK-DISTANCE, BY
THE STEEL RESOLVE OF WILL. THE OTHER GIRLS
DREAM AND SWOON, FROM AFAR. BUT SHIRLEY
PLOTS TO MEET THIS MAN, AND REDUCE TOM
GERVASI FROM HEAVENLY STAR TO ORDINARY
DAILY HUSBAND. BUT HOW? SHE'LL FIND A WAY,
IT'S NOT IMPOSSIBLE. SHE'LL PLUCK A FABLE, FOR
HER OWN. CUT THE HERD DOWN, TO HER QUITE
ADEQUATE SIZE. OR IF NECESSARY, RISE. JUST *GET*
HIM—THAT'S THE PRIZE.

Shirley heard about Tom Gervasi. Immediately, her skin began to prickle. She went through hot and cold faint, like sweet and sour park on the Chinese menu. She felt hot all over. Then she got the cold chills.

She pieced together snippets and cullings, tidbits and fragments, of stray scattertalk for her Tom Gervasi scrapbook, pasting light strips into clever montages, compiling all the oddments. Tom Gervasi was on the prevailing tongue, that season. He was women's favorite topic. There was no end to fascinating near-anecdotes that filtered through the buzzing gossip air, incomplete, alleged, spawned of fantasy and wish, hearsay, rumor, dragged in by the ants of busybody myth, giving Tom Gervasi a stained-glass reputation in a makeshift shrine from people's random donations. He was a fever. Shirley caught it. Cherished it. And nursed it back to ill health.

Then she got fed up, with sheer air. She wanted to meet the real man—in the concrete. And kiss him, on his real face.

Tom Gervasi was in great demand, that year. He had no time for Shirley, she was such a small fry. He was on the top echelons of their commercial industry world, while she clung barely to the bottom—if that. Still, a cat may look at a king. Shirley had caught a glimpse of him. Her fantasy filled in the rest.

She threw away her *actual* boyfriends a spindly youth with marred complexion and defective grammar. Then she felt pure and devoted to her Tom Gervasi cult. Now: how to make him notice her? She was in earnest. Her goal: to marry him.

A nice goal: but hardly unique. All the other girls in her commercial industry world entertained the same dream. They sighed, in virtual unison, as the gossip circuit kept Tom Gervasi tales in circulation, with new variations freshly battering against stale repetition. Why was he such an idol? How did his hero status come about? Because he was popular: not too exposed; a mystery man. Because everybody admired him; yet few saw him. He was the rage. He was a kind of folk celebrity. Yes, but why him? Why not *another* hero? Well, the consensus tolled for him. It was he. He was the one. Yes, but why him? No "why": it *was* him.

Shirley, like the other girls in their commercial industry world, either succumbed to this logic, or stood in no need of it. What rhyme or reason does love ever require? Love *is*. Simple as that. Tom Gervasi *was*. By acclaim. It was a stampede bandwagon. Of all his "followers," the surging growth of his "fans," how was Shirley Shirley, and not just an anonymous face in that herd of female sheep that went "baa-baa" in one woolly swoon at the mere mention of that magic name? A sense of intense desire singled *her* out: the rest would love him hopelessly; but Shirley—as Fate would have it, for want of a more plausible explanation—would become Mrs. Tom Gervasi! Sleep with him, scold him, tell him what to eat, remind him what time it is, criticise his clothes, and joke with him—all these intimate things, to fall to *Shirley's* singular lot, as Tom Gervasi's familiar, his equal, his spouse! She believed this. It would happen. But she must *help* it happen. No-one would win Tom Gervasi *passively.* Effective steps must be taken. She must *make* her glory; bring it about; cause it to happen. Yes, but how? "How" will take care of itself. The confident goal is set. Concentrate. Bend every act to it. It's willed. Now, go about it. Fit the right "ways" to the firm "will." Achieve no less than success. Now, *do* it. The "how" will fall into place. There *are* means.

Determination, an iron resolve, bent Shirley to her task. First, how could she *meet* him? Not just *look* at him, but *meet* him? A face-to-face encounter; not just in passing; but long enough to *establish* something *between* them: an understanding; a promise; an arrangement; an appointment for a date. Something substantial. Not a hero's flight past screeching admirers.

The other girls in Shirley's Commercial Industry World just screamed and swooned like sheep; they *knew* they couldn't get him. None of them the least suspected that Shirley's was not a flighty ambition, but a dread solemn one: as serious as death. The rest were fanatical; but Shirley was *the* fanatic. "Dream" must not do; "do" itself must do. She *meant* it. She'd snare an idol. For keeps. And wed him, in permanent captivity.

The other girls in their Commercial Industry world, had they known her thoughts, would have termed Shirley "nuts," accused her of "putting on airs," and mocked her endlessly, with mob cruelty against the individual visionary. But she kept it a silent secret; nursed her intention; plotted like an assassin; brooded, like a stern avenger. She meant business. Not Commercial Industry World business; but the private sort; restless in her dreams, not content and silly: till they convert to bold realities, and leave behind their flimsy dreamstuff. Only realities would do. The day-to-day life, as Mrs. Tom Gervasi. *Strictly* down to earth.

But before she could carry out her well-woven plans, and obtain the great man, the fashion for him changed. The season of idolising him had ended, and other idols replaced him in the fickle trend. So Shirley abandoned her plans. Tom Gervasi was "out." This called for a major revision of her will. Why want *him*, any more? No has-been for *her* husband. She's not *that* unfashionable. She stopped loving him. She'd betray her ideals, now, to marry someone she no longer loved. So Tom Gervasi became nothing: a historical footnote, in regressive nostalgia. He's "out." Shirley was calm. Her hysteria vanished. She remained free. Not tied-down, to a fallen idol. She's her own girl. Her world is the Commercial Industry World. She has a humble job in it. She's clear-headed. That Tom Gervasi fog has lifted. The veil has dropped, the film or mist left her eyes. She's clear-sighted. She's practical. She's realistic. She doesn't waste her time. She knows her limitations. She doesn't want in vain. She's level-headed. What *was* that Tom Gervasi craze? It was but a dream. She blinks wake. She casts about. Who's a marriage-candidate, for her? Not that pimply spindle she discarded once. Who surges to her horizon? Who'll sweep her over? She'll make the party-rounds, and go out dating, and "play the field." She'll find her man—or he'll find her. She's in no hurry. She has time. She has good sense. She has good looks. She's good enough, for anyone.

IV.

(A title so transparent, that what follows it has already been disclosed:)

ROSEMARY RESISTS TOM GERVASI, THE MORE SO, FOR HIS MAKING NO ADVANCE WHATEVER— WHICH IS MOST IRRESISTIBLE, TO HER VULNERABLY FORTIFIED HEART THAT HAS NO DEFENSE WHATEVER AGAINST HIS PASSIVITY.

SHE'S DETERMINED, NOT TO SUCCUMB, TO HIS NON-ASSAULT—WHICH, HOWEVER, PLAYS ON HER MOST DISASTROUS WEAKNESS: SHE RESISTS LEAST, WHERE THERE'S NOTHING TO RESIST. THUS OVERWHELMED, SHE SURRENDERS. TOM GERVASI HAD INTENDED NOTHING, BUT INNOCENTLY TRIUMPHS.

Rosemary was determined to resist Tom Gervasi, at all odds. In fact, she even told him so.

"Resist me? Resist what? I've put no pressure on you, nor demanded anything of you. What *is* there to resist?"

"You. You're menacingly attractive, whether you have a design on a woman or not. You're dynamite. You're high-risk explosive. A woman has to watch her step, or she'll wind up getting hurt, however innocent your intentions are.

"In point of paradox, the less you intend toward a woman, the more innocent your indifference is, the less there is to accuse you of, the more, in fact, lethal you are, in damaging a women's heart. It's your very indifference that must be resisted; your innocence, your *lack* of design on a woman, are a greater peril, as a passive attack where her vulnerability is most delicately poised and an imaginary threat causes real discomposure. So I'm on my guard, Tom Gervasi. I'm armed, to defend the more for your launching not the slightest offensive. You've been loved; you will be loved; but never by me.

"I'm impervious to you, Tom Gervasi! Unassailable! Do your least, and I *still* won't succumb! I'm steeled, to fight to the end; to ward off your quite peaceful passivity. Do your least; and still, I hold firm, through might and main, and not give up my heart's tattered flag for all that my fortress is unadvanced upon, for all that you forward one no aggression, making no incursions upon my embattled camp. I'm up in arms. I've made costly preparations: committed staunchly to resist. To the very *end,* I'll resist."

"But what if I *do* make a pass at you?"

"Ah, I'll welcome you, with open arms. I'm resisting your *not* making a pass. For in your passiveness, or passivity, I'm most heavily assaulted. My heart dangles tenderly. Pluck it, please. Make hold, to grab it."

"No, Rosemary. I'll do no such thing."

"In that, you're totally irresistible. *Not* attack? Then I surrender. At once."

V. AN IDEAL LOVE BETWEEN PERFECTIONS.

Frances was loved the world over. There was no end to how fabulous her beauty was—it was fabled into legend even before her prime had yet turned its peak. Men slobbered over her, drooled, went hysterical, babbled at their drinking. She was the beauty queen and the movie star and the dream siren, the sex symbol, love's very emblem, and even survived the blaring vulgarity of publicity organs that usually destroy validity at the human level. Her beauty was actual, not just fabricated. It moved men to tears of unmanliness. She was so idolized, that remoteness preserved her loneliness. A pedestalled statue, she was a sublime dream figure. Mass men venerated her. She yearned to be loved by one individual man. *As* one individual woman. As herself, Frances. Real, in the flesh, a particular woman. Not as a merely adored legend. Not as a press agent's dream, a televised personality, a cinema apparition, a photograph in a magazine. *Personally*—to be loved personally. By whom? Someone who didn't succumb to a myth. Who didn't swoon at her sight. Who didn't estimate how he would boast to his friends. Who didn't work her into all fantasies he had ever woven, as the missing central piece to perfect the pattern.

At a cocktail party, this star who was envious of becoming a person, this celebrity who yearned for the common touch or a specific understanding with a co-traveller through this living human sphere, met—yes, she did meet—the man. The very one. Her real, spiritual equal. Her consort through the spheres. The one who answered Yes to all she most looked for. Through whom she'd turn alive, as simply the woman Frances—not this built-up gigantic magnet of derivative secondary adoration via films and glossy packets for the public. Herself, simple Frances. The one underneath expensive publicity's sheen of glamor. The beauty beneath the professional beauty. The woman who needs love.

They met, and fell in love! Just like in movies! But it was *real—real*! It really *was* real! *So* real, that reality just couldn't comprehend it. Reality fell back, on known images.

They're in love. Give way to them; make room. Don't jostle. Let them breathe.

Frances, and Tom Gervasi. Ideal, and ideal. Ideally together. The ideal pair. Two separate ideals, in one ideal joining. With nothing to sunder them. Time and Death, keep far away. Keep your dreadful distances. Don't dare disturb. You're positively unwelcome. Frances and Tom Gervasi exclude you. From their charmed circle. Their select company. The closed oneness of their two clasped choices.

Tom Gervasi loves Frances. Frances loves Tom Gervasi. Two loves form one, without beginning or end. All solidity is there, from the borrowed earth. A solid love. And at the core, pure fire. And outside the sphere, only air. The air swims around that sphere; sprinkles water on it; is warmed by it. The sphere is closed. Yet nourished, from outside. Wide open. To everything.

VI. BERNICE HAS DESIGNS ON TOM GERVASI. MEETING HIM IS TO BE THE FIRST STEP. THAT WOULD GIVE LATER STEPS THEIR ONLY CHANGE.

Bernice said, with forceful logic, that if a person can grow up and one day become the president of the country, *she* could grow up and marry Tom Gervasi. Growing up was essential, in both cases.

Well, already she was grown up. So she had already earned the right.—To be a *candidate*, at least.

Now that growing up is out of the way; already—so to speak—behind her; the necessary next step, of course, would be to take her chances on *meeting* him.

How *does* a girl meet Tom Gervasi? At a party. Yes, but not at *any* party. It's got to be a party where *he's at*. That, of course, narrows the field.

Now for a contact, a connection, in the person of an invited guest to one of the parties where Tom Gervasi will be. Then she can ask to "be taken along."

She found one! He agreed! It's a Saturday night! She has three days to prepare.

She saved her bath till three hours before the party, in order *freshly* to be clean. She bought seductive perfume. And decided on a gown that reveals her shapely form to its many nooks and contours.

She went to a hair specialist; and in short, was groomed "to kill."

She'll slay him! The most wanted non-criminal male in the non-Oriental world! Hers! *If.*

If *what*? If me no buts. Bernice felt the tug of destiny. It had "Tom Gervasi" written all over it. In gold letters. Specially embossed, in Heaven's Printing Shop.

The night of the party! To give destiny its long-awaited opportunity.

But Tom Gervasi is surrounded! A press of women, hemming him in. Who'll break through the mob, Bernice in hand, to do the immense introductory honors?

Someone—not her escort—*did* know him; but slightly. But this would-be saviour felt timid about "forcing himself" on the magnet. He wouldn't "presume," in the teeth of such ferocious popularity.

So many women were in the competition. Bernice would win—but she must *get* to him, first.

Her perfume was wearing off; her hair messed up; her dress all crumpled; her makeup, by now, stale. Worst of all, her optimism was losing its confidence, her confidence was losing its hope, her hope its courage, her courage its pluck, her tenacity its endurance.

The tide is turning against her. Has she already too wilted? Or should she press on, *now*?

Her object was completely covered up from sight by the clothing and skin of surrounding people. She *could* plow through, on her own, like an unruly tank, driving people from her path. Such uncouth aggression, though, would create an unworthy impression. It could hardly recommend her in any positive sense to the *goal* of such crass and boorish brusqueness. A more delicately cunning strategy would better be pursued. But when? He might leave soon.

He's making ready to leave. He's going over to give a goodbye to one person, another to another. He's saying to the host and hostess goodbye, now. Bernice is sharply observing to see whether he's taking any one woman along *with* him. Many hopeful *possibilities* for such a candidate are exposing their postures of availability to Tom Gervasi's possible impulse-choice, in passing, as he goes out. None wants to force herself on him *too obviously.* Yet, all are obviously hoping, making themselves, in subtle unmistakability, all too evidently available. They're looking conspicuous: selectable: willing, in a not-too-surprised way, to be asked, abruptly, to "come along," by that voice which opens women's ears to their own dreams.

He's going out *alone—alone!*

Bernice rushes alongside. They're out in the street, now: the building, with its enormous party-apartment-rooms crowded with competitors and other people, with noise and clinking drinks, is behind. She's walking step-by-step with him, in the rushing dark.

"I guess you know who *I* am. What's *your* name?"

"Bernice."

"That's as nice as any. Did you know the host and hostess?"

"No, an invited guest took me along."

"Good. You were no crasher, then."

"Where are you going, Mr. Gervasi? May I go there too?"

"I'm going to a woman's apartment. No, you may *not* go there too."

"Is it on private business, you're going?"

"This is Saturday night—in fact, past it, it's Sunday morning. It's not an hour to be conducting business, ordinarily. I'm going strictly for pleasure, if you must know."

"Why didn't this woman come with you to the party?"

"I preferred being on my own, at this party."

"It had a good result—you met *me.*"

"That's a bit bold. What are you suggesting?"

"Break off your middle-of-the-night erotic assignation with this woman you were intending to visit, and switch it to me, instead. I'll make the switch prove itself a worthwhile one, for you."

"How do you know what it would be like for me if I kept my original appointment?"

"I *don't* know. But I offer you my body as a sumptuous feast, and my fresh new love."

"I can't resist. All right. Take me home."

"You can phone the woman who's expecting you, from my apartment, to tell her you were unavoidably waylaid and are very sorry."

"I'd better not phone her at all. I told her it was possible that I'd never arrive, so that she wouldn't be *definitely* expecting me. So she won't be *too* disappointed. My warning assured that."

"I'm glad you 'covered' yourself. Let *me*, now, cover you. With a big warm skin-blanket. It might keep you awake. In fact, you might reach an *extraordinary* wakefulness, when covered by my big warm skin-blanket. It may cause you to thrust sleep aside, and do temporarily without it.

"But tomorrow is a non-working day: good old Sunday. Have a late night, tonight. Will your mother object?"

"She won't if I don't tell her."

"Then don't tell her. Squeeze me. I'm your Bernice."

They embraced on the street, before paging a handy taxi. The night was dark, moonless, cloudy. It even started to rain. Bernice lived a long way away. But they got there. Tom paid the fare. Then, up the elevator. Now, in her apartment, a dim light on. The day had turned out well, for Bernice. Or rather, this all-confirming night.

✳

In the morning, she looked at him sleeping. "Last night's vague hope is this morning's reality. He's there! In my bed!" Next goal: to get him to marry her. If someone born in this nation could grow up and one day become president of it, then couldn't someone grow up to marry Tom Gervasi? Stranger things have happened, to mankind. Men flew to the moon. They took a photo of Mars. They built Chartres. They built the pyramid, or sphinx. They invented Shakespeare. God created Darwin, who made evolution. The airplane was invented; the spinning wheel; the sewing machine; the printing press. Sports and games evolved. Empires were won. Joyce wrote *Ulysses*. Mozart made operas. Astounding feats of magic have been performed. Christ was resurrected. There *is* such a thing as the Occult.

Tom Gervasi *may* be married. Bernice is a woman. Therefore she may marry him.

She'll go far, with that logic. With her body. Her face. Her lucky little determination. It already swerved mighty Tom Gervasi from his intended path, some hours ago, and put him in her bed. Now, for the rest of his life, to swerve him. She'd try her wings of power. It's mid-morning, he's still sleeping. The light streaks through the bedroom. He stirs. He'll be awake.

Bernice is ready. To *try*, at any rate.

Their futures. Together? In what form? How consistently? Or not together? Their futures. He's waking. She's waiting. Toward what, his waking, her waiting? They've only just met: her doing. She'd will the rest. Given his consent. She knows what she'd like. What will *he* say? Or will she wait? And let things develop? Of their "natural" course. Toward *her* direction. To his increasing consent. To *them*. From the her, from the him. To their own them.

VII. MYRNA LEARNS THE HARD WAY TO LEAVE
TOM GERVASI ALONE. HE DOESN'T LOVE HER ANY
MORE. IT WAS HARD FOR HER TO TAKE. *SO* HARD,
SHE NEEDED HARD FISTS, FROM HIM, AS A SORT
OF PHYSICAL REINFORCEMENT. THIS WEAKENED
HER INSISTENCE, AND SHE ACCEPTED HIS REJEC-
TION. IT TOOK SOME CONVINCING, BUT NOW SHE
ABANDONS THEIR PAST TO ITS CUT-OFF FROM
HER DIM AND DESOLATE "NOW."

"Tommy," said Myrna; "do you still love me?"

"Look Myrna, I'm annoyed that you call as Tommy. *Mother* used to, when I was a little boy. But I want to feel I've grown up, by now. 'Tommy' sounds too sticky-familiar, from you. You're presuming on some cute intimacy, which embarrasses and irks me at the same time."

"All right, I'll call you Tom. Anyway, do you still love me?"

"No."

"Oh. That's exactly what I didn't want to hear. I half-feared as much. Yet I risked hoping you'd say yes—a risk that now I regret . . . Maybe, when more time goes by, you might rechange your fickle heart's mood and revert to loving me again?"

"Unlikely. Don't wait on it. Give up now, you'll feel better later."

"But Tom, what about our sacred past?"

"It's still sacred. But now it's past."

"Then, it's goodbye, this time, for all time?"

"Yes; we're dealing with the whole future, by my now 'no.'"

"Tom, I'll miss you."

"Be sloppy in private. Endure the pain. The worst is now. Once over *that* hump, you're on the peaceful road (though not all at once) to burial and oblivion. No, Myrna, no more kiss. A formal handshake, will suffice."

"Why not rescind your decision? One more fling, between us."

"Don't be tedious. I want done with it, with you."

"I'll phone you tomorrow."

"I'll change my number to a private listing."

"Then I'll phone you at the office."

"I'll tell the switchboard operator to ignore calls from you. To you, I'll always be busy or out. If you persist with bounding me, I'll take court action, on a harassment charge, and privacy invasion, and nuisance grubbing. Myrna, consider your dignity. Consult your self-esteem, pride, honor, decency. Together, they cry to you, 'Desist! Don't drag yourself down. Take his "no" nobly. Or you'll earn the pejorative, "Fool," to tag on to "Myrna" in epithet.' "

"That's impassioned rhetoric, for appealing to such qualities in me that will assist you in getting me off your back. However, I refuse. I'll plague and haunt you, and put pressure to bear, ignoring your legal rights to an unmolested privacy in your peaceful goings and doings. To disturb you, to hurt you, to get revenge, I'll forgo pride and decent convention. I'm already low, by your rejection. I can get no lower than that. Willful spite, angry defiance, I'll play with now. You're my steady victim-to-be. I'll focus on you, through the funnel of venom; and as a target you'll be in my sight, sighted, my hatred's object. Here's a trifling start: I'll call you 'Tommy,' again."

"My mother called me that in innocence, and innocently I let her call me that, while still in infancy and soon after. Myrna, you're desperate in your revenge. *I'm* desperate, to *counter* it. Physically, I'll beat you to a pulp, as though you were a *man* berating me. Conversation can't stop you. But a pummeling might."

"But, I'm helpless, I'm a woman. I warn you, Tommy."

"There's that 'Tommy' again. Myrna, helplessness doesn't *warn* people: *power* does. If you take power in helplessness, then use it: Ward off these blows."

They rain down, and he beats her badly. She presses charges, of assault and bodily injury, from her hospital. The case goes to court. Tom Gervasi wins. Myrna must pay his legal costs, as well.

It shuts her up. She leaves him alone now. She's learned a little lesson. He *means* it: He doesn't love her any more. He's broken off with her. And he'll break *her* off, in justified physical violence, if she doesn't keep to herself.

She has a broken jaw, and other damaged bones. And she's out of pocket, with hospitalization and legal costs.

"Yes, he doesn't love me any more. Poor Tommy, did he have to go to *that* extent, to prove it? He enforced his word, with harmful deed. I learned the hard way. His fists are harder them his dear cock was. But the latter was in a preferred *place*, with gently approved violence. His fists were *out* of place. But put me, finally, in my place. So I desist. I give him up. He's gone, to our sacred past. As Tommy."

VIII. TOM'S LOVE FOR VALERIE EBBS DEAD. THE REST IS HEARTBREAK, FOR HER. SOLITARY, SHE'LL SEE HER LIFE DECLINE IN SAME VEIN AS HIS OLD LOVE FOR HER: SHE'LL PURSUE ITS COURSE, WITH HER OWN BODY.

Valerie easily sensed how close Tom Gervasi was to the end of his love for her, and thought how she could recharge it, rekindle it, revitalise it, and restore it to its flaring peak of their earlier courtship rapture. She'd better hurry. It was dwindling rapidly, and soon there wouldn't be enough to revive. She had to inject a shot of plasm serum, or something, into the bare remaining vein of that meager love.

But the love was draining away. "Tom! Tom!" Valerie exclaimed. "Recover yourself!"

"What on earth from?"

"The lassitude and languishing, the near-expiring, of your love formerly for me."

"Oh, I'm too lazy. Let it run itself out."

"*Please* don't practice inertia on what means such a great deal to me!"

"Sorry, Valerie. I'm overwhelmed by indifference for you. While we were speaking, my love had a croak or stroke and stopped breathing. How parallel to an entire person's mortality, itself"

"Oh Tom, you're dead to me?"

"No, *you're* dead to *me*."

"But this is too, *too* sad!"

"But Valerie, that's what happened. It's done. My love, no more than a corpse, can be revived. Thus, for us, it's goodbye."

"Tom! Tom! It *can't* be!"

"It *is*. It all too definitely *is*."

"Tom, Tom, I'll never survive."

"In *time* you will. Time's been a known healer."

"It's a *heel*! In time your love stopped."

"It died. It's dead. But *you*'re not; *I*'m not; only the *love* is dead."

"*Your* love is; but not *mine*."

"Then yours might just as well follow suit. It does no good, any more, since *mine* is extinguished. *Your* love for *me* is folly, obsolete, once mine for you has died."

"But Tom, how can I stop?"

"I'll be gone. Your love will starve, for I was its nourishment. From that starvation, it'll die."

"Will my dead love and your dead love meet in a dead love's heaven?"

"Heaven is for dead *people*; not for dead loves."

"So is this the end?"

"That's what I've been saying all along."

"Oh Tom, I can't bear it! Hug me, Tom. Hold me, don't let me go."

"But Valerie, my heart just isn't in it, any more."

"Oh Tom, my life is ruined."

"Sorry that it had to turn out this way, Valerie. What a grand beginning our love had! It knelt in the stars of romance. Little did we foresee . . ."

"Tom, Tom, stop! My heart is breaking, as you're saying that!"

"Sorry to torture you. But *I* feel *fine*—if that's any consolation to *you*."

"Tom, for *my* sake—*please* be miserable."

"I'd have to love you, in order to be miserable. As I don't, I'm not."

"Oh, you're so heartless!"

"I *have* a heart: but it's *loveless*."

"It's loved by *mine.*"

"But *from* it, no love *issues forth*. It's a dry well, there."

"Behold my wet eyes."

"Let's not prolong this. I can't bear how you suffer."

"I can't bear my own suffering! Tom, I still love you."

"Stop. Then your *suffering* will stop."

"Turn it off?! Just like that?! I'm not a *faucet*, you know."

"Well, let's part. There's no good in our lingering. It only makes things worse."

"Is it, then, goodbye, Tom?"

"It finally is. But our love lived a long, brave life. We'll mourn its passing. But *we* must survive. We must survive our own love's death. Valerie, I'm moved to tears. Our love was brave, and led a long, noble life. Long live our love, in the hereafter. But this is earth, not heaven. Earth is time's field. Our love has been shuffled off it. We'll remain, but separately. Our final kiss. Goodbye."

"Tom Don't leave! . . . Oh, he's left. He's gone. Here I am— Valerie. That's my name. It stands by itself, now. Friends had coupled it with Tom's. The 'Tom' half has been ripped away. There's only me, left. To finish my days. To live them out. To see them down. To follow, fast. Alone. To go the way of Tom's love for me. To dwindle out. To decline, past reviving. In grosser imitation, of Tom's love's demise, its draining away.

"That's what's left. That's what I face, and follow. In frenzied replica. In hollow mockery."

IX. CLARA WANTS THINGS TO REMAIN THE SAME, WITH TOM GERVASI; NOT HE, HOWEVER.

"I'm used to you. So don't desert me," Clara instructed Tom Gervasi. "I've made you a habit. You're necessary for my habit. Let's keep it this way."

They were in her bed. It was morning, after a night there. Clara was laying down the status quo, to arrest, freeze, and fix their state of affairs in perpetuity forever. Toward such reactionary conservatism, Tom Gervasi felt radically rebellious. Their private political polarity would be strained and stretched in opposite tuggings.

"Clare, life is flux. So is our affair. I'm restless that it should end soon. You calmly expect to keep what's between us the same. But *I*'ll make you *struggle* to *try* to keep what's between us the same. Not because I want to see you struggle, will I make you struggle, but because, from from my side, I'm eager to end it between us. My will matters here. That will force you to struggle, in an effort to maintain things as they are. You'll squirm, you'll fail. For *I*'m determined. *Against* the retention of our bond. It needs *both* our wills, to retain it. Therefore, I can only win, and you can only lose. What I want being in my power, I'll win. What *you* want being in my power, you'll lose. Our tussle already has that foreseeable end. Prepare *now*, to lose me."

That long speech, in a voice she loved to hear, used words and meanings hateful to Clara's ear. Her ear couldn't bear it; passed it to her eye to make tears drop from it; and to her mouth, angry with words of reply.

They dressed, and Tom Gervasi said goodbye. He used the door, and left. Clara was left. She was all that was left, of all that former love. She was the guardian, the archivist, curator, maintenance crew, of all that former love. He had left it all to her. Entrusted it, to her capable hands. That once-to-be status quo. She'd dust it, polish it, it was a museum specimen. It was her brilliant antique. Her keepsake. Her memento, well rounded off.

It was as though they had had a child and separated, with the mother bringing the child up, and the father off, to parts unknown. That child was their love: nursed, warmed, and well-kept by Clara, who ever brooded over it. She watered it and kept it alive. She kept Tom Gervasi, in his precious absence. She fondled his absence, like a religious relic. She became a fundamentalist, to that devout creed.

X. THELMA STOPS LOVING TOM GERVASI, AND THEY AGREE TO PART. TOM GERVASI STANDS REVEALED, TO HIS DOOM, BY THE TRUTH THELMA HAS EARNED, IN KNOWING HIM TILL THE KNOWING CRACKED THE UNION, LEADING TO HER SELF-PRESERVATION, AND AN UNIMPAIRED FUTURE.

Thelma exasperated Tom Gervasi, and for good reason. Without warning or explanation, she cooled off to him.

She used to have a continual fire blazing for him, and she'd add new logs every minute till the chimney almost caught fire.

Well, what made her stop, so abruptly? Had he lost his effect on her? Or had she decided that her passion was going to waste, down the drain, since he was disinclined to perpetuate it with a vow of constancy and a proposal of marriage? He'd ask her. That's the simple way.

"Thelma, why did you cool off to me? Has your love stopped?"

"I got tired of enjoying you by the moment and not fortifying it with the security of a future to rely on.

"Realizing that at any moment I could lose you, I felt unstable, vulnerable, tentative, precarious.

"*Assurance* would have kept me loving you. Receiving none, in self-defense I had to stop. Now, I'm out of danger, should you decide to reject me. The peril, the risk, is removed. Your loss, now, wouldn't hurt me."

"Well, Thelma, I do reject you. Unless you love me, an affair with you is fallen flat. Too matter-of-fact. Its backbone, romance, key to glorious sentiment, has been taken out. What's left? Mechanical sex. Too cut-and-dry. Sterile. Routine. Lacking soul, between us."

"Had *you* loved *me*?"

"No."

"Well, it was uneven, then. I did the loving; you the taking. It's over, now. We're through."

"Goodbye, Thelma. I won't miss you. We part at the right time."

"Goodbye, Tom. You were selfish. I'm glad it's ended.

"I loved you, *hoping* for a return. For a future. For stability. For assurance. For security.

"None forthcame. So I gave up. I'm not destroyed. I survive, intact. I'll look for a new fellow. The *right* one. Finding him, I'll find his future constancy, and rest secure. And marry. And be a permanent bride. Uninterrupted, except by death. Flowering full. A ride up time's glory, in rich maturing. Toward that, I go. And leave *you*, Tom, to a rhythm riddled with staccato, with uneven turns, fallings off, fickle change, a fluxed frenzy, successions of women with dynamic instability. That's *your* pace. It may run you down. And nerve you out. On wild crosses of chaos. On droppings off. To alteration's fever. A motion of ceaseless women, in an endless night."

"What prophecy, Thelma! You see my dark side."

"I see no *side*—only *sides*. Your facets number you out. You're stretched beyond a center. And wild nothing cries inside."

"You prophesize doom. You've cast a cloud over my cheer. Is *that* your farewell gift?"

"The truth, from my view. I *earned* the truth of this view. Learned it *hard*, from *you*. It's *your* gift. And *my* truth."

"Your truth to speak; mine to be. With that, adieu."

XI. THE *TIMES'* OBITUARY PAGE. AUTOPSY: A BROKEN HEART. MORTAL CAUSE: TOM GERVASI.

Glancing one non-working morning (but non-Sunday as well) at a newspaper called the *Times* (as opposed to the *Spaces*, which it was *not* called), Tom Gervasi happened to run his eye down an obituary column in morbid self-congratulatory idleness, when, to shock, horror, and surprise, he found listed the name of a former girlfriend. "An autopsy revealed that death, at such a premature age, was owing to a broken heart. Bedside witnesses and auditors were questioned. They testified that the last words uttered by the dying girl as her life was ebbing away and her breath breathed its last, were the following: 'Tom Gervasi, we'll meet in heaven. Don't hurry. I'll have plenty of time (or is it "non-time"?) to wait for you, with bated breath. Live out your slow life fully. Die a natural death, then join me.

" 'I wasn't able to die a natural death, since I'm dying, now, of grief that you're no longer with me. Why, oh why, deer Tom, did we "break up"? I never really recovered. I pined away, in my collapsed world; since you were the prop and mainstay of my life: then you let go, and all life drained away in drive and will. There was nothing to sustain me physically, for you were at my core and provided my soul with its special diet. But this is not a reproach, dear Tom. My dying words secure you in my hope. You are my immortality; I presume to be yours. We'll prove it, won't we? To the last, our proof must wait. Complete your sojourn through life. Then round your eternal voyage out, with me.'

"Those were her last words, according to her bedside seers-off, who verified the accuracy of their report after lengthy consultation with each other. One of them was a speed shorthand expert, and thus recorded, with faithful fidelity, the above quoted final words by the offgoing deceased. Copious weeping on the part of the scene's survivors gave rise to the surmisal that the event was most moving, in its melancholy drama: spiritually optimistic, through its mournful pall. Grief-laden, the witnesses plan to get in touch with Tom Gervasi and apprise him of the stirring address rendered him in circumstances of extraordinary leavetaking. Funeral services will be at . . ."

Tom Gervasi just couldn't believe his eyes, reading that. The phone rang on the table alongside him, where one elbow was propped. "It's probably a bedside witness reporting to me," was Tom Gervasi's swift guess. On the third ring he lifted the phone up, and found his guess to be correct. "I just read about it," he said into the phone. "The *Times* left nothing out, did it? That was thorough coverage. Through the *Times*, through you witnesses and auditors, she spoke straight to me at death's point. Now, she's there already. Her love haunts me, from the grave.

"It would be sentimental of me to say that my love has been revived by her vanishing speech. I don't give a fig for her. She attempted an 'immortal union' bribe—an afterlife blackmail, as it were. But it failed. I'm unmoved. *Let* her wait, eternally. All in vain, poor dear. I loved her once. I stopped, so we 'broke up.' She *didn't* stop, so she died. She's asking for my soul, in heavenly matrimony. She wants God-supervised love, approved from on high. Well, I deny her that. My rejection still stands, in full, firm force. My rejection crosses dimensions, from this to the other world, but remains intact in passage.

"I don't unreject her, just because she's dead. Of course, this sounds heartless. Crass. Pitiless. Devoid of any humane mercy. Cold. Unmoved. Well, it is, all that. Her plea, timed to the utmost boil of drama, is turned down. But where she is, she won't know it."

Tom Gervasi hung up. The message won't get through to her—his heartless reply. She died already, by the first rejection. Were she to receive this confirmation that the first rejection still stands to its complete extent, thus becoming, in effect, a second rejection, it might so break her heart already broken, as to cause it to unbreak, if two breaks make one unbreak. That might bring her back to life, in a burst of anticlimax. Then she'd say, "Dear Tom, I'm back again. In life, once more. This time, please marry me."

"And I'd reject her for the third time: a rebroken heart, and her second death. All over again! No! I'm rid of her. Her first death is enough. It protects me."

XII.

(Title later.)

Tom Gervasi saw what a hot, lovely day it was going to be, from his morning window and his yesterday's memory. Work was slow these summer months. He wouldn't be missed today. He phoned in to the office and told the receptionist he'd be taking the day off today. She more then took the message. Being enamored of him from an undeclarative distance, she went beyond office protocol in being so bold as to hope that he'd enjoy his day off most thoroughly—what was he planning? "Going to the beach, lying on the sand, soaking in some sun, warm drowsy indolence, peaceful serene thoughts, lazy as the wooly stray clouds that relieve the sweet burning blue."

"Tom Gervasi, you're so poetic," gushed the receptionist. "Will you take me with you next time? I wish I could be there with you today. You'd be summer infinity's ideal guide."

"Of course. Next time." And Tom Gervasi signed off. He knew she had a crush on him. But he had more women than he could handle at the moment. Should things go slack, he'd take her up on her shy, undeclared interest—which waiting might intensify. Meanwhile, he had his hands full. Women, women, everywhere. He had to hold more off than he could let in. He needed privacy, and time to work, and time to think. Women took precious moments away. They hemmed him in, and closed up the air, so to speak. He needed space for thought and work. He had to hold them off. They crowded in with pressure. He had to keep them off. They'd nip off too many precious moments. He needed solitude, peace—they always offered to share it with him. But then it wouldn't be solitude or peace. It would be talking, kissing, flirting—"doing things together." His life *could* go by that way, if he let it. But then he'd be untrue to his own soul. That's what counts, *first*: truth to his "inner self." The rest had to make room for that: to give in, take second place, and wait. Women were the invading world; they'd "take over," if they could. He had, gently, to fight them off. But not totally to discourage them. He'd be lonely without them. But he had to temper, moderate, the roles they'd play, within these exquisite years of his life's prime.

He was riding the subway to the beach. Now he was walking from the station to the beach. Now he was walking on the sand close up to the shore. Now he was lying down, half-dreaming, in his bathing trunks, with his civilian clothes in a briefcase close by. He dazed off. He lazed on. He found a favorite dream. To that, he fastened himself. He settled off, under its floating spell.

Three girls cut the sun off, bending over him. No more private slow lyrical prolonged bliss of thought drifting off thought in lovely long distillation of wide open dream space grazing the wooly gown of God. Instead, three faces of eager love. They had recognized him. He was a mild celebrity, of sorts. His reputation was locked in the private hearts of women. Here, now, were three such hearts. He wanted the sun, but instead received their love-beams. Divine light was blocked off. Love shone on him instead, three-sourced. The girls shed their sweetest rays. But it spoiled his day. *Divine* love was what he prayed for. Under the endless sun. Instead, the love of three girls: opaque, finite. Commonplace (for him). They were like a secular intrusion into a sacred temple where God, after a two-thousand-year delay, was launched on a Revelation, before a blessed congregation of devouts, whose prayers and fasting had culminated in the rarest of visitations. But the spell was cut short. An interruption by three love-proffering vulgarians, with their teasing bodies all bulging for view in brief beach attire. The spell was broken. Back to day. The beach. The girls. Their blazing love. The lofty sun. The blocked-off meditation. Unwelcome shades, bent over him. With love pouring forth. From three singing hearts. From their local own divine suns. "Well, this beats the office, anyway. I'll take one of these home with me straight to bed. I'm roused with sexual anger, being divinely frustrated from my communion with a deity of this beach; sand, waves, sun, clouds, blue heaven, the marine horizon. I was on the verge. I was just taking off. I was bound heavenward. Instead, here are three pagans, with a blunter invitation. They were most unwelcome. They ruined my unreal day. Now I'm back in the office dimension. I'll get carnal consolation, with the heathen of my choice: with lower sights, cling in lower bliss."

(Title now:)

TOM GERVASI TAKES A DAY OFF FROM THE OFFICE TO BE ALONE ON A SUMMER BEACH, CONTEMPLATING INFINITY. INFINITY BECKONS. BUT THREE GIRLS INTERFERE. THEY BREAK THAT DIVINE SPELL. WITHDRAWN FROM NEAR GOD, HE RESUMES IN THE OFFICE PLANE, BEACH DIVISION. THE HOLY SUN IS BLOCKED FROM VIEW. INSTEAD, THREE BODIES.

XIII.

(Title beneath text. Otherwise, text is pre-told.)

Nina and Fleur were the chief rivals for Tom Gervasi. The rest of the field was far behind, and bookmakers quoted hopeless odds of five-hundred-to-one for the closest contestants behind the co-favorites, Nina and Fleur, who were now closing in on the home stretch neck-and-neck, being spurred on by their supporters, in full stride toward a photo-finish. This was the race of the age. The states were vast. Tom Gervasi had announced, earlier in the afternoon, at a packed press conference, to the flash of television bulbs, that the winner of this match would be designated his official girlfriend for a year. An uproar, then a hush, descended upon the assembled journalists; when the news was released, it went around like wildfire. A book contract and a movie contract were being offered, and already there was a controversy on a rights clause. Sensationalism was rampant, in Tom Gervasi's private love life.

Nina was trying with all her might, going all-out, come hell or high water. But Fleur kept pace right alongside; not a step behind; nor one in front, either. It was as close as contests could go. They were nearing the finishing line. Tom Gervasi—both judge and reward—kept his eyes peeled, for a decision was nigh. Who would it be? The excitement was dense. You could have knocked anyone over with a feather. They came across the finishing line.

Yes, but who won? Wasn't there a winner? Was it Nina, or Fleur?

Who? Who won?

The suspense, theoretically, is over. Or *will* be: when we know who won.

Has time stopped? Are they *still* crossing the finishing line? Is the race undecided yet?

Either Nina or Fleur won. But who?

Motion is arrested. The flurried media hasn't reported the result yet, to the expectant world.

As yet, neither has won.

When will time go on?

When it resumes. But not before.

Time waits. *It* wants to know, too.

(Title, a repetitive variation on the text, now follows:)

NINA AND FLEUR LEAD THE FIELD. THE WINNER GETS TOM GERVASI FOR A YEAR. THEY NEAR THE FINISHING LINE. THEY GO ACROSS. WHO WON? THERE'S A BLUR OF EXCITEMENT. TIME STOPS. DID IT PANIC, WITH THE ISSUE SO CLOSE? WE DON'T KNOW WHO WON. YET, THE RACE IS OVER.

XIV.

(Title not here: It comes as aftermath.)

Tom Gervasi lived in a "female" apartment. He hadn't known that at the time he had rented it. He had assumed that all apartments were "neuter"; that only a person or an animal had a male or female "gender."

He knew that, in some languages like French, something which in the natural world itself has no "gender" whatever, is *given* a gender—very arbitrary, often; such as "la mer," meaning "the sea," in French.

Quite fanciful, to attribute femaleness to the sea—which, in the objective universe, rages totally genderless.

The sun—"el sol" in Spanish—was given a male gender. Quite meaningless. Apollo is the Greek sun god, but he's a *personified* deity. Neptune is the old sea god, but he's a man—contradicting, in advance, the French language "*la* mer." It all sounds so gratuitous.

God, of course, at His Creation according to Bible fundamentalists, made some people male and others female, when the "world" was given its earliest population. That was good for reproduction, according to later theories of evolution.

"La plume"—"the pen," in French, is female in gender. So is "la maison"—"the house." Whereas, "le chapeau"—"the hat"—is male; even if it's a woman's hat, it's still male. That, of course, is ridiculous.

And why should "la plume"—"the pen"—be female? It's shaped so phallically! But that's a Freudian reading-in, later.

Anyway, language is silly. And gender—sometimes that's comically absurd.

So Tom Gervasi was in his rented apartment—not knowing it had an actual gender: female.

It so happened, that in the course of his residing there, his "female" apartment gradually fell in love with him.

Ordinarily, it was female *humans* who fell in love with him. Tom Gervasi was so used to that, he even expected it. And female humans obliged, so abundantly! It got to be embarrassing, those inordinate numbers of human females who all seemed to have the common "fall"acy, or weakness, of falling for him! More than he could handle, in a month of years!

Whereas, other chaps were lonely—they weren't loved by *any* women, or maybe by one or two ugly ones. It just wasn't fair. But Tom Gervasi was fortunate.

It was a long time before he realized the state that his apartment was in—not cluttered or tidy, but its *emotional* state: toward its resident.

The chairs seemed to fondle and caress him, as he sat on them.

The windows seemed to dilate widely, to let in more light, when he wanted to glance out.

The doors seemed to open by themselves for him; he didn't even have to use the knob.

The bed seemed to regard him sexually. And it acted jealous when a human female happened to be sharing it.

The kitchen seemed to cook for him automatically: to prepare and serve his food, and do the washing-up afterwards.

The bathroom welcomed him, with its deeply confiding intimacy.

The tub practically ran the bath water for him itself: warm, soft, with foamy suds. He sank into the tub: how sexual!

The carpet seemed to flirt at his feet sometimes: curl up and nip him, or roll awry, like a pesky pet dog being perverse and playful.

Tom Gervasi realized, he'd made a mistake—in French it was "*le* mer," not "*la* mer." He had confused the sea with a horse. "La *mare*," of course, is a female horse.

Well, linguistics were hardly his strong point. Nor was etymology.

What *was* his strong point? Apparently women. For them, he always managed a "strong point."

So such for that sexual allusion. But back to his apartment.

Was it because so many women had appeared in it, drank in it, ate in it, and slept in it, that the apartment itself had conceived the idea of emulating their love for Tom Gervasi? That's a plausible theory, but difficult to prove by conclusive scientific standards.

When he switched on the electric light, the bulbs were pink and perfumy, with love-beams, whether sheltered by lampshades or semi-incandescently "naked."

The wallpaper peeled and flaked off, when Tom Gervasi was near it. What an odd way of demonstrating infatuation!

Yes, the whole apartment was in love. Or was it a projection of the possible narcissism of its resident? Had the apartment "taken on" Tom Gervasi's high self-regard, since apartments in time become extensions of the human feelings contained therein, the human feelings themselves being extensions, feelers, put out by the person who feels them?

Surely, the apartment "reflected" Tom Gervasi—his character, habits, the kind of person he was? Or did the apartment go beyond reflecting: did it presume to *react* to him, on its own, as a "living" unit: the reaction taking the form and shape of female love, imitating the female love of his girlfriends who often "slept over"?

All this is speculation. There's no official, scientifically determined bill of factual goods on apartments who love with female love the man who pays the rent and lives there.

We're dealing with a novel phenomenon: an inanimate interior of rooms and objects, furnishings and fixtures, all assembled under the unity of "apartment," having conceived a perfectly humanly femininely animate complex of responses called "love," for their male inhabitant.

Can this he explained? Or is it only a miracle?

Tom Gervasi, on second realization, saw that after all it was as he had originally thought: "*la* mer," not "*le* mer." If it was "*la* mer," was Neptune secretly a *woman* in mythology? And did he ride a female horse called "la *mare*," a sea-horse or dolphin, across the sudsy waves, the billowing breasts of the deep?

This mongrel bastardisation of mythology, linguistics, and etymology in intermedia crossbreeding, was harmful to plain scholarship, a sort of horseplay, which just didn't hold water. Tom Gervasi was all at sea, and up over his head in an element in which he was every bit of "all wet."

What could he do about his apartment loving him? It began to harmfully sabotage his girlfriends, misplacing their clothes and other effects, tripping them up, leading them into domestic accidents, minor household upsets. All in spiteful fits of jealousy against human females that enjoyed an unfair advantage in sharing the human race species with that *par excellente* specimen, Tom Gervasi.

He decided he'd have to move. Move into a neutral apartment that had no gender-fixation upon him.

But how would *this* apartment ever survive? It would mourn and grieve, and never really recover. It desperately depended on his being there.

When he was overnight away sleeping in some girl's apartment, or weekends away out of town, or weeks away on a holiday, or a few days away on a business trip, the apartment would miss him, frustrated in its helpful household acts of devotion to his well-being, comfort, and convenience. It really *looked after* him, like a devoted wife, attending to his every need, when he was there.

He lived a bachelor life. Well, his *apartment* acted as his wife. With an old-fashioned sense of duty. Of ministering to him, with deep care and loving concern.

It *wouldn't let* him move to another place. It would somehow *keep* him here. It would make him *dependent* on it—or her.

It tried, but failed. He made ready to move out. His books were stacked in cartons, all his belongings were packed. A moving van would soon park outside the building, and strong men would come in to help him move. The new apartment, not far away, was rented and ready. It was moving day.

The apartment went through a female crisis, had a hysterical fit, and went to pieces, collapsing bit by bit. Tom Gervasi barely managed to escape.

But he took some surviving articles of furniture and other objects with him to the new apartment. These remnants, like linen, cooking utensils, dinnerware, lamps, tables, chairs, desks, sofa, bed, pillows, drapery, curtains, rugs, bathroom articles, correspondence, books, pictures, decorations, towels, bulbs, and whatnot—they were part of the crew that had loved him, within that total unit, the apartment.

They'll form the hard-core nucleus in the *new* apartment, for loving him?

No, Tom Gervasi had taken precautions. He made sure that his new apartment was *male* before renting it and signing the lease.

Yes, but what if it's *homosexual* male? Oh, what a problem *that* would be!

But who heard of an apartment having a "male" gender?! An apartment is *neuter*: *everyone* knows that.

No, Tom Gervasi doesn't. Gender spreads everywhere. Even inanimate objects bear one sort or another of "gender."

"Gender" implies potential love. And who can be without love? Objects must kindle with it. They must reflect it, or impart it, be imbued with it, dyed and coated with it. Love was impersonal, too. It spread everywhere. It burst into gender, here and there.

Gender is *suffused* with love. Being gender, it must be.

Love is all over the place. In *la mer*. In *la plume*. In *el sol*. In *le chapeau*. In any shelter, any residence.

Love is necessary. The trees bow down, when Tom Gervasi passes. Who cares what gender they are?

The grass nibbles at his feet. Indoors, the rugs do. Love, from beneath.

The sun loves him. The air loves him. Women and other people love him.

The world is in love: with Tom Gervasi.

Everything in it loves him. The plants, the creatures, the spirits, the tools, the wood, the clay, the soap, the wet, all metals, glass, stone, precious objects, humble worthless objects—they join, in serenading him. They ring him, in a chorus.

He loves back. He loves everything. The world, and all therein.

(Title as aftermath:)

TOM GERVASI FINDS THAT HIS APARTMENT HAS A GENDER—IT'S FEMALE—AND IT LOVES HIM, AS A *HUMAN* DOES. IT JEALOUSLY SABOTAGES HIS FEMALE HUMAN GIRLFRIENDS WHO SLEEP OVER. IT TREATS ITS RESIDENT WITH WIFELY DEVOTION. IT SMOTHERS HIM, WITH DOMESTIC EMBRACE.

BUT HE'S A BACHELOR WHO LIKES To MOVE FREELY. HIS APARTMENT IS CLOSING HIM IN. IT'S WARMLY LOVING HIM TOO TIGHTLY, CLOSELY, INTIMATELY. IT'S ACTING TOO HUMAN—LIKE THE *OTHER* WOMEN. IT HUGS HIM IN A BREATHLESS HOLD OF LOVE. HE'S OOZING INTO ITS VERY FIBERS. IT'S HEMMING HIM ABOUT. IT CLOSES HIM IN. HE'S STUCK! HE MUST GET OUT! TO BREATHE THE AIR, OUTSIDE. TO FIND FREEDOM, FROM THIS FEMALE RESIDENTIAL EMBRACE.

TO BREAK FORTH—TO BREAK LOOSE. FROM DOMESTIC TIES. FROM HOUSEHOLD WIFELINESS THAT ASSUMES THE MANTLE OF GENDER FOR BETTER IMPLEMENTING THE TIES OF POSSESSIVE LOVE.

ESCAPE! UNDER THE *WORLD'S* ROOF! WHERE LOVE IS NOT SO *PERSONALLY* DIRECTED. WHERE LOVE IS MORE DIFFUSED, AS LEAVES, GRASS, AND STARS.

XV. HYSTERICAL FEMALE MOB STAMPEDE, LOVE-CRAZED, SET ON BY SYLVIA'S INFLAMATORY SPEECH, TO HOUND TOM GERVASI AS A MASS LOVE IDOL WHOSE PRIVACY IS RIPPED AWAY TILL HE TAKES REFUGE IN HIDING OUT OF TOWN. BUT HOW RETURN?

Sylvia took the tough line: "Love? Scientists have proven that it's just sixty-five percent romantic hogwash, with the remaining thirty-rive percent given over to sentimental bosh. That's a hundred percent. Anything left over from *that* is compounded of mere drivel, sheer air, and idiot twaddle. In short, it's not what it's cut out to be by those who have been driven out of their minds by it. In fact, it doesn't even exist. My skepticism is well borne out. Have you ever *seen* love? What color, shape, texture, is it? What does it smell like? What sound does it make? Like God, its existence is highly exaggerated by those who've made it a cult and who are lonely for fellow converts. Well, I won't be taken in! I'm well padded and layered over by protections of doubt, amour-proof armor. Once, I *nearly* succumbed—to a most heavenly man! I recovered in this, thanks to his coldness to me. I was fortunate. But billions of women are not. Nor are, as the legends would have it, billions of men. Love is a craze of reason. It softens our fibers from the inside, and makes us easy prey to diseases that stray in from the social fabric, of which I number delirium to be one."

Her audience was a group of women. They had banded together as "The Women's Defense League Against Love and Other Reactionary Phantoms." Sylvia was the principle speaker for tonight. She was renowned for the eloquent dogmatism of her point of view, and the vehemence of her rational approach. On *her* tongue, love had no chance. It waited in hiding, till the rain should stop.

In real life, however, Sylvia was—deep down in her utmost secret privacy where the public would never suspect there was anything that *had* to be hidden—in love: in the very love she had just spoken against. The object of this underground activity was Tom Gervasi, who was the only one to know about it. Unfortunately, his heart wasn't free. Twenty-five other women, at the time, loved him as well. Sylvia was along his least favorites of that batch. She got nowhere with him. The privilege of sharing his bed went to a certain few. The closest Sylvia had ever gotten to her idol was when once he shook her hand. She tried to preserve the memory by not using that hand for a few days. But then she forgot herself, and did him the disloyalty.

Loving Tom Gervasi was leading Sylvia on a royal road to nowhere. She phoned him asking for dates, but was refused, with ever diminishing courtesy; for his impatience only made Sylvia more silly and desperate in courting his unwillingness.

"Sylvia, don't phone me again, ever. I'm plainly trying to discourage you. Please take no for an answer. I never did, do not now, and never will, love you the least. Phone any more, and I'll take out a police warrant for harassment, invasion of privacy, coercion, badgering, hounding, nagging, and nuisance. Give up. Find a man who *will* love you: he's apt to co-operate more than I have. Let this be our final goodbye. Goodbye." A click: he had hung up. But not before humiliating her. "This proves my thesis," she sighed, "that love is not such a smart idea. Look what happens."

What a torrential downpour of an anti-love diatribe she memorably delivered in her next lecture in the packed, enthusiastically-applauding auditorium of "The Women's De-

fense League Against Love and Other Reactionary Phantoms"!
It went over overwhelmingly. She owed her secret inspiration,
of course, to Tom Gervasi. She determined to forget him. But,
finding herself remembering him, she had to guard against
the lapse by reminding herself to forget him anew. But she
forgot to remember to remind herself not to forget to cease
remembering altogether. So there he was, still on her mind.

She tried to take him off it. But he stuck there, like glue.

She was scheduled for one last final lecture at "The Women's
Defense League Against Love and Other Reactionary Phantoms." The auditorium was packed and enthusiastically ap-
plauding, and newspaper reporters were there to take down
notes. This occasion had the earmarks of becoming historic.
Sylvia aroused the tumult of an uproar, at the end of her
speech, with these words of dark warning to the assembled
women: "Women, I recommend you avoid love at all costs. But
more particularly, take particular care to avoid falling in love
with Tom Gervasi. He's the worst man any woman could ever
fall in love with. The suffering is virtually guaranteed at the
outset, in some acute cases, it could lead to suicide."

This produced a sensation, in the hall. The whole audience,
en masse, proceeded, upon hearing these ominous words, to fall
in love with Tom Gervasi, every last woman there, including
even the reporters. (No men reporters, as well as no men *anything*, were ever permitted at the meetings of "The Women's Defense League Against Love and Other Reactionary Phantoms."
The very presence of a man would be regarded as an obscenity,
a desecration of that solemn turf.)

Tom Gervasi became a mass idol, the rage, overnight.
Sylvia's listeners spread the contagion everywhere they went.
Poor Tom Gervasi was inundated by phone calls from lady

strangers, begging him for a date, or, barring that, then, at the very least, a vow of marriage. Tom Gervasi had his telephone number changed to a private secret one, to defend against callers at all hours. But the new number was passed out and made virtually public, for it was ferreted by snoopy sleuths who couldn't bear being deprived of hearing his radiant sleepy voice being woken up. He got no rest. He'd have to take a leave of absence from his job, and just skip town, till things should cool down. He got wind of who had unleashed this public female storm over his head: Sylvia was the culprit, who'd warned women against particularly himself, thus rousing a perverse mob reaction, a stampede that threatened to sweep him under the careless hooves of lovesick beasts. Such was Sylvia's retaliation, for being spurned.

He wouldn't take it meekly. But how fight back, against the amorous weight of such odds?

He had taken refuge in a friend's apartment. For peace. To plot his defense. Being a mass idol, of the female herd.

But word got around where he had taken refuge. The friend's apartment building was stormed, the friend's phone rang continuously till the receiver was left off the hook. A siege from red Indian war tribes could describe the turmoil now. Tom Gervasi *had* to skip town. What Sylvia had unleashed! All for spurning her! Was her heart so broken that retaliation brought so massive a revenge in the form of these hordes who were plaguing the peace of his life? Tom Gervasi's boss granted him an emergency leave of absence from the firm for escape from town and remaining away till female hysteria dies down. Yet Tom Gervasi's *return* to town, whenever that will be, could set off a revival and resurgence of this crowd behavior in riot to love craze for the devil singled out in Sylvia's stricture before

"The Women's Defense League Against Love and Other Reactionary Phantoms." How long can Tom Gervasi safely remain away? His return would find Sylvia ready again to kindle female conformity to a cult pitch.

Now, Tom Gervasi is in exile. Smuggled messages are sent back to town, suggesting how to silence Sylvia. It urges her death as a secret act, with the trace to be covered up. Her vigilance keeps him away. She must be done away with, in an undercover campaign, to make it safe for his unpublicized return. This murder is planned in self defense. Is it justified morally? Tom Gervasi had never considered murdering anyone before— or delegating the job, as in this case. But here, he had some attenuating reasons for an exception to his don't-murder-anyone habit. Sylvia had uprooted his life. She had set the mob for him (therefore against).

But even if Sylvia *were* to be eliminated, there was this realistic possibility, brooded in meditative exile by Tom Gervasi: she had already whipped and stirred up mob frenzy of love hysteria, so that, even were Sylvia to be dead, her work would already continue. The stampede would still be afoot, rumbling over her grave and hastening Tom Gervasi's descent to *his*. Therefore, murdering her might be futile. What could he do, to regain privacy upon return to town? Hounds of publicity were *waiting* for that return. Then the mob would get amorous again. They'd root out any place of refuge. They'd come in waves at him. He'd he a haunted celebrity. The target of love's dangerous multiple obsession, grown too far out of hand for police to intervene. Sylvia's plaguing him *alone* was one thing. He could have taken out a police warrant against her, for invasion of privacy and so forth. But the police couldn't stop a city-wide rampage of lovesick women out of control.

So Sylvia's death would make no difference. So Tom Gervasi stopped planning it.

His boss is inpatient. "When will you return? If not soon, you lose your job," came the message. For too much time away had Tom Gervasi been. The boss stopped understanding why. Business had to be attended to. It couldn't wait, for mob hysteria to stop.

Disguised as someone else, Tom Gervasi returned to town. But Sylvia set upon him, leading a new mob and the old one too, as Torn Gervasi's disguise proved flimsy and was seen through. He's set upon, as by a pack of hunting dogs. He's ripped to shreds. Violent love—for him, not by him—proved his downfall.

The love has quieted down. Sylvia has stopped loving him too, and all the city's women. They did him in. What more, could love do?

XVI. SUPERNATURAL RECOVERIES FROM DEATH AND MARRIAGE; IN MYTH-LIKE METAMORPHOSES TO REMAIN EVER THE LOVE-RESURRECTED TOM GERVASI.

Having killed Tom Gervasi, it was only fair that Love should also resurrect him. With its supernatural power, Love thus balanced out the death and charged him to represent Her anew.

As Love's conduit, vehicle, delegate, agent, and commissioned public servant, her upholder, minister, advocate, and performing priest, Tom Gervasi bounced right back from one of his deaths, to resume fully recharged. Subsequent marriages and deathless romances, eternal bonds, as well as deaths, will also have a "recovery" clause, allowing Tom Gervasi to go right on beginning again, in new potency cyclically refreshed for mythic metamorphosis in novel phase-variations from the coiled spring of his richly Protean sameness.

Love's servant assumes new forms. Tom Gervasi's version self-creates a consistent identity. In guises galore, to cover all women's heart-tastes, a multiple dream-dwelling by diverse romantic ranges upon this solitary person who's universally each women's "it": while retaining himself, in being the exclusive possession of women's central lonely desire.

He's their one answer. To all private intensities, in the female sphere.

XVII. WILMA WANTS TOM GERVASI FOR
HERSELF—IN HER EXCLUSIVE POSSESSION. LOVE,
HOWEVER, FORCES HER TO MAKE A DEGRAD-
ING COMPROMISE, AND SETTLE FOR A SHARING
INTEREST ON HIS POPULARITY-DECIMATED TIME.

Wilma decided: "I'm not one of many. If Tom Gervasi wants me,
he'll have to give up the others. I stipulate that, on condition of
ultimatum. It's me and no-one else; or all the rest, but not me."

Now, to *tell* him: What will *he* say? She may have to relent, or
concede a point, here or there, in surly compromise. He might
bargain her down *considerably*. Maybe they'll settle on a reduc-
tion of his harem—providing she be admitted—to half or, if she's
lucky, a third. Even then, she'd have far too many rivals. She
detested rivals; would eliminate them all, if she could. Ideally,
exclusive rights was her dream, in property of him. It thrust in
direct counter to his rather opposite ideal for unlimited quantity and roving freedom of license.

"Look, Wilma. Though I love you better than any of the others: in the cumulative aggregate in sum of collective ensemble
as a total whole, I love them more."

"Then eliminate *some*."

"How many?"

"Eliminate nine-tenths."

"No, for my love for those nine-tenths exceeds my love for
you alone."

"How can love go by quantity? Are you in the wholesale business? By mass job-lots and unit computation? *Quality* is love's
true core. Not numbers of greedy measurement, the loveless
soul of mathematics."

"Sorry, Wilma. I choose them, over you."

"If I agree to let you have me, then how many of then are you willing to sacrifice, in gift offering to my possessive pride?"

"A third."

"Then I'm yours. Share me, with the remaining two-thirds."

"You're a very welcome addition, Wilma. You'll be a valuable item on my roster."

" 'Addition,' 'item,' 'roster'—I *detest* those words. I feel like an object-thing."

"When we're alone together, I'll treat you as though you were not."

"Many intimate thanks, for that complacent assurance, patronizing, contemptuous, humiliating, degrading, infinitely reductive. Only my love for you compels me to accept those terms—whoreishly insulting."

"Wilma: You raised your voice! Be subdued, at once!"

"I will, master."

"That's a good Wilma. You're scheduled to sleep with me two weeks from Thursday. Make sure you're not having your 'period' then. If you are, we'll switch you to a later date."

"*We*'ll switch'? The corporate 'we'?"

"Very well; *I. I* take the responsibility."

"And I take the lowliness. Subjected. Love's slave."

"You'll grow accustomed to it. In time, your rebellious spirit will fade out. Servility is more traditionally feminine, to *my* approved taste. Well, take year place."

XVIII.

(Title at conclusion.)

Suddenly, out of thin air, gratuitous-seeming, arbitrary-coming, with chilling abruptness, Rosalie stopped meaning anything to Tom Gervasi: her image turned cold; his love wasn't there, any more.

"Look for it, look for it!" she begged. "You must have left it somewhere. Love is intangible, so it's easy to lose it, hard to locate where it dropped out. *Find* it, I beg you! It's there, *somewhere*. It didn't just vanish. An evil wizard didn't make it disappear—science wouldn't allow for that.

"It *must* be restored, fully, to your heart. I demand your love's total resumption, as though nothing had ever happened to interrupt its happy continuity within the constancy of your breast."

"Look, Rosalie, I don't *want* to find it again. It's not a tangible object. It has no height, width, or solid depth: it's not empirically concrete.

"Love is a *figure of speech*, so to speak. It's a sort of poetic metaphor, if you will, or abstract emotional concept deified into an absolute by sentimentalists of non-death.

"My love died, for you. I regret that, Rosalie. It's not Just lost: it's dead.

"You're dead, as my heart's desire. Go on living, for *yourself,* and eventually for a new boyfriend; to me, you're cold and dead as the Rosalie I loved. You're reborn to me: the post-love Rosalie, to whom I'm indifferent. That's your changed meaning, to me. Your changed existence, in fact, from my vantagepoint of choice and rejection. You're dead to me; but alive, in *fact*."

This little speech hardly spared Rosalie. But sometimes *blunt* surgery gets right to the heart of the matter. While, beating round the tissue-bush, skirting the issue of affliction, messing about with little kid gloves in neutral corners, turns out to produce consequences more mercilessly brutal, with intensified agony of prolonged crucifixion, torture's excruciating spasms accelerated to a dizzying pitch that permits no release from hell's conscious devils into numb oblivion's haven.

This was Tom Gervasi's premise, in being so direct in his rejection of Rosalie.

It worked. She fainted; went into an amnesia coma; was hospitalized; and in due time (though an enormous hospital bill had by then accumulated) woke up with total loss of who ever Tom Gervasi was. No trace of him remained in her convalesced memory.

Forgetting was her therapeutic blessing. Even his name wasn't there. The spot had been razed through, levelled down, exterminated.

Rosalie lived on, met a new man, married. The husband never knew there had been any Tom Gervasi. Rosalie shared his not knowing, to the fullest.

(Concluding title:)

INFORMING ROSALIE WITH SUCH BRUTAL DIRECTNESS—WHICH TURNED OUT TO BE MOST MERCIFUL—THAT SHE DIED TO TOM GERVASI. THE CURING HEAL STARTED IMMEDIATELY. NOW, *HE*'S DEAD TO *HER*. SO IT WORKED WELL. UTMOST PAIN, THEN COMPLETELY PAINLESS. NO TRACE OF THE WOUND. FRESH FLESH ENJOYS ITSELF, ON THAT SPOT.

XIX.

(Title after, not before.)

Mary, Elizabeth, and Catherine, of whom neither knew any of the other two, all loved Tom Gervasi, from a hopeful distance, waiting for him to break up with Audrey, a painful breakup protracted in torture and throbbing with grief. Painful? Torture? Throbbing grief? Who was feeling those things? Audrey alone? Or Tom Gervasi too? Audrey mainly, Tom Gervasi somewhat. Tom Gervasi could bear his own, but worried about Audrey and tried to help her get over the breakup, accept it, before it conclusively occurred.

Mary, Elizabeth, and Catherine knew what Audrey was going through. They knew it could happen to them, as well, if they persisted in their intentions of becoming involved with Tom Gervasi. How could they help but persist, being in love with him? Yet, there was Audrey's example, of what could happen. Poor Audrey was a horrible warning to them. Were they about to follow into her process, poor thing? They'd risk it, for love. But much depended, of course, on Tom Gervasi. He wouldn't accept all three of his waiting-in-the-wings adorers from afar; most likely, not even two of the three; maybe even not one. They might *all* be spurned. Being spurned seemed to be the only thing that would prevent them from following Audrey's dismal fate. Audrey *hadn't* been spurned: till so late, it really hurt. Mary, Elizabeth, and Catherine were love's eager victims, martyrs all, if *permitted* to be. Would Tom Gervasi save them, by saying no in advance? Their Audrey-like ordeal could only happen if Tom Gervasi first accepted them. Only he could save them—from themselves. They were so pathetically willing—as Audrey had been, the poor dear, suffering so greatly for it now.

A moth might be attracted by a burning light, thus costing it its life. Mary, Elizabeth, and Catherine are all-too-willing victims—potentially. Will Tom Gervasi ratify their voluntary martyrdom? For one, two, or all three? Or spare them all?

Audrey is going far away, to try to forget. Who's next? To the execution chamber? The chopping block? The viper's den? The lion's cage? The eagle's nest? The snake's pit? The land mine bomb? Courting disaster?

Please spare them, Tom Gervasi! In spite of themselves. Save them. Reject then *now.* Now, would mean mild pain; later, great.

Audrey is gone. Who's next? Don't let them, Tom Gervasi Say no, right away!

(Now for the title. It seems better placed, here:)

MARY, ELIZABETH, AND CATHERINE WANT TO FOLLOW AUDREY'S FOOTSTEPS, TO SUFFER FOR TOM GERVASI. MAY TOM GERVASI HUMANELY SPARE THEM SUCH AGONY, IN SPITE OF THEIR ALL-TOO-WILLING MARTYR-COMPULSION TO BE THE CANDLE-LOVING MOTH AND BE BURNED AT LOVE'S ALTAR. PREVENT THEM, TOM GERVASI. SAY NO, RIGHT AWAY. LATER, IT'S TOO LATE. AS IN AUDREY'S HORRIBLE EXAMPLE. CUT DOWN HUMAN SUFFERING. SAVE THESE BRAVE VOLUN-TEERS FROM AUDREY'S FATE OR WORSE. LOVE KNOWS NO LIMIT, AT PAIN'S POLAR BARRIER.

XX.

(A title of ambitious dimensions follows this text:)

Tom Gervasi reasoned thus: "What was God up to when He stuck women into His world creation? He must have had a plan in mind for them. They weren't just appendages, ornaments, frills. They served some real practical function. There was a purpose, an intention, to God's scheme. He wasn't just letting things appear idly. Now, what part were women conceived to play? Probably, to give men pleasure, as well as birth.

"Well, one woman *already* gave me birth, and the rule is that once that's done, no one else can do it for a fellow, it's a one-time-only proposition as far as any given fellow is concerned, in his once-only lifetime—the one life he has, to ruin or build or play with or all those things he does with it. So I *already* had my mother. Dear Mom, she's irreplaceable. She did her job, and that's what counts. First I was inside her, now I've been out, out to stay. Well, thanks, Ma. I'm eternally grateful. I can never thank you enough. Thanks a million, Ma. I'll take care of you when you're helplessly feeble and senile, I'll be a devoted son, you bet. I really appreciate it, Ma. Of course, Dad gets a bit of thanks, as well. Without the two of you, where would I have ever been? It's inconceivable, to imagine.

"So that takes care of one primary, principal, major reason God stuck women into the universe. Birth. One should never underrate it. So far as life goes, it's pretty essential. *Damned* necessary, in fact.

"Well, and the *other* reason God made women? To please men. Now, I really praise God for that. Women have done all right, by me. When they take their clothes off, a bit by bit, lingering at the underwear, slowly teasing me visually, my lust knows no bounds, and my excitement rushes out with eager joy.

"Then, when I'm actually stuck *into* them, with all that friction and motion that novelists have described in detail, or hinted at at least, or al'lude'd to, or intimated the intimacy of, well, God sure knew what He was doing, if men's pleasure was the scheme of the intention, the plan of the design, the purpose of the pudding.

"What a great sculptor-architect God was, in molding women to their form and function! Women are some of God's proudest handiwork. Real masterpieces, like any that Rembrandt or Breughel ever made. That's why I'm so religious. I owe it all to God. I've enjoyed mere of His women than most any man I know has. Therefore, I've got more to be religious about. Atheism is ingratitude, agnosticism is irresponsibility. Religion is recognition, and heartfelt thanks, and deep thanksgiving, of and for the pleasure women have afforded a fellow. Not just the carnal sort, but the wonders of love, the glorious romance of souls melted to a devoted unison of sweet and loyal concern for the absolute existences of each other. Women really complete the picture. God must have been inspired, or lecherous, when He had *them* in mind! What God gave, I take. And take. And take. And give. And give. Life is just simply terrific, this way. I hope it keeps up. But God tossed Death into the scheme. Too bad. It mars the picture. It's an unsightly blotch, on our Divine prospect."

(An elaborate title, fully spun out:)

THE RELIGIOUS PAGANISM OF TOM GERVASI, THANKING GOD FOR STICKING WOMEN INTO THE WORLD CREATION SCHEME. WHY HAD GOD

DONE IT? BY THEORIZING WHY, TOM GERVASI REVEALS HIS PERSONAL THEOLOGY: THE CREATION, ACCORDING TO SAINT THOMAS, APOSTLE OF LOVE, LECHERY, AND LOTS OF LATITUDE WITH WOMEN. THIS INCLUDES A DEVOTIONARY HYMN TO HIS MOTHER, WITHOUT WHOSE EARLY SERVICE LIFE WOULD NOT HAVE KNOWN TOM GERVASI; NOR WOULD PLENTY OF WOMEN, EITHER, AS IT TURNED OUT, LATER, RIGHT UP TO NOW, AND, FORESEEABLY BEYOND. THUS THE FUTURE OWES A LOT TO THE PAST. GOD BUILT LIFE ON A TIME SCALE. THIS PROVIDES THE POSSIBILITY OF MANY WOMEN, FOR TOM GERVASI'S SINGLE LIFETIME, IN SLOW STAGES OF INCOMPLETE MOMENTS. THUS, GOD DREW IT OUT, FOR HIM, FOR PLEASURE TO EVOLVE SHAPES OF VARIETY. WOMEN, AND MORE OF THEM. GOD'S GIFT, TO TOM GERVASI.

XXI. GRACE AND JOY—SELF-DECLARED CANDIDATES FOR THE POST OF MRS. TOM GERVASI. WELL, HOW DOES IT TURN OUT? IT'S UP TO HIM. ON HIS DECISION, DEPENDS THERE GRACE AND JOY.

Grace and Joy shared the same ambition: to become Mrs. Tom Gervasi.

However, that would depend a great deal on what, of course, Tom Gervasi himself thought, on the matter.

Grace and Joy wanted to *influence* how Tom Gervasi thought on the matter.

Each sought to impress herself so favorably upon his romantic heart's lust, as to favorably impress him, to the extent that he'd press his suit to woo for her hand with dashing courtship. Such was their identical goal. Two girls, with but one Tom Gervasi to win.

But what did *he* think? Yes, what did *he* think?

He gave not a damn for either! Not a pence or a fig. They were "outside the running," and had as much chance of co-featuring in a wedding with him as Tom himself did with that fabled heroine of yore, Helen of Troy, who attracted Greeks and Trojans alike, so universal had she been, in those dim old days of modern pre-history celebrated in epic style by that bard of bards, Homer, the all-seeing blind man.

Back, however, to Grace and Joy. They really felt the "hots" for Tom Gervasi! They'd squirm in their panties, just drooling to think about him.

What *he* thought, of course, mattered more. His was the vote of weight. His was the power, to decide.

How'd he *use* that decision? Unfavourably, in the case or both applicants. "Thumbs down," in brutal rhetoric.

Grace and Joy wept. That was what was left to them. Big, rolling, juicy tears. Each tear mirrored Tom Gervasi's sacred image, enshrined in miniature. Then it burst.

Poor Grace, poor Joy. Dead hopes. No ideal marriage. Gervasiless, for life.

Doomed Gervasiless. Too widows, gazing at their long-lost hope through the darkening, raindrop-stained, dim windows of their souls. Gazing, into lost remoteness. No grace, no joy, for either. Nursing virgin grief. Next stop: the tomb.

XXII. MARJORIE AND JENNIFER MEET. IT'S TOM GERVASI'S DOING. LOVING HIM, THEY HATE EACH OTHER. THEY HAVE A SHOWDOWN. *FOR* HIM? NO, *AGAINST.* THEY PREFER EACH OTHER, THANK YOU.

Marjorie and Jennifer didn't know each other. Well, *most* people don't know each other: especially the ones who live in different cities or countries, or even different centuries.

Marjorie and Jennifer lived not only in the same century, but in the same city. But still no chance brought them together; but not for long. They're "bound" to meet, and quite soon. Their meeting will have Tom Gervasi to thank, as its catalyst.

Tom Gervasi shares their city and century. Also, lately, their beds. He's been alternating them as girlfriends over a simultaneous spell of time. As both love him, they hate each other unseen. "Who's this other woman?" Marjorie asks. She's answered only with the name: "Jennifer." Jennifer asks the same; she's answered, "Marjorie." Tom Gervasi is discreet, he respects privacy and doesn't betray confidences. He protects each from the other. But not to the extent that he can prevent their mutual hatred, sight unseen. They *imagine* what each other must be like. Marjorie imagines Jennifer to be quite unlike the way Jennifer really is. Likewise, Jennifer imagines Marjorie to be *one* way, but in actuality . . .

They demand a showdown. From two sides, they force their lover-in-common to bring them together. They'll clash, settle, resolve, this stormy issue.

Tom Gervasi is their link, their broker. He's their point, their angle, their circle. He's their fulcrum, lever, pivot, or seesaw. He's the odd one, whereas they're even.

At the meeting, both turn against him. From combatants, they've become allies. From loving the same man, they've gone to hating him. Jointly. As a pair. Together.

Marjorie said, "So you're Jennifer! I had imagined you as some ogre, some man-eating monster. But now I've encountered you, I think highly of you. We have an affliction in common: Tom Gervasi. He's been our bane. He played us off, for his erotic delight and romantic vanity, against each other. It perversely stimulated him, like a wicked fetish. Let's gain some measure of revenge. I detest him, now. Don't you?"

"Oh darling Marjorie! I agree with every word you said. He's our nemesis, our curse. We were destined to meet, but he kept us apart. He delayed the friendship we were fated for. (Although he was the agent, the catalyst, for bringing us together, I prefer the grander notion that we were meant for each other, and would have met, anyway.) Well, let's deal harshly with him. His being our mutual adversary will of course cement our new friendship: having an enemy-in-common is great for making alliances firmer. Let's kiss each other, and beat him up."

And that's what they do, in his own apartment. They quite "manhandle" him. They mete out a stern measure of punishment. Their love for him is transferred to each other. Have they become Lesbian lovers? That's a bit immodest. Let's say that they're *platonically* homosexual.

Are in arm, without so much as a glance back, they leave Tom Gervasi lying there in some daze of stupor, and storm out or his apartment, matching strides, in glee and joy for being liberated from Tom-Gervasi-tyranny, concurrently with their mutual discovery of Jennifer as Marjorie's Saviour, Marjorie as Jennifer's, the double deliverers of each other from travail, servitude, and misinformed enmity for each her glowing best friend now.

Tom Gervasi staggers up. "Two losses, in one night. Both my girlfriends. But what a blissful gain *they* made! They have a double find, I have a double loss. Well, I've done it all for *them*. Why be selfish?' I made them happy. It was my *duty* to. As their lovers, both."

XXIII. THE SELF-PUNISHED TRIGAMIST.

Jane, Boss, and Lynne: Jane's face, Bess from shoulders to waist, Lynne from hips on down. Jane's face was ideal; Bess'es middle the ideal; Lynne's lower the ideal.

All loved Tom Gervasi and wanted to marry him. He requested that each submit to death, to the surgical table, and to the three being reincarnated off the surgical table as one freak ensemble of the ideal parts of each, a crossbred montage mongrel jigsaw stained-glass collage combining the superior parts of each and eliminating—rather ruthlessly—all the rest. Would they agree?

That one incarnated supreme survivor of three deaths would embody the select taste of Tom Gervasi in face, middle, and lower parts; Jane, Bess, and Lynne: all deathlessly represented, in one magnificent specimen.

They wondered, before agreeing: would each one retain her own conscious identity as a personal unique self, after dying and being woven as a third into two-thirds foreign matter? The surgeon said yes. Tom Gervasi beamed. He, the surgeon, and the three guinea-pig girls were in a high-level conference, to decide the latters' fate—or rather, fates.

They gave the go-ahead, then, and went to the operating theater. There, the surgeon killed all or them (Tom Gervasi winced, as the only spectator), and on the surgical table, grafted, with skillful dexterity, Jane's dead face, Bess'es dead shoulder-to-waist section, and Lynne's hips-on-down section.

The result: a magnificent monster. The ideal parts of each just didn't match, when put together into an attempted single unity as an all-embracing woman. The new creature lived, but she was a monster. Tom Gervasi regretted this experiment, but had pledged, alas, to marry it.

He was as good as his word, being a man of honor. The monster wouldn't let him out of it. So with revulsion, with repulsion, with a shudder of "ugh!", he married the loathsome creature—was it a "her," or really an "it"? "It" seemed more likely. Ugh!

Now, he's stuck. He's mocked, by those who used to envy and respect him, admire and esteem him, for that dreadful "wife" of his, who's accepted nowhere, as a unanimous social outcast in all respectable circles.

Oh, Tom Gervasi's regret! He tries to sue the surgeon; but loses the case. He's stuck. With a foul "wife." Like Caesar's old Gaul, she's divided into three parts. None fits. They're all warring. Internecine, civil warfare. No inward grace or radiance.

Three clashing egos. In one foul machine.

※

Divorce. That's Tom Gervasi's next step. The monster refuses. He's stuck. He *made* this awful bed: now he lies in it.

The whole is different from its parts. Learned the hard may, this lesson sinks in.

Too late. The deed is done. He can't *un*do it: by making this monstrosity robot into its three original constituents, all of Jane, all of Bess, and all of Lynne. It can't be done. The surgeon says as much. It can't be done.

No restoration. The damage endures. One horrible wife. Of three women, in a drunken, three-way squabble of endless discord: with each other: and with their bright victim, their husband-in-common, their open scapegoat, the repentant fool, whose foolishness endures in this perpetual creature.

What a mess! "Till death do we part."

Will all three die at once? Or one by one? Either way, it's no treat, this wait. The *waiter* might die, ahead of the waited-for-to-die. Husband Tom Gervasi. The self-punished trigamist.

XXIV. DOLORES RESISTS TOM GERVASI WITH INDIFFERENCE. BEFORE FINDING OUT WHY, HE PRACTICALLY WRECKS HIMSELF. THEN SLOWLY RECOVERS, ONCE THE WHY IS KNOWN.

Dolores, damn her, was so different from the other women: she was able to resist Tom Gervasi! By what means did she accomplish that extraordinary thing? That unassailable defense: Indifference.

Infuriated by that resistance, where all the other women had sooner or later succumbed to his heralded irresistibility, Tom Gervasi rose to it like a challenge, and vowed to rip it apart.

How dare Dolores be calm in his presence? It insulted the solidity of years of reputation. He'd go to work on her, with the wrath of vengeance, till she sings a different tune: the love-cry.

He'll melt her resistance down like the sun of spring to thaw the stubborn ice into rivulets of oozy ooze. Her icy indifference fortress will run and drip, and give way to glaring holes that widen till all the structure has gone. She's so beautiful! She's lovely. He'll work her into his spell. With his magic charms of the King Male that rules the top city's densely overlaid sexual jungle. Dolores will he brought to heel.

He pursued her, he pursued her. Dolores was immune; impervious; icy; disdainful.

He tried harder, he tried with all his might. He tried so hard, that *he* fell in love—with *her.*

Deaf people often talk loudly in the attempt to set a volume standard which other voices would rise up to, thus making it easier for the deaf person to hear. Tom Gervasi fell in love with Dolores in the process of attempting to persuade *her* to do so with *him.* He thus fell into his own trap. While he wriggled in there, Dolores calmly overlooked him. While he struggled, Dolores smiled. "Why Tom Gervasi! Can *you* be in love with *me*? With all your might, you had tried to get *me* to feel that for *you*. Well, you turned your table upon yourself. I refuse to love you. Love me all you will, for all the good it'll do you. I'll not follow suit, nor at all reciprocate. Suffer, you fool! Your own weapons miss-shot, and damaged you: backfiring, it's called. Live by the sword, and die by it. Well, well. You're in my power. You cast your net, and it went over your head to hold your own arms fast. Too bad. I reject you, firmly. And that's final. Love on, in vain. Ha! No mercy. I'm quite enjoying it."

Dolores was cruelly playing with him. Why, having succeeded with so many women, had he failed with her, though turning on his charms full blast and training them powerfully against her? To what was his failure due? She was in love with another man? Therein is the probable answer.

He did research, and found, no, no other man. Further investigation brought this to light: Dolores loves women, not men: a lesbian.

Then, he fell out of love, with that finding. Now, he's recovered: Wobbly, unsteady, semi-convalescent, unsure on his feet: but the worst is over. He's surviving her. A lesson well learned: don't get riled if a woman should resist him, with tepid, cold, or lukewarm indifference. Don't construe it as an all-out challenge. It could wreck him. First, see if she's a lesbian. That would explain it; and leave his honor intact; and be no slur, on his private pride or public reputation. Look and find out: *then* leap.

XXV. TOM GERVASI, WITH LINDA AND MURIEL (BOTH RECENT) AND HELEN (A RELATIONSHIP GOING FURTHER BACK), ALL THREE OF WHOM LOVE HIM WITH COMPETITIVE ARDOR AND DESPERATE DETERMINATION TO OUTRIVAL EACH OTHER. BUT IT EXHAUSTS HIM MOST. HE REBELS, AND BECOMES TRANSFORMED. LOVE, SEX, AND THE THREE WOMEN ALSO ALTER. READ HOW ALL THIS COMES ABOUT. IT'S INTERESTING, ANYWAY.

Linda loved Tom Gervasi, but in secret. Muriel loved him in secret as well. Linda and Muriel, however, didn't know each other. And both barely knew Tom Gervasi. A woman who *really* knew Tom Gervasi was Helen. But Helen knew neither Linda nor Muriel. Helen worshipped Tom Gervasi—not from afar, but from up close: they were in a scorching affair. But Tom was tiring of her. He heard that Linda and Muriel secretly loved him, from their shy distances, and decided that the Helen bond was growing stale and tedious. He'd give Linda a try, then Muriel. Or maybe both in the same overall time span, alternating one night with one, another with the other. However, Helen wouldn't let Tom go. She sensed his increasing indifference to her, but grew more desperately attached to him. Tom met Linda, asked her out. Then he dated Muriel as well. The better to get rid of Helen, he told her of his double infidelity to her. She became terribly jealous, but doubled her insistent possessiveness over his reluctance and unwillingness. Tom's life got really complicated. He was seeing two new women and trying to unsee a third; and he wee loved by all three. It was more than he had bargained for. It kept him dancing on his toes. Helen did some research work, found out how to contact Linda and Muriel, and arranged that all three should meet to try to thrash out the Tom Gervasi problem between them. The three rivals met. No two of them had ever met before. Neither had all three met before, of course. Each insisted that Tom Gervasi was *hers* and hers *alone*. They made no progress, whatever.

It degenerated into a shouting match. Helen maintained, as the ringleader and instigator of the meeting itself, that Linda and Muriel should both back off, resign from the competitive fray, and leave the field free, by their voluntary double-elimination, for Helen herself to fully reclaim the rightful prize that the two newcomers had kindheartedly renounced in fair abdication to Tom Gervasi's true owner by seniority of long-love possession, Helen, whose queenly reign had kept him equal throne. Linda and Muriel, however, vehemently disagreed. "He needs new blood," they stubbornly maintained. In spirit, Tom was there, surrounded by those Three Graces. They fought over him like cats, not noble goddesses. They raged and scratched. They were demons, made demonic by the demon who possessed them, the Tom Gervasi demon, who gives quiet women claws of rage and teeth sharpened to ferocity's blood-scent.

The meeting became a shambles. Instead of peaceful arbitration to determine who should lawfully walk off with Tom Gervasi (as if he ever would have abided by *their* decision!), it degenerated to irrational screech and undignified scream. Even hair-pulling was resorted to! Lucky for all three that their idol wasn't invisibly watching them be reduced to a common puddle of disgrace.

The meeting broke up. Actually, it broke down. The result: inconclusive.

Helen said to Tom Gervasi, "I won't let you go. You're mine. Go on, take out a police warrant on me. I have my own key to your apartment, which I'll use freely. Even if you change the lock, I'll go on haunting you. I refuse to be gotten rid of by you. It's a clash of wills. But mine is charged with love, and will relentlessly defy yours. I'll never be ousted, from my customary hold over you. I've thrashed it out with Linda and Muriel. *They* oppose me, too. Each wants to be my successor. I just won't let them. I refuse to be replaced. I've grown accustomed to you. How can I relinquish the Lord of my Heart? I venerate your shrine, and have squatter's rights there. I've rented a permanent home, in the Temple of You. I reside by divine right at my Master's hearth. Evict me, if you can. As tenant, I'm *your* landlady: I'm the porter and superintendent of the premises, and own shares in our real estate. I go with the land: that is, I stay with it."

"Oh, go home!" Tom Gervasi replied, somewhat peeved.

"But I *am* at home. You *are* my home." Then she seduced him, and they made love. Then the phone rang. It was Linda, asking him for a date. Tom made one with her, right on the phone, within hearing distance of the livid Helen. *That* business concluded, the phone again rang. It was Muriel. "I rang before, but your phone gave a 'busy' signal. Please, let's make a date." So, again within hearing of the even more livid Helen, Tom eagerly obliged. Quite a busy man! Loved by three active women, who fought like tigers over him. His cup ran over, at both ends. His candle waxed at either side. He burned his water, and ate it.

He dated Linda, and she sexually exhausted him in her apartment while Helen waited in *his*, in vain, all night, sobbing, for his return. Next night, he saw Muriel, who wouldn't let out of *her* apartment, and drained him dry of all his sperm. He was not the Sultan in the Harem. Three women were Sultans, in *their* harems, to whom he was the only slave. He loved none of the three. But Linda and Muriel were of greater interest to him than Helen, being excitingly new. But their exciting newness would in turn, in time, wear off dull. Then younger women would appear, over Tom Gervasi'e juicy, replenished horizon. He'll never age. Not with ever younger blood to nourish him vigorously young.

He changed the lock to his apartment, so that Helen's key to it become obsolete. But she stalked him, and hounded him, in person, waiting outside his office building, or inside his apartment building's lobby, to waylay, intercept, molest, harass, the object of her obsession, the destroyer of her pride. She couldn't afford pride. She had two eager, active rivals. She wouldn't abandon the fight to them. She'd carry the fight to him, anywhere, everywhere. She even waited outside *Linda's* apartment, and outside *Muriel's,* exposing herself to scorn, contempt, embarrassment. She just couldn't desist. She was driven. Their love *couldn't* be over! No, it was just a temporary mistake. Soon to be made right. Just a momentary aberration, now, to interfere with Destiny. Soon to be set to rights. Redeemed. Made whole, purified of this current corruption, this insane violation of the Lawful Scheme to Be. She'll reassert her dominion, and re-establish her rightful claim. It's just a drunken dream, now. The focus has gone mad. She'll wake up serene. When, oh Lord? And how long?

While Helen went through her interminable tunnel of grief, life wasn't *too* much more fun for either Linda or Muriel. Their *holds* over Tom Gervasi were too slight, too tenuous, too ever tentative, in light of their drastically increased, deeply dependent devotion for him. They were in agony over each other, in the keen outcry of jealousy. And they were tormented about Helen, who, both feared, would wield the magic of tradition and sacred memory as weapons of winning Tom back through nostalgic regression. She once *did* own him. And that, at least, enlisted Time's Past, as her invaluable ally, in case Tom should weaken in his present life and revert to deep sentiment of far ago, presided over by the comeback-bound ghost of the once and possibly future Helen. Thus, relatively recent Linda and Muriel had to contend with Tom's unpredictable memories, some of which could bind him to dear old loyalty and to former enchantments. To oppose which, they would insert their vigorous, persistent presences to keep his consciousness busy and his ardor ever occupied. They were building future "pasts" with him themselves. Now after now after now, are deposits in the bank bound to bear interest upon the maturing of the bond.

The newcomers concentrated on his body. The sooner any new sperm was secreted into the buds of potency, the sooner Linda and Muriel, by turns, pumped him dry of the last sweet drop. How could Tom manage to keep it up? Sex dwindled to stale tedium. So repetitive, so dreary! Ah, for the golden life of a eunuch! Chastity and abstinence loomed high, in Tom's altered ideals. To mortify the flesh became his monkish aspiration. Lust became disgusting. Delight dropped out of sensuality, which was now associated with stern, solemn duty, with moral obligation, with bondage, repetitive servility, custom's tyranny, stale hypocrisy. Carnality was repugnant. He prayed for Pure guidance. The Soul, disembodied. Cleansed, of women-vermin.

It was a revulsion against fleshly sins. He refused carnal intercourse, in horror, with Linda- and Muriel, neither of whom could coax him to rescind his stern prohibitions. As for Helen, she enjoyed a revival—but platonic. He became "friends" with all three. No more manhood toward them. "Just friends," now.

It worked! All three stopped loving him—though it took quite a long time. Linda had a new boyfriend, Muriel had a new boyfriend, and Helen, in fact, consoled herself with several. All three were "very fond" of good-old-Tom. They thought the very world of him! But passion, romance—both struck off, for Tom's name. He was their "brother." All three confided in him, about their current love problems with other men. They kissed him—like sisters. He had cured them—and himself. Too well, in his own case. For when he met other girls, he found himself impotent with them. Not just impotent, but harmless. Sweet, kind, gentle—but undangerous. He had gone too far—to the other side—in rooting out ugly lust. Just a temporary imbalance? To be, in due time, straightened out? He'll see. But he can't function, in bed. He's a dud, there. And, for once, he's unloved: How strange!

XXVI. TOM GERVASI AND THERESA DUNN: A LOVE MATCH? WHO'D WIN, WHO'D LOSE? THEY'RE BOTH TOPS IN THEIR LEAGUES, WITH PERFECT RECORDS. WHY DON'T THEY MEET, FOR THE SUPREME CHAMPIONSHIP?

When the irresistible force meets the immovable object,—well, it depends, on *which* force, *which* object, *when, how,* and other specifics in the particular case. If two irresistible forces meet, you'll have a championship combat. It would be a showdown, and *one* of their records of continuous success would fall. Only one can triumph, if two oppose. There's a tournament of competitive elimination, until just two unvanquished ones remain. They collide head-on. One supreme victor will emerge. That's the sporting result. But in the *romantic* arena . . .

Tom Gervasi had a perfect record. But so did Theresa Dunn. *He* knocked out all the women; she all the men. Each looked for new fields to conquer. Tom *exuded* mastery over women; Theresa over men. Both were at the top of their game. Both were at the peak of their skills. They were in winning form. The odds always favored them both. Most women were pushovers for Tom; most men for Theresa. The *difficult* women, Tom aims found a way of edging out, to retain his victory record; likewise with Theresa, and the difficult *men.* Each was surpassing, whoever the opponents, so far. But they had never met *each other.* Who would "give," in *that* event? It would be a fight to the death. Tom would *never* lose; but neither would Theresa. Neither had ever tasted the pall of defeat. But if those two champs were to meet—this tussle would go into history. It would be a rare event.

The world will never know who will have won. That's the loss for all us fans. Theresa Dunn slayed her adversaries in Great

Britain; Tom Gervasi ruled in North America. Each occasionally traveled to the other's vast territory; but they never ever met. Alas. We'll never know.

What would have happened? Let's guess, and record our conjectures, concocting a hypothetical romance. It would have been the dream bout, the pace-setting standard, a love affair to end all love affairs, in the annals of recorded history, as the top *our* age should boast of. Or would it have been a lop-sided contest? Would one *easily* have toppled the other? Idle speculation. We'll never clinch a positive result, in the deep awe of our wonder. Tom Gervasi. Theresa Dunn. King and Queen. On separate thrones. In separate kingdoms. In separate reigns. Majesties both. Unscathed on field of battle. Love has never claimed either for victim. Love loses. For neither has ever lost. Love falls, for them both.

They vanquish love. They're indomitables. Love is no match, for either. The only chance it ever had, never took place. Who's supreme? Love loses, for failure of proof. Their full test, that would-have-been, drifted off to dark myth. To fantastic mystery. To unbelievable fable. To an impossible legend.

Create it. Give it a shape. *Invent* what happened. We *need* this invention. we can't serve two Gods. Which? Either, but definite. Complete the tale. The season *begs* to conclude. As is, it's suspended. It's frozen, in deadlock. Arrested, in mortal grip.

Provide a thaw. Is it Tom Gervasi, this side's champ? Or Theresa Dunn, who rules that side? Matchmake them! Promote the event! To a decision! To the death, of all doubt. To a reign of one ruler. Supreme, in fair contest.

XXVII. A TIME-BENT TRIANGLE: MIKE BUCK, MICHELLE BELL, TOM GERVASI. AN INNOCENT TRIANGLE, DEVOID OF TRADITIONAL CONFLICT.

When Mike Buck was a little boy, his father warned him that he'd beat Mike up unless Mike grew up to be a real, rugged, brutal he-man. As it turned out, Mike became an effeminate homosexual. But his father died too early to be able to carry out his promise to beat Mike unless . . .

Anyway, Mike felt guilty toward his father. He was desecrating his father's memory, by posthumously proving to be such a disappointment. How could he "make it up" to his father, by way of a propitiatory act of atonement for an unmistakable crime in identity? He was too "gay" to he a great athlete or warrior. So what was left? He thought hard. His father could wait, being dead.

It would have to be something momentous, drastic, what with so much to make up for, this single act. It would have to be an earthshaker, within the world of Mike Buck's life. A complete upheaval, a forcible break with the past. It would have to crack open his father's grave, and apologize to the grim old ghost: "Beat me up, Pa; I didn't become the man you said I had to be. But I'm so contrite, Pa, this is what I *did* do . . ."

Finally, he knew what it should be. He took out his bank savings from years of office employment, and got on a plane to a Scandinavian country. There, he entered a special hospital, to undergo major surgery that would totally reverse his sex. He came out a woman. He was no longer Mike Buck. He was Michelle Bell. His father would never recognize him. Just as well.

The new woman returned to ex-Mike Buck's old city in North America. To *prove* herself a woman, she had to have a man. A *real* man, the man of all men. The one her father would have wanted her to become. She got a new job in a new office, using her old skills as a man: typing, filing, expert clerical work, with a good business head. An office boon, at *any* sex.

She made friends with some of the other female workers. She confessed that she had no boyfriend; that she was from out of town; that she knew no men in this city. She concluded that, being quite glamorous, she could reasonably expect the Prince of Men for her boyfriend. Did the others know such a rare specimen? If so, could they arrange an introduction? Matrimony was her covert aim, she readily admitted. With no less than the Prince of Men. Who knew him well enough to produce him? Michelle Bell was lucky. One of her office colleagues did know such a man. "He's a friend of my husband," said the knower. "He's the idol of women far and near. Wherever he goes, he leaves a cloud of romance behind. But he could break your heart. It's *your* risk, Michelle; do you want to take it?"

Michelle said yes, she'd dare it. So a dinner party was arranged, at the apartment of the couple who knew this great Prince of Men. Michelle was all prepared to fall in love. She had loved men before—but never as a woman. She'd make her virginal debut, as Michelle Bell with her first beau. She was all in a fluster. She blushed with immodesty. Her excitement, as the hour for the dinner party approached, mounted in pants and gasps. She was in womanly heat, for the first time in her turnover life. What would it be like—her first "normal" date? Ah, her father would be proud—of the Prince of Men. Not having been able to *be* him, she'll do the next best thing: *acquire* him, as her own. That should be ample compensation, for her absurd disobedience to her father's brute command.

When the dinner party concludes, this Prince will take Michelle home. She'll seduce him, and have her first unperverse experience in the ancient history of sexuality. She'll be a *normal* woman; not an abnormal man. She'll be frankly accepted, by the whole world.

When she had been Mike Buck, she had never come to terms in accepting her "deviation." It was her secret shame—or "his." Now, she could qualify. She'll have made a proud conquest, of . . . the Prince of Men!

He turned out to be Tom Gervasi. Michelle was beautiful. He *did* take her home. She *did* entice him. To his acute surprise, he found himself deflowering a virgin. "Why were you a virgin so late?" he asked, later. (They were lolling in bed.)

"To save myself for *you*," Michelle coyly replied. "The men who came along before you wouldn't do. It *had* to be you. So I waited."

This flattery practically knocked Tom off the bed. "Then marry me," he said. She agreed. They were engaged. In time, they *did* marry. Tom never found out that his bride was the former Mike Buck. No one from her past was around to inform him. Her mother had died a bit after her father. She had no brothers or sisters. They lived a long married life, with several children into the bargain. Tom was never told. He never need know. This true story cannot be published till Tom Gervasi's death. He's close to that now. So am I. I'm Michelle Bell. Hello, reader. I'll be dead, when you read this. Tom will be, too. Our children will find out, when this is published. If it shocks them, they'll recover. They're worldly, mature. Well, I'll attend to Tom, now. He's in a wheelchair. He'll never walk again. He's old, crippled, infirm. But in his prime—what glory! I married him, I know. He *was* the Prince of Men. The man *I* should have been, had my father gotten his wish. Are you satisfied now, father? You lost a son—but, in the end, gained one. As good as—or better than—you would have had me be. I did the right thing. I obeyed you, in the end. Forgive me, father. In *his* name.

XXVIII. KATEY GETS A TOM GERVASI CURE FOR INABILITY TO LOVE. WHEN THAT CURE TURNS OUT BAD, SHE NEEDS A CURE FOR *THAT.* THEN SHE'S *REALLY* CURED. BUT LONELY, ALAS.

Katey was cured of a cold heart that had never loved anyone before. The cure was in the person of Tom Gervasi. But now that Katey was cured, with her new found ability to love, the cure became a curse, when her love went unreciprocated, to give her pangs of pain.

What could cure the cure, then? For the first cure—loving blissfully—had turned to a broken heart.

The cure's cure would be a healed heart of indifference. Time provided that cure, much to Katey's relief.

Now, she's *so* cured, she's overcured. Man after man after man—all of them non-Gervasis—asks for her heart in love, for marriage. "No more love," she replies. "I'm overcured, of *that* disease."

Moral: Love at your own risk. In learning *not* to love, through prior injured love, take the risk for *not* loving, as well. It's a deep risk: a loveless life, alas.

XXIX. TOM GERVASI AND HIS JILL, JILL AND HER TOM GERVASI, BETWEEN THEM THERE'S A ONE-NESS, AND THEY BOTH RUSH IN TO FILL IT, LEAVING SEPARATE SELVES BEHIND, TO FEUD AS THEY WILL. CONVERGENCE IS TRUE LOVE'S OWN MOTION.

Tom Gervasi was confused: he wasn't sure whether Jill loved him, or he loved Jill. That's how entwined they were, all wrapped up in each other. It had been going on for so long, that by now they felt like incestuous Siamese siblings stuck permanently together by a rich confusion of their flesh.

Their four legs and four arms would be twisted like pretzels through, around, and between each other. Tom sometimes thought that an arm of Jill was his, or her leg, or even her face. That's how all knotted they were, within their two joined bodies, as though a *third* were made thereby, with extra snake twinings putting out multiple tentacles like a narcissistic octopus.

It was, of course, erotic confusion. Sometimes they couldn't tell their pleasures apart—who was feeling what. If Tom sneezed, Jill would feel her own nose quivering as though it had been her sneeze from which joint vibrations were slowly subsiding.

"Where's the old Tom Gervasi?" he asked himself when he was alone. "I'm getting dragged into Jillness. I'm one of her extensions. I'm going though a compounding. I'm so intertwined, that I dread the irrecoverability of the unique me I once was.

"I must disentangle myself. Jill's scent is on my person. Her hairs cling to my body, even after a hearty shower. My mouth is still rinsed with her words. Her personality sometimes uses me as a spare outlet. Her ideas sometimes percolate through my own pre-articulation process of thought refinement. Recently, one of her fingernails was on one of my fingers. I'm even growing a breast, on the right side, akin to hers. Even my family history is being welded to hers.

"We're like two separate trees who've joined roots and partake of the same earth nourishment. We're welded, we're wedded.

"I want my individuality back. If I don't get it back soon, then soon I *won't want* it back; for my *will* has been coupled with Jill's.

"We're a close pair. *So* close, we're at one.

"That's love's ideal, isn't it?

"But the *cost* is too great. I don't want, in the process of this total enmeshment with her, to wake up finding I'm no longer me as a self, but merely a part of 'Us.'

"If the Government is too Federalized, then States' Rights are endangered. But if the states are given too much autonomous power, then the federal unity is endangered. Either way, loss accompanies gain.

"Do I want to lose myself into Jill? Or to regain myself by withdrawing from the Jill union? Gain and loss, with *either* decision.

"There's the key in the lock: Jill's. She returns. I'm lost."

"I'm back again, Tom. To be one with you."

"Jill, where am *I*, if I'm at one with *you*?"

"You *still* have your*self*: I won't eat it up, in our unity process. It won't dissolve, as a weaker catalyst in our compounded chemicality. You'll be every inch *you*. That strengthens the *Us*."

"You swear that?"

"Don't take the liberty of seceding from our Union. It would grieve me so—I'd be lost, without you; unbuttressed, moorless, floating, a pin shot loose from the magnetic field, the Fallen Angel from Miltonian Heaven.

"Let's wed."

"I'm afraid, Jill. Will I *still* be *me*, if we're married?"

"No loss of liberty. Rather, freedom's broad gain, solidified by background and rich context.

"You and I are the axis of a universe. We're a solar system, a whole galaxy. As a star, you'll twinkle brighter, in firm place, in the Firmament."

"All right, Jill. If we're *that* close, and yet are still apart, and I won't lose my 'me' within our system of 'us,' then, indeed, let's wed."

"We *are* wed; but you mean officially—in social convention."

"Yes. *We* mean that."

"Did I put the words in your mouth?"

"They issued from *your* mouth."

"Tom, it's *our* mouth."

"Then we have two mouths?"

"Yes, count them: two noses, four ears, four eyes, two sets of hair, two necks, four arms, two groins, four legs, one male set of genitals, and one female."

"With all those assets, we could go into business. They'd be our capital stock. We'd enjoy a low overhead. And profit, in our partnership."

"Those were *your* words, Tom? I *thought* them."

"Jill, are we really *us*?"

"Yes; you and I are."

"Only we ourselves, alone."

"Yes, my dear and only."

"Is *this* 'love,' then?"

" 'Love' wasn't *before* this; 'love' is defined, *by* this."

"So essence follows existence; existence precedes essence."

"Yessence. *We* make reality. Concepts are derived from *that.*"

"Let's be married, in social terms."

"I'm *with* you, Tom. Let's stand together, on that."

"A united front?"

"*And* back. My dear half."

"Am I your dear half? But you're mine."

"We're a whole, Tom; wholly so."

"On the whole are we; not partially?"

"*Wholly*, by all that's holy."

"Now holy matrimony."

"As a way of letting the world know. To make our private oneness a public matter. Like *publishing* a book, instead of burning a diary."

"I agree."

"*I* agree."

"Then we *both* do."

"We don't do things by halves."

"Yes we do: by *double* halves."

"So we're the halves—as opposed to the haves-not."

"Yes, to halve and to have not."

"Let's kiss, and put all our lips in operation. Our mouths had been speaking. Now let them speak *for* us. And into our kiss let's pour our mingled breaths. Our souls dance on admixture, and so do join."

"Did *you* speak that?"

"Did I? And you thought it?"

"Who know? It's from our same business. And goes back in."

"For your business *is* mine. And *I* mind yours."

"Then it's the corporate 'we'?"

"And royally, the 'us'?"

"Jill and Tom together. Dancing the light fantastic. And in slow degrees, to merge."

"*I* said that."

"Did you? Oh. Then *I heard* it."

"*I* heard it *too.*"

"Our functions, our faculties. Our talents, our capacities. Virtues and vices. All our attributes. Qualities, properties: A Joint Stock Corporation."

"Let's float our stock: to float our private bond on the public's open water. And sail out, on the bold sea's venture."

"For we're in the same boat."

"Don't rock it, now."

"No. Our journey's smooth *and* rough. A swim-or-sink double-risk. And at the opposite shore, two deaths."

"Two? From one life?"

"We'll diverge in dying. As we converged in living."

"Well, I'll miss you, when we die."

"I'll miss you too."

"Let's, then, *not* die. Isn't love immortal?"

"Yes, but not our bodies."

"We'll *become* love, then: and join its immortality."

"*I*'m game for *that.*"

"And *I too* . . . Who's talking? Is this a dialogue?"

"No: it's *our* monologue: by halves, of two."

"And is this a dream?"

"That we're awake to."

"And we *are* our love?"

"We embody it. It's our doubled soul; an indestructibility composed from elements unseparated within one indivisibility. That's us."

"Me?"

"And me."

"Oh, you're so selfish!"

"For *you* I am."

"And I for you. Books may have separate shelves; we, our separate selves; the separate shelves belong to one bookcase; our separate selves are articled together, in the same soul structure. We're its sole parts; but change places, as children may change beds, in the strangely combined night."

"We switch our parts around. I'm *you,* on occasion."

"And *I* do *your* things, too. But is it too messy?"

"Let it all mix together; it'll hold up."

"What *is* the 'we'?"

"It's Tomjill."

"Jilltom?"

"No name. Why have a name? Let's be and do what the name can't catch up with. We elude our name. Our name won't tag us. We're running it ragged. It falls behind. It gives up. We're nameless."

"In that case, undefined?"

"We're always *being* defined; but then *re*-defined; it's all a *becoming.* On the run."

"A stable *being* has a name. But our *becoming* doesn't. It's on the go. We're in it. It's moving us. It's our motion. It's love's re-arrangements, with only its fluidity the same. Not a static mix. But heaving along an organic transition. From you to me, me to you, and us to All."

"Labels chase us, but we outrun them. Terms can't affix themselves, nor brands have title, nor values lay claim, to this wild flight that dizzies us in distance from established definitions. We're making us, on the go."

XXX. LYDIA PRETENDS NOT TO LOVE TOM GER-
VASI. IN EXPOSING HER BLUFF, *TOM* GETS IN DEEP.
ONLY MARRIAGE CAN SOLVE TRUTH'S TUSSLE
WITH LOVE'S UNMEASURED EQUALITY; BY TIME'S
STERN TEST, RISKING, CHANCE BY CHANCE, ALL
FUTURE FAILURE IN A PERILOUS IDEAL. CAN
LOVE HOLD UP? IN BOTH CASES? SUBMIT IT, WAVE
BY WAVE, ACROSS TIME'S ENTIRE OCEAN. IT'LL
DROWN, OR SURVIVE ON THE OTHER SIDE, ON
HEAVEN'S HEROIC SHORE. HENCE THE OLD SAW,
"TAKE THE PLUNGE." TRUTH IS MORE THAN NOW.
IT'S WHAT'S TO BE.

Lydia pretended she didn't love Tom Gervasi. But the latter saw
right through her, as though she were made out of a transparent
gown.

But he pretended to be "taken in" by her act. "So you don't
love me, Lydia? I admire you for your restraint. Other women
haven't so much self-control. They're so self-indulgent! What
they need is some discipline. They should take a leaf from *your*
book, Lydia: your discipline is very talented. I'm delighted you
don't love me. It puts me at my ease. I feel free, unthreat-
ened. Thank you so much, Lydia, for your gift of these liberties. To show my gratitude, I'm going to requite your gift, and
return the compliments, by refraining from being in love with
you. Fear not. I'll spare you from that affliction. I'll impose on
you no such burden, of having to suffer the insufferable, bear
the unbearable, put up with the unputupable. I'm generous in
my withholding. You need not endure, deer Lydia, the unen-
durable. Does your gratitude measure my generosity, for what,

in all consideration, I desist from inflicting? *Do* thank me. I've taken pains."

"Tom, I pity your holding back so. *Do* relieve yourself, a little bit, by relenting somewhat, and easing your spartan hold on your straining self. Give slight vent to that love *bursting* to course through you. Or, dear Tom, you'd explode. I fear for your health and sanity, if you keep it all pent in."

"Then *you*, dear Lydia, must, in *your* turn, give vent to *your* inhibited love, as well."

"But Tom, I have no love to inhibit. I feel no love—and I can't hold back what I don't feel. I feel *nothing*, toward you."

"Lydia, is that true?"

"Yes, my dear love."

"Are you sure?"

"Absolutely, my dear love."

"You're cold-hearted?"

"I am, adored one."

"Well, I am to you. I was only bluffing, when I said how much I'd be holding back. There *is* nothing to hold back. I don't love you, Lydia."

"*Please* do, Tom. *Please.*"

"But you won't reciprocate. I don't *dear* love you, if I'm not guaranteed of being loved back."

"I *promise* to, my loved one."

"Very well. Then I agree."

"To *love* me, adorable?"

"Yes, my dear Lydia."

"Oh Tom! I *adore* you!"'

"I feel that way toward *you*, dear Lydia."

"Then it's a *mutual* love?"

"Yes, dear."

"I'm happy, Tom."

"So am I, Lydia."

"Marry me, Tom."

"Of course, Lydia."

"You're snared, Tom."

"I am, Lydia. I was glad to see you undisguise your love. It was transparent, from the start. You were faking indifference, but I saw right through it. I'm glad to have exposed you."

"And *I*'ve exposed you."

"I needed your love for me to be declared. At the time I needed that, I hadn't loved you. But *now*, that you've *declared* yourself, I *do* love you."

"It's out in the open, now. We're both frank about it, candid, explicit. I loved you first, but hid it. You, Tom, saw through my hiding of it. You wanted me to confess. In getting me to, *you* fell for *me*. Our love, now, is on equal terms."

"So equal, we'll *un*equalize it. Through marriage, and slow time that turns odd."

"I'm your bride-to-be, Tom."

"And I'm *grooming* myself for the marriage."

"All fair and open. We'll take a double step, on love's firm mutuality."

"You and I, Lydia. Love, betrothing itself: On that exalted altar, of divine equality. You love me, I love you. Two loves, weighed the same."

"But a love is intangible: how can it be measured? Or compared?, which is a measurement."

"We'll *assume* the same measure. And that way, take the step."

"Oh Tom. It's really us?"

"Together, Lydia."

"Is it true?"

"Who knows? Let's take the test. Truth gets *proven*. We'll go ahead. The future may falsify our vow, and prove *one* love false, or *both* loves false. We'll risk it. We'll chance it. As a wedded pair. Time's vulnerable twins."

XXXI. TOM GERVASI INTERVIEWS GIRLS WITH BOY-DERIVED NAMES WHO APPLY FOR A LOWER VACANCY IN HIS CROWDED LOVE LIFE.

Georgina, Philippa, Maxine, Daniela, Josephine, Roberta, Johanna, Laura, Martha, Stephanie, Michelle, Patricia, Frances, Veronica, Nicole, Alberta, Henrietta, Paula, Jacquiline, Eleanor, Isabel, Irene, Christine, Louise, Emily, Karen, Sylvia, Ann, Alice, Geraldine, Adele, Wilma, Frieda, Sheila, Claudia, Sandra, Felicity, Leonora, Theodora, Bernice, Julia, Georgia, Charlotte, Sally, Gabriella, Carol, Rose, and Grace had all disappointed their parents by being born female. Their various parents by token compensation, then gave these offspring names approximating the boys they had hoped would arrive instead: Georgina, for George; Philippa, for Philip; Maxine, for Max; Daniela, for Daniel; Josephine, for Joseph; Roberta, for Robert; Johanna, for John; Laura, for Lawrence; Martha, for Martin; Stephanie, for Stephen; Michelle, for Michael; Patricia, for Patrick; Frances, for Francis; Veronica, for Vernon; Nicole, for Nicholas; Alberta, for Albert; Henrietta, for Henry; Paula, for Paul; Jacquiline, for Jacob; Eleanor, for Elliott; Isabel, for Israel; Irene, for Ira; Christine, for Christopher; Louise, for Louis; Emily, for Emile; Karen, for Carl; Sylvia, for Sylvester; Ann, for Anthony; Alice, for Alfred; Geraldine, for Gerald; Adele, for Adam; Wilma, for William; Frieda, for Frederick; Sheila, for Sheldon; Claudia, for Claude; Sandra, for Alexander; Felicity, for Felix; Leonora, for Leonard; Theodora, for Theodore; Bernice, for Bernard; Julia, for Julius; Georgia, for George; Charlotte, for Charles; Sally, for Salvadore; Gabriella, for Gabriel; Carol, for Carl; Rose, for Ross; and Grace, for Graham.

In good time, these girls won their way into parental accep-
tance. When they grow old enough to become mothers themselves, or at least to turn men's heads (much more common
then becoming mothers), they all uniformly flowed through the
one-way street leading to the foot of the vault of Tom Gervasi's
heart. They hoped to be admitted. They jointly presented a petition to Tom Gervasi, beseeching him to pity them for their birth
handicap: their parents had punished them for not being born
boys: which was more their parents' faults than their own, or really nobody's fault at all, or really not even a *fault* at all, because
what's wrong with being born female? In fact, they were *proud*
of it, now. Why were they so proud? Because, by being women,
they were qualified to hope to be accepted by Tom Gervasi as
girlfriend, mistress, or wife, in that ascending scale of rarified
preference.

Furthermore, the petition of these birth-afflicted women
beseeched Tom Gervasi to choose from among their natally stig-
matized ranks, his next girlfriend, mistress, or wife. That would
be immense compensation for having been nominally slighted
for daring to presume the wrong birth gender.

Surely, wouldn't *one* of them please him? They'd take off
their outer clothing and pose for him in tight underwear, as
well as submitting to a personal interview, to help him decide
a nice warm choice for himself. Would that appeal to him?
Yes, it would. It sounded delightfully lascivious. So he admitted
all of these poor unfortunates into his apartment, where they
crowded the living room, where there was plenty of wine to en-
tertain their theoretical thirst.

First, down to business. Their spokeswoman asked, now,
was there a vacancy in Tom Gervasi's sex life for girlfriend, mistress, wife? "Well, if truth be told, I've been quite active lately.

All posts have been well filled, in my—as you call it—sex life. But I protest that that's a cheapening term. Sex is only one aspect of a man-woman involvement. Why reduce it to that, merely?"

Having made this delicate point, before his admiring throng of supplicant visitors who were all dying, one by one, to strip down to their tighties for his private view and lecherous titillation, Tom Gervasi cleared his throat, and went on, with a light touch. (The women, who had fantasized about him before, adored him more now, in his casual approachability, his stunning presence with its disarming note of equality before his assembled fans.)

"Let's not say 'my sex life,' with its reductive simplicity, but 'my love life,' rather, which broadens the connotations of relationship, as opposed to mechanical physical mutual exploitation. Pardon, if I seem too pedantic."

(An appreciative murmur indicated that he had, indeed, been pardoned: fulsomely.)

"I see you're all keen for my services and favors as boyfriend, lover, husband. I'm duly flattered to be held in such esteem. Other men would burn with envy, could they behold us here now, and hear what's going on. I deem myself *most* fortunate."

The supplicants applauded. The occasion had become rather formal, despite the early, misleading note of breezy ease.

"Yes, I have one vacancy." (A joyful stir, in the room, an eager gasp, the hush of suspense.) "Not for a wife; I'm sorry to say." (Moan of disappointment, in generalized chorus.) "However, I do have a position open: for subgirlfriend, or junior mistress. Any applicants?" (An enthusiastic roar of "Yes! Yes!" made the chandelier tremble.)

"Well, now it's time for interviews. I'm my own personnel director. I'll take on the most qualified applicant. Résumés, or curriculum vitae, are unnecessary. All your background data that I need to know, you can fill me in on when you're interviewed. These interviews will be private and confidential. They'll be conducted in my bedroom: where I expect an atmosphere of impeccable decorum to be observed," he added, on a sharp, rising note. The girls venerated him with complete attention. Not a pin could be heard dropping, in this intense aura of concerted female concentration. Every word by Tom Gervasi took on, thereby, the prophecy of an oracle, or the uttering of the Ten Commandments, or the Sermon on the Mount, or a voice from heaven. He had woven a spell over these girls. Their servility was breathless with hope. They would have carried out any orders, from his oracular tones of authority.

Tom Gervasi was "the Boss." Those meek creatures craved for any opportunity to prove obedience. Who would be so lucky, as to be put in that position?

Now, the interviews would begin. Each girl would get about fifteen minutes, alone, in confidence, with her prospective Boss. The rest would remain, drinking wine, comparing notes, trading outlooks, in the livingroom. One at a time, the applicants would be interviewed—in the bedroom. There, they'd be asked to strip, and would undergo a series of questions, vocal rather than a questionnaire to be filled out. The examination would be, in each case, designed to bring out each girl's special aptitudes, and suitability for the post offered. They were asked not to be nervous or embarrassed, for that would distort the findings and partially invalidate the test. Tom Gervasi couldn't promise impartiality. He was only human, after all (and *before* it, too), and naturally would have personal preferences, idiosyncratic taste, for playing favorites according to private predilection. He warned the girls that all but one would be a loser. There should be no bitter weeping, at the end, when the final decision would be announced. To assure that, they would all have to go home first. He'll inform each one, personally by phone—in all but one case, endeavoring to cheer the loser up.

The tests were conducted with airs of secrecy. Being interviewed by him constituted, for each girl, so far, the major highlight of her young life. Each girl went home to wait by the phone. Tom Gervasi promised them all that he'd phone—one by one— them all within two hours. With this farewell warning: "Girls, don't elevate your hopes to the desperate suicide pitch. All the failures can apply again in about two years. By then, many of you will have improved your chances. So to all of you, but one, farewell for two years. Meanwhile, don't be nuns."

Each was at home waiting. All those girls, named begrudgingly after the boys their parents wished they had been born as. As promised, each got the call—from the Boss: "Sorry." The final call was to the winner. The winner wept the hardest. "Finally, I'm glad to have been named after the boy I was wanted to have been. For that qualified me to be among these self-pitying petitioners who called today on the Boss. With this result: I'm now his subgirlfriend, or junior mistress. I'll do so well as a beginner, I'll be promoted, till one day I'll be his wife: Mrs. Tom Gervasi. The greatest name, for any woman to have. The name I wasn't born with: but, through audacity, perseverance, hard work, observance of duty, and great good fortune, may acquire. I commit my life to that end. The true goal, for any girl born in this Tom Gervasi Century. The Crown of any female endeavor. The natural heaven to redeem common earth. Sublimely to end what my dubious birth began with grudging compromise.

Mrs. Tom Gervasi. My parents never realized this improbable prospect innate to my inherent start as a female disappointment. Tom Gervasi makes females proud of themselves. But if he were homosexual, I'd turn male. He's not, so I stay female. For thus he'd have me. And make me his."

XXXII. DIANE LOVES TOM GERVASI. HE YAWNS, FROM THE STALE AIR.

Being loved upon. By someone, who's shedding it from her source, radiating a glow of love. Its beams fall across Tom Gervasi. Soft rays of sweet love. He basks in it without convulsions. So mild, like the shine from the Star of Bethlehem. Coming at him in soft waves. In fluid ripples. To tinkling tunes, from a chiming mandolin, semi-muted. Effusions, subdued. Seen through a glass darkly. From Diane. Dear Diane. So dearly, does she love Tom Gervasi. How lovely, to be loved by her. Her kiss flows over him. It washes over his lips. Leaving froth. A delicious spray of foam. Gentle reminders. The endless source, of true love.

Unfortunately, Diane is beginning to bore him. In alarm, she recognizes on his face these signs of indifference. What she's been doing ceases to have the desired effect. She should change her tactics. Revise her approach approach. Not display love so openly. Hide it, and feign something else.

But what? She's already declared herself. Tom Gervasi is no fool. He'd see straight through her pretense not to love him. He'd see that love is *behind* the pretense. Meanwhile, he represses some yawns. But he's growing less polite, with greater boredom, to the point where now his yawns are not covered, stifled, or checked. Diane reads that coarseness for what it tells her: she's not cared for, any more, by him. He'll soon drop her. Other women are pressing in to take her place. Tom Gervasi flirts back with them, in bold signs of encouragement. Diane is slipping out of his life. She's lost her hold over him. Her love had peacock-spread its fullest flung feathers of lyrical outpouring. Just then, his interest waned. Now love bleeds sorrow. *Why* did he fold in? Just as their souls were on the quivering verge of contact?

"Is it over, Tom Gervasi?"

"I'm afraid so, Diane. I hate to tell you this. I can see that look of woe, in your terrified eye. It hurts me to tell you this. But not as much, of course, as it hurts *you. You're* the suffering one. I'm seized with guilt, but briefly. You'll recover slowly, if ever. Your love for me, Diane, was so complete: it had achieved perfection. For me, that was static. It limited my field of action. It stifled my invention. It made even spontaneity seem stale. There was nothing more for me to *do.* Just sit there, and be loved. I became a perfect object: a still one. A still-life, as in a painting hung with an old frame. There was nothing left for me to prove. Your love took over. Why, I could have *retired,* on its steady funds. I could have settled into sterile peace. I would have faded, into your love object. I would have died, as Tom Gervasi. No more fields to conquer, problems to find solutions for. I would have turned mineral. And you would never have known. You would have been the same loving Diane. On and on. Love oozing from you, like milk from mother cow. You were secreting love like a machine, in dull motion, on a perpetual horizon. I yawned: my only defense."

"All right, then I stop loving you."

"Stop lying. You're only saying that. To change my tune."

"Can I keep on seeing you?"

"No. I want to make room for the new women who've been petitioning my company. I don't want any hangover from the past. I want to do a thorough spring-cleaning job, get rid of what I can't use anymore, air out the place, renovate, overhaul, start afresh. An influx of new women. To stir me up. To unyawn me, of stale air."

"Is *that* what I've been?"

"What you've become. Poor Diane. You meant well. Love *is* full of well-meaning. But it sucked up all my animation, and dimmed me in a pall of tedium. I yearn for fresh adventure!: new women."

"I'll always love you, Tom Gervasi."

"I know, Diane. But I want some excitement. Your love is a dusty old museum, with cobwebs left in corners. I'm no antique, just yet. Bring on the new women! Goodbye, Diane. Preserve what I was. It's in your keeping. I burst loose, now."

XXXIII. DAISY *THINKS* SHE CAN GET TOM GER-VASI. SHE APPEALS TO SUPERSTITION, AND GOD, FOR ASSISTANCE. SHE'S SO PLAIN, SHE NEEDS GREAT LUCK. SEE NEEDS MAGIC, MIRACLES, FATE. SHE NEEDS ALL THE "BREAKS": AND GOD, TO BACK HER UP. IMPOSSIBLE? SEE.

Daisy felt lucky: she *might*, just *might*, win Tom Gervasi as a wedding prize.

Astrology; palmreading; handwriting analysis; skull bumpery; table-rising; prayer; fasting; meditation; breathing exercises; saying "Hail Mary"s; worrying the rosary beads; guru-consulting; the Chinese *Book of Changes* (*I Ching*) reading; crystal-ball gazing; alchemy; witchcraft; black magic; Judaism (with the Torah); Zen Buddhism; Mohammedanism; Church of Englishness; star-gazing; playing-card-reading; miracles, known and rare; soothsayery; prophets; clairvoyants: she resorted to all these things, with auspicious omens and the most unscientifically verifiable superstitionism, to confirm that, with luck (*good* luck, actually) on her hopeful side, *plus* (an *essential* plus) Tom Gervasi's falling in love with her, she'd have a terrific outside chance, to beat the odds, and win, as lawful wedded husband (to domesticate him forever to the marital yoke, harness him to his conjugal oath), that wild romantic man, Tom Gervasi. Himself, no less.

But Daisy wasn't just going to sit back and *passively* wait for the fates to bring this about. No, she'd take active steps, to promote this phenomenal event from its mere dream status to rock-bottom real actuality as a verifiable phenomenon within solid existence as having world-occurred in the concrete universal, uncontroversial, empirical, ascertainable in the sanity of social framework.

What will she *do* with Tom Gervasi, once she has him? Make him hers, forever. Clip the bird's wings. Unsoar him, trapped in an earth cage of routine fidelity, duty, industry, devotion, steadiness, unshakeable stability; dependable, reliable, he'll do her bidding, support her with high standard, and never leave her side, except when going to, coming from, and being at that carefully tended-to temple of commercial enterprise, his office, where he chases success for home and hearth.

This was Daisy's plan for Tom Gervasi: what she had in store for him, once he was snared, and officially pinned down.

She needed luck, pluck, initiative, persistence, and God's help, to accomplish what she had in mind. She believed that her *wanting* it so badly fully entitled her, with well-deserved merit, to *get* it, God willing.

She'd be helpless, without God's aid. Yet God, in stern majesty, required that *she* contribute, too.

Tom Gervasi, as yet, didn't know of Daisy's existence. She loved him from a distance.

But she'll close that awesome gap, and nab him, up close. Snatch him (or is "rescue him" the right term?) from the conniving clutches, the fell talons, of an undeserving mob of what could charitably he called "other women."

Daisy's star, Tom Gervasi's star, were one twinkle. The firmament's celestial pride.

To let him know of her existence might be practical as a first step. This would afford him the opportunity (necessary at this stage) to fall in love with her, if not at first sight, then later, eventually, somehow.

A disadvantage distinctly not in her favor: she was plain. "Just plain Daisy," she had been called, by her cruel classmates.

Tom Gervasi was known to prefer beautiful women—all other things being, of course, equal.

Well, what had Daisy to offer, instead of beauty? More precious, valued higher, than more beauty?

No extraordinary intelligence; no special brilliance; no brilliant career; no highly select breeding; no wealth to speak of: *what*, then? *What*?

Her own pure self. Daisy, plain and simple.

If *that* didn't suffice . . . well, it had *better* suffice.

What more, after all, in all fairness and in mighty modesty, could, in his right mind, Tom Gervasi ask for?

Plain Daisy. The earth's crowning achievement.

To meet him: first step.

She got herself invited, as an acquaintance of the hostess, to a party of which the guests would include that special one dream man.

She arrived early, well-perfumed, wearing a most becoming gown. Designed to knock him down. And raise him up again, clamoring to get inside.

It was a huge party—over a hundred people. An after-dinner party, featuring drinks mainly, but with food bits to pick on at strategically located tables where stops could be made for solid refreshment in the course and flux of flow and to.

Tom Gervasi was present—but surrounded. *Women*, mainly, were milling about him. Daisy's dangerous rivals.

But she'd have a surprise for them all. For *her* the prize. For them, that negligible consolation, dregs of a dubious solace: nothing. Nothing, for them; him, for her.

In order, at the moment, in the prime of ripe time, was "the introduction." To bring truth to its critical tide, face-to-face with its crucial development, so far.

Daisy asked her hostess-acquaintance to please do the honors, by providing the suitable trappings of an introduction.

To take the moment by its hand, and lead it to . . . Fate, in its final form.

✳

"Tom Gervasi, this is Daisy. Daisy, Tom Gervasi."

The crowd backed up, gave way, gave them room, in an ample pocket of space.

They spoke softly. No-one else could hear.

"I had been *hoping* to meet you, Tom Gervasi. I'd heard, of course, so much about you.

"You'll reform, from your profligate ways, once you marry me. Propose now."

"But Daisy, I'm not inclined to. I never heard such spontaneous nonsense, so baseless a caprice, a giddy whimsy unfounded on manners or good sense, as what my ears, in all diligence, report most echoingly.

"You're plain. You don't attract me. You're rude. Forward. Unsound in mind, perhaps. Aggressive, to a violent fault. Rash, reckless, and uncouth.

"Do me the courtesy, now, to leave my presence.

"This party swarms with other women. *They*, not you, interest me. I'll step away."

"Wait, Tom—wait!"

"What urgency is this? Why should I wait?"

"*Fate* brought us together."

"Fate? *That*'s not the name of our hostess."

"Cut out that civil levity. You're mine, do you hear? You're mine!"

"I'm not."

"You are. I *compel* you to be.

"I have delicious hips, a lovely ass, full of round flesh, and large thighs. Try me. Try me. Try me."

"You've excited me. Let's leave the party and go to my apartment. For privacy, of course."

"Tom! You're panting!"

"I'm just drenched with lust. I never 'wanted it' so badly."

"You're aroused sexually? Then you're in my power."

"Let me be in your body, too. I'm begging for it."

"*Contain* yourself, you bad boy. Patience, discipline, that's what you need! Maturity, and restraint."

"Later, later! Right now, I want *you*!"

"Let's inform the hostess, and leave the party. Control yourself. Your pants are on fire. Don't ejaculate *now*. Save the fun, for later."

They left the party, to everyone's surprise. Plain Daisy had taken him away, early! How did she manage *that*? Was it some personal bribe? Something fishy was afoot. It all looked too strange. So weird, it defied nature.

"We're in bed, Daisy."

"Yes, Tom."

"Daisy, will you—"

"Yes, Tom."

"Just a small ceremony. I don't want a lavish wedding—one of those vulgar affairs, blatant, bombastic, flamboyant, to a fault.

"No: plain and simple—like you."

"Yes, Tom."

"Daisy . . . ?"

"Yes, Tom."

"What did it? What hooked me? What do you have?"

"Sex appeal?"

"Don't talk like a textbook. *Other* women are sexy, too. *Plenty* of them. How did *you* get me, and not they?"

"I appealed to what's most direct, simple, and basic in you."

"That sounds like mystical nonsense, oversimplistic, a stupid sort of cosmic 'oneness,' undifferentiating that from this, or this from that."

"I *am* truth. I don't speak it."

"You're plain-talking, Daisy."

"I'm plain all over. That's the plane you see me in. Need I further explain?"

"I'm bewildered. How did you get me?

"Was there some trick? To which no other women is privy, but which, somehow, won the day, and me as well?"

"God helped me. I dabbled in the occult, until I deeply penetrated it. Some divinity rubbed off on me, of supernatural dimensions; I traded in my ordinariness, in return . . ."

"For what?"

"Power. Spellbinding power. It took away your resistance. And it won you over."

"Sounds mystical, to me."

"It *is*, Tom; it *is*."

"But it sure did work! I'm your slave. I'll work hard for you, till we become rich. You'll have every luxury. I'll be yours, stead-fast. Deviating never an inch, from our pure union."

"That's acceptable. You'll do. I find you satisfactory."

"Our wedding?"

"Tomorrow, if you wish. *You* handle it, won't you? I have no knack for detail."

"I'll do it *all*, for you. All that I am, all that I have, all I'm capable of, rests at your service. Use it."

"I have every intention to. I wouldn't waste all those pre-cious assets or yours. They'll prove of sterling worth, to my many requirements. You have quite a value. I'll convert it, to practical necessities."

"Use me well, Daisy; don't *abuse* me; nor exploit in a way of violating me."

"No, Tom. You'll do. Just as you are."

XXXIV. THE NUN LOSES FAITH IN GOD, BUT GAINS IT IN TOM GERVASI, HER SECULAR SUBSTITUTE FOR HER DIVINE FIRST HUSBAND.

Brigit was a nun who began to have a few theological misgivings: not many, but enough. Doubt coursed through her, as once faith had. This dismissed her from grace, and led her, lonely, to her "self," outside God's umbrella. She'd shunned sure salvation. She'd reneged on a holy vow. The secular, not the celestial, became her immediate future.

She'd had a Vocation, once, in Christ: a divine calling, for which she commanded the adequate aptitude, within her unfailing capacity. She led the other novices, in Devotion.

Now, the world. Off with the old habit. She donned civilian dress. Got an office job, in a commercial outfit. And, to complete this perverse conversion transition, and enlarge the dangers thereof, she, as ways went, by the grim lot of chance, met, and fell in love with (and she was a virgin intact), Tom Gervasi.

Tom Gervasi didn't represent evil, nor embody it, as the Devil's hard-working advocate commissioned to tempt good women to slip and slide down to sin's slush.

No. All he was, was a simple male. With a hedonistic appetite for good hearty fun, on the carnal carnival's happy-go-merryaround. He needed partners, and women loved it.

Brigit had become a woman. Despite having been a nun, her organs were all in the same place (places) as any *fallen* woman's.

Also, she was attractive. That pinned her quite up on Tom Gervasi's notice board. She spinned his head around. Who more exotic, than a virgin former nun, as sophistication's arch foil?

"Let me initiate you: into the sacred rites of the fertility ceremony. I'll be your High Priest. I'll lead you, to the body's holy temple."

"Stop satirizing religion, you unblemished heathen. I'm not a nun any more, not because I stopped taking religion seriously, but because I *did* take it seriously. I love God, above life, above nature. But I take the *worldly* road toward Him; not the nunnery's remote hermitage.

"You're a pagan, unrepentant. I, though doubts relieved me of the coif, do still, and do always, believe. My faith is doubt-riddled; as our bodies contain worms and germs and such vermin, cankerous parasites. I'm God's. But not as a nun. As a woman, so test me. *Confirm* me in my womanhood. Bring out the full woman in me. With lust-covered love, and base bodilyness."

"Sounds fine with *me*, Brigit, Come visit my apartment. Test my bed's bounce. And *my counter*-bounce. *You'*ll be bouncing, too."

"I have an apartment, and a bed. Come *there*, with me."

"Yes, but why?"

"Is your bed old?"

"Yes."

"Then *other* women have been on it. But *my* bed is *new*. As new, to the 'game,' as *I* am. Let *two* virginities fall, by your one stroke."

"What an order! Suddenly, I feel impotent. For years, I've been seeing experienced women, none but non-virgins. Now, there's you. I fear I'll fail. Why, it's so momentous! So sacred! Not just frivolous fun. Not just an easy, automatic, fornicating lark. I'm treading in the garden of de-flowering: holy ground."

"Does it cow you? Unman you, quite?"

"My powers are fled. I cower."

"With *your* reputation!"

"What has *reputation* to do with *us*? It's just you and I, Brigit. And heaven, for a witness."

"Why, Tom! *You're* the serious one!"

"I'm solemn. Impotent, too."

"It remains to be proved. We'll put it to the test."

"To the testicle. Off we go. To your bedroom: clad in stillness."

✳

He was right: he couldn't do it. Her nun's preserved virginity overdaunted his manly resolve. "Do you still love me?" he asked.

"Yes, but I love God more."

"God's omnipotent; I'm only impotent."

"*Now* you are; later maybe no."

"I'm humiliated. I've disappointed you?"

"Just on the physical surface. My *soul*, though, has been deeply penetrated."

"Yes, by mine. I have a soul in love with you. Shall you not *remain* virgin, in the puritanical convention of another generation, till we, Brigit, wed?"

"But I'm *already* married: to *God*."

"Oh, that's on a different plane. Remain constant to Him, on *that* plane; devote *this* plane's fidelity, please, to *me*."

"I take the vow, as I once did. *Not* as I once did. I failed the *nun's* vow; my faith wavered; but *this* vow I'll keep: in conjugal holiness."

XXXV.   KATHLEEN IS LOSING TOM GERVASI. A MARITIME NIGHTMARE.

Kathleen kept holding on, holding on, like a drunken sailor to a sinking ship, which heaved to and fro; while surging from Tom Gervasi came, over and over again, "It's over, it's over"; and the ship was badly lurching; lurching worse than the drunken sailor; and Tom Gervasi seemed to *hiss*: "It's over, it's over"; but he was practically weeping it. And Kathleen was sinking. The sky was raining. The waves tossed *up* their foam, while the sky poured it down; the metal was clanking; the nightmare was rocking, jolting; Kathleen held on; she couldn't let go; Tom Gervasi was weeping, sobbing, "It's over, it's over." Was Tom Gervasi's sobbing Kathleen's sobbing? Who could tell what? Light came from the sky, but it was night. The ship was listing, all its lights were struck out in the whirling, slanting storm, that kept blowing through the dark; coldly blowing through Kathleen. She said, "No, no . . . No, no . . ." while the night got drunker; everything was shattered. The deck was whirling about. Inside the cabins, furniture was sliding about; in the big dining hall the tables were sliding; in the engine room, the clanking was clanking; in the control direction motion area, the stations were abandoning their men. The captain was on his back. The little boats were packed out, frantic passengers grabbed at them; the waves were pouring in; the ship was plunging; it was tilting; it was listing. The rain ran down. It was running down Kathleen's face. Tom Gervasi, where was he? No more "It's over, it's over" from him. Instead, the silence that follows those words. The silence that completes those words. The end is crowded with that silence. The space is groping for itself.

Kathleen can't find Tom Gervasi. His prophecy has gone. "It's over, it's over." He doesn't say those words any more. The sayer is lost.

His presence gave no comfort. His absence has no comfort. There's no ship, no storm, no night. No Tom Gervasi. It's so still. There's no water. Kathleen has no one. The lights are out, but it's dry.

"Tom Gervasi. Please, where are you? I'm forsaken, I'm abandoned. I'm dry. It's too still. It's still dark.

"No metal clank. No lurching ship. No water, coming up."

XXXVI. TOM GERVASI AND JIMMY BAGNO: BOYHOOD'S FRIENDSHIP, IN MEMORY'S DEEPENING PRESERVATION.

Tom Gervasi yearned for his ball-playing boyhood. Disorganized, makeshift, inventive, improvised, casual, but intensely contested, were these variations on the basic game of bat and ball.

He had a special favorite playmate, Jimmy Bagno, and they'd have great times in schoolyards, gutters, wherever there was some undisturbed space.

Now, Tom Gervasi was grown up. He had a responsible job in an interesting business. He had married, divorced (childless), and was now a few different women's simultaneous boyfriend. He did grown-up things with them, not just neck, kiss, and pet and have sodas and malteds and hold hands in the movies.

He did with them what heroes do with heroines in adult novels or in movies that children are advised not to see.

He had gone to college and graduated. He read books and thought a lot. In social circles, he was regarded as quite the intellectual.

He was analytical, critical, imaginative, inventive. He spoke with forceful eloquence. He commanded respect—of men. And he won women's love, without half trying.

Still, through the triumphs and industry of his current life, he visits the nostalgia of days gone by.

Ballplaying, with Jimmy Bagno. They were great pals. Still are, but meet only once or twice a year now. Jimmy Bagno is living a different sort of life, than Tom Gervasi. Less glamorous, more humble. Wife, kids, job in factory out of town, lives out of town. Hadn't gone to college, wasn't intellectual.

Tom Gervasi is in the highest social circles, with a glittering reputation, as a brilliant wit and ladies' man.

But he thinks back, longingly, to those Jimmy Bagno days. They were great pals, though already embarked on separate paths.

Now their paths had widened, further apart.

But loyally, they remained steadfast. They were sworn pals forever. Their roots had entwined early. Their most lyrical hours were spent playing together. So long ago. Yet now, as well: through visual memory.

Once they had had a falling-out. Jimmy Bagno's sister, at fourteen, became infatuated with Tom Gervasi, age fifteen. Tom had taken advantage for a few little thrills, but far short of ending the girl's virginity.

Jimmy Bagno, in a similar situation then, would have tried to go even further than Tom had, if given encouragement and opportunity. Jimmy wouldn't have blamed Tom if it had been with any other girl—but it was Jimmy's sister, and there was a family code of honor.

Jimmy refused to talk to Tom for quite a while. But then the sister gave up on Tom and was cured of her romantic obsession. This cleared the air for resumption of Tom's and Jimmy's friendship—which became keener than ever.

The sister, mercifully, could be forgotten. It never came between them again.

Jimmy was building up his body; he was becoming an athlete. Tom was big on the books, and was becoming a literary scholar. Jimmy had some flings as a professional ballplayer: successful, but he was injury-prone.

Finally, he had to give up his budding career as a very promising ballplayer, since his body balked, and couldn't perform up to the high standards.

To console himself, he would have loved to become a manager. But he hadn't built up enough of an established *playing* career. And he had no connections to influence authorities of teams.

So his great promise faded behind him. He worked at a factory trade, married, accumulated kids.

Tom Gervasi made a splendid college record, and landed a good job upon graduating, in an important literary establishment.

Tom and Jimmy would have reunions, and play ball, for old times' sake.

But those reunions got fewer: finally down to one a year.

They're old buddies. They're still playing ball, and going to the beach together, and joking and talking—still doing those things, in their separate (but bound together) visits to nostalgia's shrine, the holy temple of friendship kept up by prayers of memory.

Tom revisits their old haunts, their old playing grounds, the routes of their long old walks, the benches of dear old talks, in parks and grounds and hallowed places.

It all comes back to Tom.

Separately, Jimmy does too. And to *him,* it all comes back.

They're friends. They've overcome time, educational and career differences, circumstantial differences.

Those differences make no difference.

They're young again together. There's the bat and the ball, and they're playing.

They'll do it all over again, some day. Go through youth again together. Resumed, to full detail.

Re-enacted.

Before, was rehearsal. To make a pattern.

There they were, on the boardwalk, with their amusement games from arcade machines. They walked far to get there, it's night.

They have, ahead of them, two grown-up lives.

But the ocean has the moon on it. They'll grow up, but not yet.

They *are* growing up. More and more. Toward separate paths. But prolonging all their playings and walks.

Lingering, in late adolescence, in the early twenties, full of vigor.

They're diverging. They're going separate ways.

Yes: *officially* they are.

Unofficially, they're boys, With their ball and bat. With their apartments and mothers.

With time bearing down. The opening out. The claiming world. Women. Work.

They had fun. They're old pals, now.

But no more bat and ball.

The *rhythm* is still felt—the playing. The running. Catching, hitting, throwing.

An unused rhythm. It's now just a "thinking back."

To all that once was, whose meaning has kept up with them, through conditions remote and foreign to all that.

They talked about the professional ballplayers endlessly, in those days, and wove such talk into their own playing.

They also talked about girls—at first furtively, with reluctance.

Those days will never go.

However, they're gone.

Yes, but they won't ever go. Not from Tom. Not from Jimmy. Not from the big now of the future, or the little now of the present.

Tom and Jimmy. Walking and playing. Old talking.

Their occasional reunion, now.

They had met in the same junior-high-school class.

Time took them on. And bound them, forever.

Tom looks back, and salutes.

The old Jimmy. Where the former Tom still is.

Jimmy *is* his youth. With ball and friendship. And talking of players. Of girls, too: with increasing prominence.

Now is so far away from then!

But now *contains* then. And holds up their bond.

The bond of old and new. New musings, on the old that's renewed, by chosen memory. The link of young and old. Of young Tom and Jimmy. to old Tom and Jimmy. Who dwelled in the same place, for enough time, to set up a flow of permanence.

The places are *still* the same, but past. The time remains. It's always old.

XXXVII. TOM GERVASI IS CAROL'S CURE. BUT SHE NEEDS A CURE FROM *HIM*. BUT DON'T WORRY, IT ENDS WELL.

Carol went to the doctor. "What's wrong?" he asked, since she looked so healthy.

"I'm worried about myself."

"Who isn't? But what *about* yourself are you worried about? After all, I'm not a mind reader."

"Doctor, maybe you're the wrong doctor for what I'm worried about. It doesn't have to do with my physical body. It has to do with a feeling I never had. All other women I know have had it, especially long before the time they've reached my age, which is in my late twenties. I'm worried because maybe I'm deficient in that feeling. It's not normal that I never had that feeling. I feel I *ought* to have had it. But I've never yet had it, and that's what worries me."

The doctor looked serious. "What *is* this feeling you've never had?"

"How do I know? I never had it."

"Yes, but surely you must know what it is anyhow. Otherwise, how could you even refer to it? And how could you tell that other women *did* have it, and that you never had it, unless you know at least what it is? So, in spite of your not having had it, do tell me what it is that you've never had."

"All right, doctor. You win."

"Very well. Then tell me. After all, I'm a doctor. I'm a busy man. Other patients are waiting. Don't waste my time."

"You want it straight?"

"I'm too busy for it crooked. Tell it now, and directly. What is it?"

Carol paused. Then she came straight out with it. "Doctor, though I'm in my late twenties, I'm terribly worried. *Why* am I terribly worried? I'll tell you why. In brief, here it is. I've never felt love. Not for anyone."

"That's very selfish. Why not? Didn't you meet a man you found irresistible, romantic, handsome? Didn't you have a crush on him, become infatuated with him, daydream about him, fantasize about him, moon about him, sigh about him, laugh about him, and bear him in mind with an imaginary hug? Didn't you *ever* have that experience, since you're already in your late twenties? No? Not ever?"

"No, doctor. Never."

"That's very distressing. I'm worried about you. Do you have normal genitals?"

"Physically, they seem to be normal, though I haven't really been using them. Tell me. Is the heart the seat of love?"

"Only as a poetic figure of speech, a romantic metaphoric liberty in anatomical misuse. The heart is really for blood circulation, it's a pump, and has to do with veins and arteries. Your heart is in perfect working order, biologically, for I gave you a pulse and a cardiogram test recently. Love is a feeling, and it's located intangibly. In fact, it's located nowhere. You only feel it."

"Doctor, I long to feel it. But how?"

"You need a man to get smitten by. Someone who'll turn your head. Who'll inspire a fatal passion. Is that what you want?"

"With all my heart."

"The heart *isn't* where it is."

"It was only a fanciful term. I know you're a scientist."

"I *must* be a scientist. Otherwise, I can't cure people of what ails them."

"Doctor, you now know what ails me. Can you cure it?"

"Yes. I think I have the anecdote."

"You'll cure me with an anecdote? a story? A tale?"

"No, I meant *antidote.* The therapy, for what you complain of."

"Good. I'm glad I came to you, even though you're a medical doctor. You *can* treat me. With what prescription? I'm determined to be cured. I'll do whatever you say. What do you prescribe?"

"Carol, I want you to meet someone."

"Really? Who?"

"Tom Gervasi. *That*'ll cure you."

"I'll fall in love, for the first time in my life?"

"It's inevitable. It's bound to happen. It's a physical law."

"Is he *that* attractive, is he *that* irresistible, is he *that* romantic?"

"He's all of those things, plus more."

"Oh doctor, I'm thrilled. Where can I meet him?"

"I'll arrange it. I'll arrange an introduction."

"And it's guaranteed to work?"

"I assure you it is. There's ample testimony that other women could give you. They fall victims to his fatal charms. You're human, you're a woman, and so will you."

"Oh doctor, you give me hope!"

"I know the workings of the human heart."

"But you said it's not located there."

"I was speaking in a poetic figure of speech. It's the subject of love that does it. Love drives people into metaphor. It plays fast-and-loose with mere accuracy facts, for it disperses words into combinations highly imaginative. It makes us want to lose our hold, loosen our tight grip, on the tough logic world, and so we become playful. We wax fanciful. We take liberties. We exaggerate. We resort to poetry. Our world is transfigured."

"Oh, I hope to experience all that. I'd be eternally grateful to this Tom Gervasi you speak of, if he can provoke all that in me."

"He will: and more."

"Oh doctor! Will I be cured?"

"Yes. But you might want a cure *from* it, after you're cured."

"Really? Can love *itself* be seen as an ailment? And not just the inability to love?"

"I assure you, it can."

"Oh, then I'm *afraid* to meet Tom Gervasi. Doctor, what are you getting me into?"

"Trust in me, Carol. I'm your doctor. For your *present* ailment, take the Tom Gervasi cure. That's the only sure way of treatment for it. If, in your being cured, you acquire the opposite affliction to your current one, why, come again to my office, and be treated for *that*. But one illness at a time. Let's not get ahead of ourselves."

The doctor duly arranged the introduction, and Carol was cured. At first, her love was a blissful release. She felt relieved to have the ability to feel it. It was a Godsend. She thanked the Lord. In kneeling down, she thanked Tom Gervasi instead. Her saviour! She really had the ability to love! She was cured, forever.

Then her love became unhappy, since it demanded that he love her in return, which he didn't feel like doing. She became miserable, and wanted a cure *from* love.

So she returned to the doctor. "Doctor, please, it's urgent. How can I stop loving Tom Gervasi? It's a disease plague, since he doesn't requite my love. I've never been so depressed. I'm on the verge of suicide. Cure me, quick. Or I'll just die, I tell you."

"Oh, you're desperate! Be calm. Here, take this pill. Swallow it with this cup of water."

She followed the doctor's orders. In joy: "Oh doctor, it worked! I'm cured of my love! I no longer feel a *thing* for him!"

"Good. That's a relief. But you're not back where you started. Though you don't feel love *now,* anymore, at least you know that you have the *ability* to love. Apply it to some other man, next time, who'll love you back. *Mutual* love is the ideal. Your love for Tom Gervasi was only one-sided. That's why I had to cure you from it."

"Oh doctor! You're so wise! What's your fee? I'll pay you."

"My fee is steep. It's extreme. Carol, I've fallen in love with you. So please marry me."

"Oh doctor, I'll be only too glad to! Already, I love you back. Now, I'm *happy* in love! For my first time! Oh doctor, you're a dear! I positively *adore* you!"

"And *I* adore *you*! What could be better? *Mutual* love."

XXXVIII. TOM GERVASI IN A DEMOCRATIC SOCIETY. WHERE THE MODERN WORLD TAKES PLACE. AND WHAT HE HAS TO DO, IN SELF-DEFENSE. AND WHY, AND ALL THAT.

Carmen from Spain, Deirdre from Ireland, Pamela from England, Ingrid from Germany, Olga from Russia, Nicole from France, Betsy from Canada, Maria from Italy, and Liz from the United States, have this in common as well as their gender: all love Tom Gervasi. This puts an international burden on him. It's really more than he can handle. He mustn't show any prejudice or discrimination against nationality. He must be fair, to all applicants, in unilateral bipartisan neutral nonfavoritism. Yes, but how?

Simple: He must reject all in the same manner; so as to slight or offend none. Easier said than done. Is he to make a printing of identical rejection slips, and distribute them with silence and a blank expression? Each girl, of whatever nationality, cries alike: tears know no language, and break down international barriers.

They'll *all* accuse him of being unfair. Explanations will be unacceptable to all alike. He's bound to hurt all those national representatives. No way out.

Well, they *risked* being hurt, by loving him in the *first* place. It's *their* responsibility. Not his.

He'll be internationally unpopular, by that down-the-line action of negating their affirmations. He's a scoundrel, in any language, for causing sighs of grief, pants of woe.

As if he didn't have enough problems, this handsome adult male meets up with more: complaints from major representative minority and ethnic groups of his prejudice and discrimination against them: that an insufficient ratio quota of his history of girlfriends were members of those ethnic and minority groups.

An angry Jewish organization complained that Jewish girls had complained that so few if any of them had ever been accepted as girlfriends by Tom Gervasi.

An irate Puerto Rican organization complained that none if any Puerto Ricans had ever managed to become Tom Gervasi's girlfriends.

An indignant Italian-American organization complained that girls of Italian extraction had been unfairly treated by Tom Gervasi insofar that he rejected the love offers of all, or almost all, of them.

A bitter Black Negro organization complained that almost none of all of Tom Gervasi's girlfriends had ever been or are black or Negro.

Letters from Congress began to flow in, offering to help balance out the proportions, percentages, ratios, and quotas of various group representation in the girlfriendhood of Tom Gervasi's love-life, which now was becoming a matter of public debate, political controversy, social concern. His love-life used to be private. Now, democracy and equality had invaded it.

Maybe he should get a manager to put his affairs in order.

"These are *my* affairs," he attempted to say to the various political action groups, democratic watchdog societies, Minority Defense League, Social Equality Bureaus, Women's Protection Organisation, and The Modern Society for the Promotion of Fairness in People-Interactions; but they vetoed him, and he was scandalized as a celebrity. "Who's Tom Gervasi going out with now?" was a frequently prominent headline in a tabloid of sensationalist caliber that was reputed to expose the truth for what it really was, give the lowdown, and liberally debunk where necessary. "Who's Tom Gervasi going out with now?" This was picked up on by rival newspapers and less frequently published periodicals of a competitive, muckraking nature battling to come up with "the inside dope," "the real story . . . come to light," unearthing sordid facts and other salient information.

Public speculation on Tom Gervasi's love-life: endless rumors, unconfirmed. Alleged quotes. Private detecting. Interviews with current or former girlfriends of Tom Gervasi. The rumor mill. In-depth analyses of "recent trends" (illustrated by graphs and charts, photos too on occasion) "in Tom Gervasi's inside love-life."

"Who's in, who's out," of Tom Gervasi's love-life. One column featured this attention-grabbing headline: "Whom Tom Gervasi is in, and whom he's out of." Copies of the paper featuring the article sold like hotfire. The public knows what it wants to read. News of Tom Gervasi sells papers—news and conjecture, psychoanalytical-type reports by prominent sexologists and a whole swarming field of love experts whose opinions have a fond place in print for the Average Mr. and Mrs. Reader of humble or no literary pretensions.

Humanly, any material on Tom Gervasi caught the reading market and held it like glue. Already, the Legend was taking over, while the Private Man receded out of view.

How did Tom Gervasi, himself, react? He was appalled. He wanted his privacy back. It was his inalienable right, for being a citizen forced to vote and pay taxes.

"These are *my* affairs," he maintained. "The public have no business with them. Let them not snoop, nor pry, into what concerns me, and the particular woman, whoever she may be. My women have a right to remain nameless; to go undetected; to hide behind a veil of secrecy; to protect their right to go unobserved. Comment about them is ruinous to their potential reputation. Let television, radio, magazines, and newspapers be herewith warned: 'Keep out. Don't trespass. It's none of your business.'"

That all *all the more* spurred publicity on. Tom Gervasi was a noticed figure. The identity of the women he was seen escorting was an open game, in an open season, for widely distributed morsels of newsworthy items. That's the price, of fame, as a "ladies'-man."

An aggressively energetic member of the journalistic fraternity "tailed" Tom Gervasi and an unknown woman to a nightclub, bent on coming up with a "scoop." He even brought a camera along, and shot it at Tom Gervasi's table, causing a flashlight blink within those romantic orbs, Tom Gervasi's eyes. The woman he was escorting, too late, covered her face with her hands. The photo was telltale, revealing. Research would be done, to come up with the identity of the woman "caught" with him, on the basis of the photographed face. The "Extras" would scream out the headlines, tomorrow.

Tom Gervasi acted swiftly. He lunged over to that photojournalist's table, grabbed the bum, shook him by the lapel, cracked him across the face with a really gripped fist, and tore away from him, out of that lousy bum's grasp, the all-valued camera, which Tom Gervasi destroyed, prints and all, much to the unenlightenment of an impatient posterity.

The reporter sued Tom Gervasi for interfering with his performing the duties of his vocation, and holding up his career advancement. The counter-suit by Tom Gervasi cited privacy-invasion, harassment, molesting of peace. The court ruled a draw. So no money was lost, or won.

"I'm too much in the public's eye," Tom Gervasi decided. "I'll go lay low for a while. I'll take a long leave-of-absence, from my good old job, but I'll be guaranteed to be given it back when I return. I'll leave the big city, to cool off its publicity on me. I'll go to some island, somewhere. In the Mediterranean, somewhere, or some other European sea, somewhere, or maybe in a coast nook off the mainland. I'll write my memoirs, like Casanova once did, that former Italian Don Gervasi—I mean Tom Giovanni—or whoever, I'm so slipping. I'll drink 'perniff,' or whatever the local drink is, at the coastal haven or resort, or island hideaway. I'll meet the local tourist women, the moneyed dance from Northern Europe or North America or other cosmopolitan places. They'll be in bathing suits. I'll ogle them, and get a few mistresses. Sex is nice. It keeps the body in fine working order."

So off he went. No-one knows where. He just took off. He left no trace, for journalists. He's maybe incognito, with dark glasses. Maybe he's drinking "perniff." Writing his memoirs. Fondling some rich tourist dame's breast. Stuff like that. That a movie hero would do. A sophisticated type, who's handy with the women, knows his way around, is worldly-wise, and is no-one's fool.

But no, he's no type at all. He's that enigma, going by the name of Tom Gervasi. As inscrutable as an Oriental used to be thought of.

He's outside publicity. In self-imposed exile, from the old rat-race of frantic knockabout in a competitive society with hypertensions in the old pressure-cooker.

Maybe he's letting a beard grow on his chin—flaked with gray hairs a bit. Maybe he's getting tan, from the good old sun, wherever it is. Maybe he's inbetween a lady's legs, somehow, doing the good-old you-know-what. Or maybe it's romantic starlight. Near the beach.

Oh, so *many* possibilities. He's beyond social detection. He's "out-there," somewhere. At his good-old ease. Writing memoirs. Doing a bit of philosophy, on the side.

Back in "town," that is, "the big city," the papers are silent about him, television has calmed down, his name isn't in radio or magazines. There's a quiet, going on. A stillness, about the man's absence.

He'll return, though. And when he does—look out!

XXXIX. LOVE CHAMP OF THE WORLD. THE FINAL TUSSLES, FOR THAT SUPREME TITLE.

Gloria was the biggest man-conqueror of all of the British Isles and Europe, while Sharon was the North American Champion in that same department. A challenge was accepted, and they met to compete for the title of Champion Man-Slayer of Western Civilization. European Gloria conquered some of the finest lady-killers of the world; but North American Sharon did likewise to an equally rated batch of world-class lady-killers. The referees and judges found the match to be going neck-and-neck, with neither Gloria nor Sharon having an edge yet, since each had annihilated the resistance of her men-opponents, reducing them to mere love-pulp.

The world's greatest lady-killers were all defeated by Gloria and Sharon, except for one who refrained from competing, in his proud championship majesty as the acclaimed single greatest lady-killer of them all, renowned and celebrated the globe over as the one undisputed king of heartbreaking irresistible men: Tom Gervasi. "I challenge the winner," he said.

The head judge reasoned with Tom Gervasi, thus: "You can't challenge the winner of the Gloria-Sharon match, because neither can be determined a winner unless she slays *you*. Each has gone undefeated right up and down the ranks of the foremost male challengers. So it's a deadlock, so far, as no challengers are left for them to beat, except yourself, the champ of all men who wilt women down to abject love-fodder."

"Well, *neither* will beat me. I'll beat them both," Tom Gervasi estimated, with the calm confidence of an undefeated winner of all love-trials against the most men-melting woman ever amorously to compete.

The judge cautioned him against underestimating Gloria and Sharon: "Gloria is undefeated against all men she's ever faced; and Sharon is too. In fact, between them both, they've beaten all the top men in the field, excluding only yourself, Tom Gervasi. Everyone has been eliminated but just the three of you—you're the only ones left, for the title of "Love Champ of the World"—of our *Western* world, at any rate: quite a sizable chunk."

Tom Gervasi said, "So I'm the top man left, and they're *both* the top women left?"

"Yes, Tom Gervasi, and obviously they can't settle their deadlock tie by opposing each other *directly*; they must vanquish equally ranked men, in compared performances. Both have vanquished the worthiest men, in proven superiority. No more men are left to conquer, save but yourself. Thus, we're reaching the climactic finale of the whole tournament. You'll be matched, first against Gloria, then against Sharon. If Gloria beats you, thus spoiling your undefeated record, you must still compete against Sharon. If Sharon beats you by the same margin of dominance with which Gloria had prevailed against you, then Gloria and Sharon must be declared co-Champs, and share the Title. If *you* beat one but lose to the other, the one you lose to is the undisputed Champ. For *you* to win the Title, you must beat them both. Is that clear?"

"I'm game," Tom Gervasi said, warming to the contest. "I'll emerge victorious. Don't bet on anyone but me."

"As I'm the head judge, I'm not permitted to bet."

"I hadn't meant to slur your integrity. Please award me the palm, in my mighty love contests, first against Gloria, then against Sharon."

"I'm impartial and fairminded, as head judge. You'll be declared the winner only on merit: not on pre-influence. You're illegally off-bounds for attempting to prejudice me to be disposed in your favor, Tom Gervasi. On performance you'll be judged. Go ahead. You versus Gloria. To the finish. Fight fairly, and good luck."

In front of a hundred thousand cheering fans in the great stadium, Tom Gervasi and Gloria met in the middle of the arena. They looked at each other, spoke to each other, and then it was obvious, to the judges and spectators alike, that Gloria was in love with Tom Gervasi, who, in turn, rejected her. Tom Gervasi's hand was raised by the head judge, who declared him the winner; while Gloria, the loser, sighed and pined in vain, in romantic despondency.

Thus, Gloria fell from the ranks of the undefeated. Now, for the climactic bout between the only two undefeated performers left: Tom Gervasi, and Sharon. The contest was in a different stadium, next night, all lit up to about a hundred and fifty thousand fans, packing it to the rafters in a new attendance record. The fans were vociferous, and wildly applauded or jeered every move between those two most magnificent love objects in the Western World. They met in mid-arena, flirted around, conversed, and soon, to spectators and judges alike, it was obvious who the winner was: Tom Gervasi. A tumultuous cheer rose. He remained quite indifferent, professionally, to Sharon, while she quite fell for him, in a heap of love.

"Love Champ of the World"—that's Tom Gervasi. He proved himself. He's the Man of the Hour. Possibly of the Age, as well. He defeated all rivals, by being loved and by refraining from loving. He's so heroically romantic! Those who were loved by others, loved him alone. *They* were lovable, but he, impervious.

The most loved human being of North America, the British Isles, and the European Continent. Long may he reign. The Crown is his. To be retired, upon his death. No more contests. He culminated the sport, making any subsequent bout irrelevantly anticlimactic. The Title is retired, in his permanent possession.

XL. TELEVISION MISTREATS TOM GERVASI, THEN APOLOGIZES, BUT EVENTUALLY USES HIM. HIS WHOLE TELEVISION CAREER, IN QUICK SEQUENCE.

Tom Gervasi was interviewed by a love-psychologist on television: "In general, would you agree that when a woman is first seen or met, she's just more appealing than later, after we've known her a long time? And that's why love affairs and marriages break up?"

"As 'a foremost authority in the field,' I'd have to agree with you. Of course, the circumstances vary enormously, and lots of other factors would tend to complicate the issues. It depends, of course, on so many things. So your hypothetical question is a very bare simplification, and only by particular cases in special contexts are we able to estimate more accurately . . . urgh, I'm lost. What was your question again?"

"Let's move on, Tom Gervasi. We've covered *that* subject enough."

"*Covered* it?! I thought we barely sketched what was hinted at."

"Tom Gervasi, let me criticize you. I take the liberty, being a psychologist. You're too fussy about truth. It's bad for television."

"I care more for truth than for television."

"Oh, stop acting so noble, so superior. Go slumming, a little bit. Won't you compromise your standards for truth, somewhat, for the sake of our national television audience? They don't want you to be so conditional and qualified. They want you to give straight, gutsy, manlike answers. Are you, Tom Gervasi, secretly homosexual? It's obvious that you're an intellectual: you betray yourself rather openly, on that score. But aren't you a homosexual, as well? You *seem* not to be. But are you hiding?"

"I find your implications insulting, offensive, and snide. I think you're a rat, you stink. Your values are sickening. In full view of our national television audience, I'm getting up out of this chair and leaving the studio, you lousy bum. To hell with you."

"Well, folks, Tom Gervasi was as good as his word. I guess I provoked him the wrong way or something, but he's abandoned this interview, and I'm left here, holding the bag, so to speak. Personally, I think he's queer, gay, a fairy. That's my instant analysis, on the spot. What evidence had I to go on? True, I'd never seen Tom Gervasi before. This was my first time. He's been renowned, in wide circles, as an authority on the special field of women. That, in itself, smells suspicious, doesn't it? Anyone who hangs around women all *that* much—why, it's transparent that he's *compensating*. What is he compensating *for*? Yes, now we're trapping him, hounding him into the corner, where he'll have to reveal his true colors. I'd swear that not only is he an intellectual, but also a homosexual. On my license as a practicing psychologist, expert enough to be a television interviewer, I'd swear that's the case, with Tom Gervasi, whom I've just unmasked. I don't intend character assassination or maligning of his integrity. I'm just playing *his* game: going for the truth. All the women in his life! They're all just coverups, that he needs, because he's a pathetic weakling, a little snot masquerading as a man's man and a man of truth at that. He's neither. He's just a sniveling sniffer up women's garter-belts, those who are wearing them. Anyway, that's Tom Gervasi, exposed. The *real* Tom Gervasi: not the legend. Tom Gervasi debunked. Tom Gervasi, revealed as be really is. That's the truth about him. Not very nice, is it, that truth? Well, *he*'s not very nice, either. How *dare* he walk off my show! In front of a national audience! Showing me up, like that! Some nerve, he has! Why, I'll sue him! For every cent he owns! For making me a laughing stock! On my own show!"

The psychologist interviewer was now uncontrollably angry, and the studio monitors were getting alarmed. The interviewer seemed insane. And he's billed as a psychologist! This reflected ill on the network channel, and was bad for public relations, since the publicity was just giving it a bad name. The network channel ought to apologize, in a public statement, disowning responsibility for that fraudulent psychologist interviewer, and announcing that he's been fired from his job. That will restore credibility for the network, and partially repair a damaged reputation. The network requests that Tom Gervasi reappear. He receives official apologies, from the President of that channel, in a special show, taped live for the national audience.

"Tom Gervasi, you went through slander. Your integrity was maligned, your name defamed, your manhood impugned, your intellectuality held up to scorn. But we fired the culprit. Would you take his place, as a weekly psychologist interviewer, choosing your own guests? You're known as a national expert on women. Perhaps you can air your views, by interviewing your own self. I offer you the job, in front of the full national audience. Salary is confidential, we'll wait till we're not on the screen, before negotiating it. I'm potentially your new boss, if you accept. You may, of course, keep the job you already have. This will sort of supplement the income from that. You'll be paid handsomely, since our advertisers know that, with *you* scheduled on the screen, the whole country's women are bound to drop what they're doing and watch. Your appeal to women is our universal wonder, here. I mean, we don't wonder *why*. Or *how*. We wonder, in the sense of 'Wow!' "

"Thanks, President of network. But no, I won't accept. I shun too much publicity. I value being a private person. I don't want anonymous women to go berserk watching my image.

"Thanks for your apology, President of network, for my being subjected to that psychologist interviewer. You fired him in your *own* interest, of course; not just to placate me. He was awful. I shudder to remember him.

"This is my final television appearance I ever intend. My life with women is private. *I*'m private. I shrink and shy away, from this medium.

"Goodbye, President of network. Goodbye, women watching me. And men too, goodbye. And the little kids. And the cats and dogs, watching. Goodbye, to the vacant brain. I'm soon off this screen. And there I stay. Off."

"Folks, that was Tom Gervasi. His opinions don't reflect any network policy. He spoke in his private capacity. As himself, in fact. Quite a guy. Well, we'll miss him. His television career was shortlived. But remember, folks—however shortlived his career, where did it occur? Here! On *this* network channel! So women, remember. We're Tom Gervasi's old television station. His only one, ever. Therefore, buy all our products. Everything we advertise. Don't stop, till we tell you.

"Women, I'm sure Tom Gervasi would *want* you to watch our network, and buy all the commercial goods advertised here. Do it for *his* sake. For Tom Gervasi."

Tom Gervasi didn't hear. He was gone from the studio, after he signed himself off to all the viewers. He was exploited behind his back, out of sight or hearing, by the network President. So television used him. Even after he left it, gone from the studio. He was used, for commercial gain.

XLI. A CHAPTER WHOSE FIRST PAGE IS MISS-ING. ITS LIKELY CONTENTS MAY BE PARTIALLY INFERRED.

. . . She'll fix him. The sweet vengeance could start by her sabotaging his business standing. She'll find a way of having him lose his job. She knew a thing or two to use against him. She'll betray him, through his weak points. Wherever he's vulnerable, she'll attack. Hate was more pleasant, more self-assertive, more aggression-venting, than her soft moping, her passive hoping, her futile loving. He'd given her years' accumulation of hurt. She was too loving to protest. Now, she'll reverse that, sharply. Emphatically. And nastily. The prospect thrilled her. She warmed to it.

Bit by bit, she damaged him. She put her heart to it. She spared no detail. Tom Gervasi was now reduced in circumstances, thanks to Carol's unremitting labors to bring Tom's misfortunes to a head. He had been a near-executive, but had been fired. Attempts to get established with other firms had misfired in every case. Tom had been forced, by a series of reversals in his career ambition, to settle for ever lower positions in the business hierarchy. His present post was embarrassingly humble. No longer able to afford the rent on his old apartment, he was now living in a rather cheap slum. He had really come down in the world. Snobs who had once courted him, were avoiding him now. His clothes were less presentable, and he was looking grubby. He gave off a whiff of squalor. He stopped being attractive to women. His girlfriends abandoned him. (Discovering this afforded Carol a gloat-crowing satisfaction. It touched off, in her, a certain sadistic glee, and a malicious righteousness.) Tom Gervasi's decline was romping rapidly. Respect and esteem for him in social circles galloped out of sight. His very dignity was dwindling. Behind the scenes, Carol presided, pulling strings where she influentially could, over this conspicuous deterioration of this former man of achievement and promise. His whole stature crumbled. He was going downhill on the bum's road. Only recently, he was admired and envied. Carol attended to these details very carefully. It was her joyful masterpiece, if destruction was her game. She achieved it. Tom Gervasi's friends watched helplessly. They were no match for the hidden hater who worked with calm skill.

An alcoholic beggar, Tom Gervasi was in rags. He was at Carol's mercy. She visited his hanging-out haunts sometimes—decrepit streets. She hissed. He remembered her. But he was weak. He couldn't fight back. He was down. She rubbed it in. With love, gone bad.

Her cruelty has alienated her friends—it's undisguisable. She still works at her office job; but she's avoided by colleagues there. Men never ask her out, except ones too puny to assuage their own guilt. They borrow her sadism, upon themselves. She's past middle age, though. She had so much wanted marriage, and children! It's all over, for her. Having reduced Tom Gervasi to a beggar, she finds herself a victim to her own process; in debasing him, her own degradation has kept parallel; though outwardly, her position is more acceptable. She's created horror and become it. *Two* victim-products are her toll. Enough, in one life's work.

XLII. BARBARA FEIGNS INDIFFERENCE AS A RUSE OF WINNING TOM GERVASI'S LOVE, WHICH WOULD BE EXPRESSED BY *HIS* FEIGNING INDIFFERENCE LIKEWISE. HOWEVER, HE SEES RIGHT THROUGH IT, AND MAKES HER CONFESS. THAT BRINGS THINGS TO A HEAD, SORT OF. TO CLEAR-CUT CONFUSION'S ACUTE CULMINATION.

Barbara had it all figured out: The way to fascinate Tom Gervasi, to intrigue him into fantasy over her, was to act as though he didn't interest her in the slightest.

She'd as much as admit, as politely as she could, "Sorry, Tom. You just don't attract me."

This was designed to provoke his gamesmanship for challenge. Then, he'd lay siege on her; bombard her with flower bouquets, telegrams, dinner invitations, gifts of perfume, telephone calls rehearsed to sound impulsive. Tom would cover up his passion With a wayward air of whimsy. He'd develop a seriously actual love for Barbara, but style it out in lighthearted levity and caprice. *He*'d pretend to having no mad obsession for her; which would parallel, with poetic irony, Barbara's own current pretense to care not a fig for him.

Make-believe *not-to* is a great betrayer of the reverse state of affairs.

Barbara's make-believe would con Tom into such love for her, that *he*'d stoop to make-believe as well.

Then they'll simultaneously unmask, in one confessional night. And their double truths, from being hushed up, will gush out, like long-delayed spouts of blood; to kindle ardent vows of mutual fidelity for the rest of all their born eternities.

This was Barbara's long-range plan. She'd play *her* role, of feigned indifference: and soon would have Tom playing the same role. The amorous theater will turn out real, when "indifference" gets exposed. Then dammed-up love will flow in mighty gusts.

Thus, with an air of grave unconcern: "Oh, hello, Tom. I hadn't recognized you. You reminded me of someone else. But I can't remember who *he* is, either. Maybe it's *several* people whom you remind me of: but I can't seem to place them . . . Yes, I *do* remember you. Is it Tom Lavelli? . . . No, don't tell me. I'm hopeless, but let me guess. Tom DeRenzi? I *know* the last name is sort of Italianate. Tom Barboni? Oh, I give up. I know I've seen you *somewhere*: who are you?"

"Barbara, you must be mad. We've slept with each other over a hundred times. We've been on vacations together. We've been intimate on many levels. Have you turned schizophrenic, gone catatonic, had a traumatic seizure of amnesia, or just gone plain 'nuts'?

"I'm worried. See a doctor, hurry. You have an acute memory block. What on earth have you been repressing? The big-city social-commercial mad rush has been getting to you. Maybe you need a peaceful rest in the country.

"I'm upset. You seemed so sound, once. Now, you don't recognize me.

"Or are you only pretending? That's it! You love me, so you're acting like you don't even know me, to insure that I don't 'taka you for granted.' What a put-on! Why, it's pure theater. Confess, Barbara: isn't it?"

"You saw through my little ruse; and caught my bluff. Well, it's true. I love you with insecurity. I endeavored, somehow, to contrive to guile your interest from flagging to keen, on behalf of my lonely, unreturned love for you.

"I've made a clean confession of it all. Are you moved to pity me? If so, show it with love."

"This all goes to strike home to me the inadequacy of my regard for you, by the scale of proportion of yours for me. It's almost comically uneven. It means I'll leave you. Then you'll recover, and *truly* forget."

"Well, it was all brought to a head. The way things were, it was getting intolerable for me.

"Now you've rejected me and we'll break up. It's better, this way. I was hoping with illusion. Better no hope, no illusion. Grim truth. Goodbye."

"Poor Barbara. I pity you."

"Poor pity. I craved your *love*. Now, just pity, on parting, is what I get. A paltry substitute. Tom Gervasi's pity. I bitterly see how easier it is to provoke *that*, than that rare commodity, your love."

"Poor Barbara. Take my pity instead. It's all I have. If I *had* love for you, you'd get it."

"How generous. What's your name again?"

"You've uttered it thousands of times, as well as a few seconds ago. You've *admitted* your bluff. Cut out pretense.

"But my name is your sorrow. Stamp *both* out, at once."

"Let a blot darken it; and raze it out. The memory and the pain are indistinguishable. I've learned to overcome hope. And, in the deep stab of time, to grow your name remote, in a poor forgotten field."

"Poor Barbara! You bleed so!"

"I bleed what I have. I bleed my love out, hope and all. And bleed oblivion in. The healing naught, that inks your name away."

"You feigned indifference, in hope to win my love. May indifference step out of the theater, and find its worldly home, in quiet, forgetful fact."

"Oh Tom—how can I *ever* forget you? Ever, in a million years!"

"Now, that's not the way, Barbara. My pity pours forth; and mingles in one mud-center with your beaten love. For the final time, our secretions combine. A bitter mix. Your love flows, and meets my pity. That compound is all that remains, of our time on earth together. I weep my pity; you, your love: let these mingling pools swim a silver way to open sea, where all things find their common end, to trade their elements in, and work out such change or rest to bring a welcome disappearance about of the former mold. My pity, your love. The sorrow is yours, but guilt is mine. Now dip them scattered into the vast vat of All: and let new tricks appear, tagged on to new names. We've mingled our selves and substances, to our separate regrets. Now let's *be* mingled, in all that's over us, beneath, within, outside. And be recombined, with other chance elements. And come out, as other beings."

"Very mystical, Tom Gervasi. Sloppy and sentimental, too. I'll forget you when I can, that name and you behind it. To *prompt* me to forget, to *cue* me to forget, I may need death's reminder. Then 'Tom Gervasi' will be the same as my indifference to it. *Till* then, though, I *am* your name: and wear it, on my widowed heart."

"I'm moved; I'm touched."

"To mere pity?"

"*Yours* the love; mine the pity. It's our bond. Let death break *that.*"

"It will: without trying. What does *death* care? It shows *authentic* indifference; not feigned, in vain love's hope."

XLIII. TOM GERVASI LOVES GEORGIA'S BEHIND, BUT SHE WON'T LET HIM ADVANCE THERE. HE'S QUITE FRONTAL ABOUT HER REAR: BUT SHE TURNS HER BACK ON HIM, TO PUNISH HIM FOR NOT LOVING HER FOR HERSELF, BUT JUST FOR THE PROTRUDING BULGE OF HER DEEPLY DIVINE POSTERIOR. THUS, HE MAKES AN ASS OF HIMSELF, OVER HERS.

Georgia interested Tom (Gervasi, that is) because of the way her buttocks curved up from the back. Her rear end reared up, and protruded, with smooth swellings that curled over, through the broad, voluminous thighs, to the front, with its "mound of Venus" and then dip-under.

But the rest of her was all thin and slender, though in proportion—*especially* in proportion.

She had but a slight waist, and thin ankles and wrists. But where it *really mattered,* she bulged over.

It wasn't a platonic love that Tom had in mind, concerning Georgia. It wasn't for reading books together that he sought her company. Nor for studying a foreign language together. Nor for discussing politics, sociology, anthropology, geology, botany, zoology, biology, chemistry, economics, psychology, art, music, literature, theater, dance, movies, sports, food, furniture, forestry, metallurgy, engineering, architecture, fashions, war, geography, history, oceanography, crime, metaphysics, philosophy, religion, genealogy, navigation, aeronautics, mythology, astrology, astronomy, trade and commerce, business management, industry, advertising, market research, medicine, dentistry, palmistry, handwriting analysis, the occult, mysticism, abnormal behavior, law, bureaucracy, typography, radio, television, journalism, propaganda, government, mineralogy, insects, agriculture, fish, bibliography, wine, linguistics, etymology, silverware, antique vases, finance, mass transportation, ecology, demogogery, ethics, or any other subject, none of which even remotely touched on Georgia's rear end as Tom's hands itched to do. He felt ill just thinking about it.

However, Georgia was married. But the marriage was dissolving, it was "on the rocks," with divorce proceedings already underway.

However, she had a boyfriend. But she and the boyfriend were on the verge of breaking up, and had already stopped seeing each other.

So what stood in Tom's way? The road toward behind Georgia ought to be clear, with free access ahead (or rather, behind). Tom should get going. What's stopping him? Some over-subtle scruple, some dire misgiving, some uncalm qualm?

Georgia herself—the part of her in front of her behind—what opinion did *she* have?

Oh, she was delighted to have Tom take such an interest in her magnificent buttocks and substantial upper thighs.

But all men were alike, in that respect. She wanted Tom to respect her as a *human being*: not to regard her as an object of his eroticism. She wanted him to love her for *herself*—and leave all the rest behind. Therefore, she'll resist him, till he shows evidence of interest in non-backward matters. "I'm not just a pelvic region," she reasoned; "I'm a whole entire person. Let him treat me as such, before I let him grab my ass with roaming caress. I'm Georgia, first. Only secondarily, am I what sticks out behind and at the hip level.

"Sex is all very well and good. But I come first. The rest will merely follow, once I feel esteemed in my whole being for all that I've been and might become. Let him show evidence. *Then,* I'll let him in, the large round way about."

However, Tom could think of nothing else but that three-dimensional section, which obscured all of Georgia's spiritual being altogether. He had a fixation, an obsession, on that voluminous area. It eclipsed awareness of the incidental person that Georgia also was—an individual, born free, with an immortal soul and a democratic equality—irrelevant rubbish, to Tom's all-consuming desire for her sweet rear bulge.

"Georgia. Please. I'm desperate. Let me at least *touch* it. I'm losing my mind. Let me have my way, so that I could relieve myself there, to release me from that fixation, and then my mind will be clear for regarding other matters, such as you as a human being, interested in books and society, art, politics, the world, and so forth. I know you have a personality, a character, lodged within you, a soul, a unique individuality, stuff like that. But I'm not free to contemplate or appreciate all that stuff. Your behind sticks in the way, it stands out and bars your 'deeper' qualities from my frustrated admiration. Let me get at that wonderful behind, please, and grovel there, wallow there, make free, free, with all that flesh.

"Then I'll feel much better. My head will be cleared. And I'll see the *you,* uneased from that more prominent attribeaut."

"No, Tom. It's your supreme test. I'm making it difficult for you, to see whether you can overcome your immense internal resistance, and love me for myself alone, while keeping your dirty hands off that glorious ass of mine. It's a way of testing the purity of your devotion, lechery-free, for my beauty as a human being. I'm Georgia, not my ass."

"You've got it all backward: You're your ass foremost. Georgia is there, somewhere, but powerfully overshadowed by the ass-first domination which grips me by the priorities. My carnal craving overcomes all decent considerations of civil decorum and even courtship's slow protocol. Turn around, please. I know where my love is. It's well behind you, Georgia: And clings to all your torso, from that supreme vantage-point, 'Mount Overlook,' where scenic tourism is graphic in the round and compels all fascination to suspend itself there, divinely arrested. I beg you, turn around. For that's the better part of yourself, dear Georgia. The seat of your soul is your ass. In such prominence, is your spirit's holy shrine. Look to where your divine Core is. Behind, Georgia, behind."

"I'm forward-looking for the emancipation of women as people commanding respect."

"My respect for you, Georgia, foremost, is back there."

"Sorry, I'm forward-looking. I'm punishing you for overlooking my emancipated women's-modernity, by depriving you of what you're keenly savage to grip your itching fingers in. Back there, it's *my* territory. My husband, and then my boyfriend, were humbly gratified, back there. They swooned in helpless delight. But you, Tom, I'm depriving of that. *Starve* your longing look: I forbid the touch."

"It's your property. I place a high value on it. Could we marry? *Then* I could get it."

"No, I turn you down, for punishment. I *have* the ass, but you *are* the ass. Suffer, Tom; suffer. Suffer!, you miserable male!"

XLIV. TWO WOMEN WHO LACK HAVING TOM GERVASI, AND A POLICEMAN WHO LACKS *BEING* HIM. THEIR DEPRIVATION SUMS UP WORLDLY DISCONTENT.

Two women fight over Tom Gervasi. A policeman tries to reason with them: "Is he worth it?"

The women are indignant. "You aren't women. And you never saw him. So you're in no position to know how strongly we feel about him to the extent that we've been fighting."

"True, I'm no woman and I never saw him. But my duty is to stop you from fighting, no matter what you're fighting *about*. It's the fighting itself that's illegal. It doesn't matter that it's over Tom Gervasi."

"Have we been disturbing the peace in a city street?"

"Yes, so stop, or I'll have you women arrested. You go free with the first warning. But resume the fighting, and you're taken into custody."

"Then we'll just go to the apartment of one of us, where we could privately fight in peace."

"I have no control over that, women. But don't make too loud a noise, or the neighbors might complain."

"We promise, policeman. Thanks for not arresting us."

"You're welcome, women. You're both so pretty, that I wish *I* were Tom Gervasi. Then I'd pick one of you, and have lots of fun."

"If you *were* Tom Gervasi, policeman, which one of us would you choose?"

"I don't know, because I'm not him. But if it were *me* to choose, I'd pick you both, and alternate you, one for one week, the other for the next week, and so on. That way, I would lose *nei-*

ther of you, and could enjoy the spicy flavor of changing off. Why don't you recommend that solution to Tom Gervasi? He might well agree with me, even though he's not me."

"We've suggested it. But he turned it down."

"Why? Is he homosexual?"

"No, but he's already been alternating ten or twelve women for the last few months; and to take *us* two on in addition would just compound his well-deserved sexual fatigue."

"I'm jealous of him. Or am I envious, instead?"

"Let's not quibble over words, Anyway, policeman, you could see how frustrated we are to be excluded from his harem, and how we're taking out that frustration by fighting with each other on the street. But your duty was to inform us that we're disturbing the peace. So we're going to cool off our fight while walking to the apartment of one of us, and then heat it up again behind locked doors of private residence."

"You gain nothing by fighting, except to relieve your frustrations?"

"We certainly don't gain *Tom Gervasi,* by fighting over him. So our fight is pure; art-for-art's-sake; rather than pragmatic in winning Tom Gervasi as reward for one of us, the prize to the winner of the fight. We'll neither get him. Thus, our fight takes on a poetic, rather than a practical, flavor. We're *both* losers. And as losers, we fight."

"Wouldn't one of you want to be a winner of me?—or both?"

"No, because you're not Tom Gervasi."

"What must I do, to be him? I lust for you both, so I'll do *anything,* to be him."

"There's nothing you *can* do. You're *unable* to be him. It's impossible, policeman. He's *already* him. And you're only you."

"In that case, *I*'m frustrated too. Take me along with you to the apartment of one of you. Then *all three* of us can fight: frustrated losers."

"We won't take you along, policeman. Because you might get perverse sexual pleasure, in fighting with us."

"You women are very bright. You see right through me, you know my game. Well, it's futile, so I give up. Have a nice fight, at the apartment of one of you. I'll resume being a policeman on my own, and walk my beat. But as a result of talking with you, I'm changed now. Before, I didn't know what was wrong with me, what was my primary lack. Now, you women have taught me my fatal deficiency as me. I've now learned to regret not being Tom Gervasi. I've lived all my life not knowing what, regrettably, was wrong with me, my true failure of identity. You've defined it now: Tom Gervasi."

"Sorry to provide you with such a basic discontent within the personality of your whole existence, poor policeman. But you had to do your duty, stumbling on us fighting. And we had to answer truthfully why you wouldn't do as the boyfriend of one or both of us, for whom you conceived a dual lust. So we women lack Tom Gervasi, grieving us with bitter discontent, to the extent that we fight with each other. Whereas, policeman, in *your* case, it's not that you lack him in terms of possessive acquisition, romantic property, an obtained bond, which creates your discontent; it's your lacking *being* him. Your lack is more fundamental, therefore, than ours. Your problem plunges to the depths of existence. You're not Tom Gervasi. *We*'re sorry you're not, and so are you. So much sorrow, can one man cause, in his absence somewhere?"

"I ought to arrest *him*, women."

"But policeman, on what grounds?"

"The sorrow and discontent, the fighting, the regret, he's causing, by my not being him, and your not having him. Yet, he's within his rights, the lucky man. He's causing us legal pain. The law can't touch him. Nor can you women claim him as your own for love. Nor am I able to *be* him. Well, there ought to be *some* consolations, left, in our three lives."

"We'll go to the apartment of one of us, and fight."

"And I'll go along and walk my beat. Goodbye, women. I wish I could have one or both of you."

"You'd be most welcome to, if only you were Tom Gervasi. But only one man can be that person. Unfortunately, you're not that one man. Unfortunately for us women; and for you, you poor policeman."

"We're all groaning. But that lucky guy is probably gloating to be the only one to be himself. Well, I don't blame him. I'd gloat, too."

"And we'd *help* you gloat, dear policeman. We'd let you make love to us as many times as you wanted."

"That's the true extent of my loss! I blame my parents, for having made me *me,* and not *him.*"

"That's unfair. They're innocent."

"What *is* fair, women? Nothing is fair. We're all so unequal in justice and good fortune. We all fall short."

"Except one: Tom Gervasi: he's the measure of *how* we fall short: you by not *being* him; we by not *having* him. Human life is finite. The earth is no place for ideals, save in demonstrating the defective degrees of falling far below them. But there's a *heaven*: where you, policeman, can fully be Tom Gervasi; and where us women can have him, fully, his whole happy heart and body. For heaven, then, let's thank God. There alone, and then, we'll make amends, to be and have."

"I agree, women. I'm going to heaven straight away, to remedy the deficiencies. Why wait? Imperfection is here, perfection is there. Here, all is wanting. There, it's having, it's being, to satisfaction. Why go, women, to the apartment of one of you, and fight? Instead, go straight to heaven, where no fighting will be necessary, where there'll be nothing to be frustrated over. Let's all three go there. I'll become Tom Gervasi, and you two can have me."

"What a perfect ideal It's just too ideal! It's a heavenly solution. But there's one flaw: we must die first."

"Yes, women. That's a difficult step to take. In fact, I'm reluctant to do it."

"And so are we, policeman. So let's linger here. And fight and mope, in plight of hope, where doors won't ope. You *be* your non-Gervasi. And we'll *have* our non-Gervasi. And we'll go on lacking. And what we lack will dwarf what we are and have. We crawl about, in Tom Gervasi's shadow. There's but little, here below. There's nothing, barring him."

"Well, we'll still live, women. If you call this life! Compared to what *could* be! If only. Poor 'only.' Our actual famine, against our prospective feast! Oh, earth is a loss. And life is finding that so. To know what we don't have. Wretched poverty, of our tiny lot."

"Policeman, we're all too sad. We live in a Tom Gervasi world. And partake, not at all."

"Nothing, for us."

"Or dreadful something, as nothing's negative equivalent. Policeman, we hate you. You're not Tom Gervasi."

"I hate *you*. If I *were* Tom Gervasi, I'd spurn you both; I'd scorn you; and delight to reject you. Then you'd fight, over *me*."

"Oh, you're so hypothetical, poor policemen. This is a grim dream. Somewhere there's a sun shining. Tom Gervasi is there. (That *could* be you.) He kisses and loves two women. (That *could* be us.) O happy sun, to shine on so happy a sight! O brightness! O truth, in its *preferred* state. The *right* truth. The *bright* truth. The truth we're not in. The shade of falsehood, we live. Feeding on a false shadow. For all is false, outside that light. We're on the wrong side. We're in a dark dearth. We're in a deprived earth. We're gripped, by negation. We want vainly. We live as lacks, as great Lack's gnome-like lackeys. We live already our prepared death. As non-Gervasi-creatures. In a creeping void. In this Nothing, by which we know of sun's heaven, and Tom Gervasi."

XLV. TOM GERVASI APPEALS TO GOD TO SETTLE THE MAY-JUNE DISPUTE. THUS MODERN TIMES ENTERTAINS A MIRACLE. PROVING THAT MIRACLES AREN'T EXTINCT, THOUGH THEY'RE A DISAPPEARING BREED.

May and June are not only months, but women's names. They're not only women's names, but in these two cases they actually *are* the women. The women being, of course, May and June.

By coincidence, though they've never met, they both love the same man. Through him, within him, they meet. He's their spiritual go-between.

Tom Gervasi knew first May, and than June. The whole world goes by that springtime sequence, as well, by any standard calendar. But Tom Gervasi knew not just the months in that order, but the women. In his case, May continued to go on after June had already begun, by amorous overlap and erotic alternation. With the months, May stops altogether just as June begins. But Tom Gervasi has now made them concurrent, within, overall, the general same time span. Even in snowy winter, May and June are quite active, even dominant, in the weather and climate of the sultry, stormy, quick-growing, invigorating currents and crosswinds, sunny or not, sometimes misty, but always greening, of Tom Gervasi's emotionally adventurous life in nature.

Now, May and June have gotten wind of each other, and without even having yet met, already are wrapped in such mutual detestation that Tom Gervasi keeps them well apart; for a confrontation between these keen rivals for his heart would be eye-scratching, hair-pulling, dress-ripping, shin-kicking, spitting, screaming, sobbing, name-calling, scene-making, traumatic, humiliating.

May says, "If I ever meet that June, she'll be taught to learn that May takes precedence, that I come first, in the love and life of Tom Gervasi. I'll enforce that lesson with nails and teeth, fists and feet, and a boiling tongue. She'll never forget it. She'll retire, in defeat, from the calendar of events. Then the coast will be clear, for Tom Gervasi and me to romp through the dear year freely in each other's arms, without June's disruptive interference. We'll be one another's own, with June out of the way. Then I'll marry Tom Gervasi. With June retired, from the fray."

June, however, is of the opposite way of thinking. "May is only the prelude, the building up, the laying groundwork for, June's triumphant entrance. She's preliminary, I'm climactic, in the spring calendar. Thus nature has it. And so it is, between us. June will *bury* May, will supplant it altogether, in Tom Gervasi's heart of spring. June's a wedding month. That augurs well. With May out of the way, having expended herself, having drained Tom Gervasi of a few wild oats in his seedy season, I'll take him over, altar-bent, to the bridal suite. Garlanded by nature, at her prime."

Thus, May and June disagreed most uncordially, the whole year around, each clamoring to be a full-time production, a year-round event, not a brief specialty of the season, in the great outside world, the universal nature emporium, of Tom Gervasi's love-heart. He did some deep thinking: "I've got to keep them away from each other. But I can't go on *forever*, dating both. I must choose one, and one alone. Her I'll marry, the other I'll reject. Yes, but whom? Both are dear, to me. But they're building up such hate for each other, I dread a cataclysmic war of months. They'll rend the calendar, and divide nature up. I must avert these hostilities. But how?"

He *enjoyed* having two mistresses. That way, he tired of neither. It kept them on their toes, each eager to find ways of pleasing him that the other had yet to discover. Like competitive airlines, one of which advertises especially delicious food for the flying patrons, while its rival may stress, in its advertising campaign, sexy stewardesses in very short skirts. The first may advertise a safety record of few crashes. The second might emphasize the great free movies to be seen during flight. So too, May and June are hustling competitors for Tom Gervasi's comfort and delight. They vie to outdo the other in providing him with unique advantages in their solicitous company. Each is enterprising, explorative, in making the greater impression. These are Tom Gervasi's splendid advantages in setting two mistresses in all-out contest for his heart. But it's cruel to them. Tom Gervasi is kind. He wants to stop this emotional carnage. It's brutal to pit adversaries that way, like Roman gladiators against lions before a decadent Coliseum audience with a cutthroat disposition; or bear-fights, cockfights, for depraved amusement. And May and June haven't even met! They're to be kept apart. They're capable of an atrocity, the blood sacrifice of each other at the shrine of Tom Gervasi sweepstakes. His choice will cause the loser misery; even—he dreaded—suicide. They loved him more than life itself. He must avert a catastrophe. The months are embattled. Whom to award the favor? His hand in prize, at a flower-bedecked wedding, which all of nature must attend. For one, grief. For the other, himself. Was he born to wield such power? What kind solution, to the savage dilemma?

He thought and thought. As yet, to no avail.

Last night he slept with May—in his or her apartment. Tonight, with June—in his or her apartment. Next night, May. Night after, June. Each one is spurred on to stimulate him sexually, to outdo her imaginary rival. Each one seduces him even with nothing left in his genitals, fearing that the other might find greater means of enticement. Tom Gervasi found this tussle between them exciting, and made great efforts to accommodate it. But it's a steeper and steeper climb, against fatigue and exhaustion. He needs a sexual rest. But neither May nor June dares to give it to him, as they equate sex to a tool for winning his heart. They wear him down. He's worn out. He's drying up, becoming thinner. But the girls ply on. For dear life. For the highest prize: Tom Gervasi as bridegroom. But Tom Gervasi as *corpse* seems more likely, at *this* stage.

He does something desperate: he arranges a high-level meeting between them both, with himself to preside, to restrain them, to have them vow civil courtesy during trying circumstances of triangular warfare. He sat between them, so they wouldn't scratch or bite, pull hair, or kick. "Behave, girls!" he warned.

And went on: "The two of you love me, I love you both. But you're ready to kill each other for me. We're all bound together most dangerously. That's why I've had you meet: to thrash it out, by peaceful means. It's hard for me to make a choice. On what basis shall we arrive at a solution? We're in tense peril of sanity, at these close quarters. We're interlocked, in a fatal grip. Let's disentangle, unwind, and resolve all this. I can't please you both."

May and June concurred, in that. But they avoided each other's eyes. They both glazed at him. They looked obedient, to his any bark.

Slavish, servile, they were. May would use anything in her power to kill off June and be sole on one stage to this man. June would do likewise to May, toward dearly the same wish. Tom Gervasi wanted to please them both. But how *can* he, at all? Only by becoming two identical Tom Gervasi's, could he. Then there'd be one for each. One for May. One for June. Joy for all.

At this point, God intervened. He invaded Tom Gervasi's apartment in a bolt of lightning, with a clapse of thunder-flash to go along, in primeval association.

May, June, and their idol were all surprised. "God! What in the world are *You* doing here!?" exclaimed Tom Gervasi, with rhetorical emphasis. God smiled, enigmatically. He had a trick up His divine sleeve. (Or was it under His beard? Or in His hanging gown? He was like a stage magician. He dazzled wonder and suspense at you.)

"Well, God," asked Tom Gervasi, ever the genial host, "what brings *You* here tonight? Just dropped by? Do stay. We're rather cozy, now."

May and June glowered, glared. They suspected monkey-business. Some mischief was afoot. It all seemed altogether just too supernatural for words. Neither could afford humor. In grim solemnity, the chips were down, the stakes were high, the moment of truth was to be faced. Who shall get Tom Gervasi? And who shall die? Winner take all. For the loser, it's goodbye.

"Well, Tom Gervasi," God kidded, "you're a greedy man. Two women at a time? You're carrying My 'love-thy-neighbor' ordinance rather far—toward sexual exploitation I hope not? Don't *obey* the Lord in vain: I'd get a bad Name that way."

Tom Gervasi smiled, at God's wit. He could *use* the Old Boy's power, now. To unravel the May-June problem, here. "Look, God, this is damned serious. You've got to help us."

"Then don't curse. I'm squeamish about that."

"Sorry, it slipped. May and June, here, both want me, and I want both of them. Whoever *doesn't* get me, will die. That's some price to pay! It's only fair, that somehow *both* get me. That's where *You* come in, God."

"*Me*! You're out of your mind! What can *I* do? I'm only little old God. My power has all been stripped away. I *used* to be great, and venerated. But I'm shorn of all that. I'm but shabby-genteel, in considerably reduced circumstances. It's quite an embarrassment, I tell you!"

"Look, God, can't you remember some of Your old tricks? All that omnipotence You used to have! Want to make a comeback, of sorts? For old-time's sake? I'd be so grateful, I'd convert."

"To what?"

"To religion. What else?"

"Well, that clinches it. I'm game."

"Good old God! I *knew* you could do it!"

"Do what?"

"Ah, that's the crux of the matter."

"The—er—what!?"

"Crux. Oh, I shouldn't have used that word. You're 'hung-up' on it?"

"No pun, now. What do you want?"

"God, You created evolution."

"Yes, but Darwin took the credit. So what?"

"Remember the amoebas? Those little things?"

"Sure. Microscopic, they were."

"And still are, God. Anyway, You came up with an ingenious device, for their reproduction. You remember what it was?"

"Sure. They split in two."

"Good memory, God. You're far from senile."

"Thanks. But what's the point?"

"Can You, just for once, apply that reproduction trick to a human being? Me, *I*'m Your candidate."

"For once only. And only in your case. And just as a special favor. But give Me one good reason for doing it."

"*Two*, Your Honor—I mean God. You see them here: May and June."

"Boy, they're both pretty! *I* see what your game is. You want them both, without relinquishing one. And they, or course, both want *you*. Right now, you're only one Tom Gervasi, to the two of them. That's not a fair division of labor, or romantic equity. By splitting you into two, there's one for each. How's My arithmetic, so far?"

"Just great, Boss! Just great."

"Let Me address Myself just now to May and June. Girls, you look like you hate each other. Is that true? . . . You nod yes, vigorously. Well, I hate your hate. *I* stand for love! *If* I can give you *each* your own special Tom Gervasi, do you swear, before God, to change that hate to love, for each other?"

"They're assenting, God! They're even smiling! Love is great, and You're it!"

"I don't need your compliments, Tom Gervasi. Now, stand still. There."

Two Tom Gervasis appeared from a cloud of smoke, where before there had stood one. The amoeba had but one cell to split. Tom Gervasi had many. But God did it! He came through! It was a grand comeback, like an aging Sarah Bernhardt, Greta Garbo, Margot Fontaine. He had His old magic back. In the same whiff of smoke from which one Tom Gervasi became two, God graciously disappeared from the scene. He'd brought love. Fourfold.

XLVI. THIN WOMEN FOR SUMMER; FAT WOMEN FOR WINTER: TOM GERVASI'S THEORY OF SEASON AND SEX.

Tom Gervasi prefers, for summer, thin women; and fat for winter. What's the psychological physiology behind those seasonal variations? Here's his explanation, recorded at a press conference from a panel discussion on the timely subject: "Sex by Season":

"Well, ahem, or, it's like this. You see, ugh, summer is hot enough, you get me? It's thick with sweat, so to speak, and we swelter in humidity, and are already well smothered. In defense, we wear light clothing, and prefer light women. I don't mean 'lighthearted,' I mean light-*weight*. Just like we like a nice cool drink, right? And eat light food, like salad and melon, whatever's crisp and cold. Stands to reason, right?

"Well, by an opposite token, winter is at the other extreme, see? That's obvious, if you get my point. Winter errs on the *cold* side, if not freezing. That's its basic flaw, inherent to its natural makeup.

"So, we've got to compensate, see? So we grab ourself a real fat women, with flesh that stores heat, like a flabby sort of radiator swollen with soft heat, all for you, not for the general public. Why, you can *wallow* in that soft, spongy heat; it's nice and consoling, for the harsh wind outside.

"Whereas a bony, lanky dame has nowhere to store her best, so with *her* you'd only freeze together. Brrh! That's not *my* idea of fun. No sir, not unless the barometer goes the other way.

"A fat dame in winter, if she gets on top of you, it's like a thermostat blanket, a multi-layered eiderdown, and she could make you mighty cozy! The kind of smothering you really need, once the temperature hits a few feet below zero. Sex conducts heat, anyway. We say, 'the flame of love'; she's 'carrying the torch for him'; 'the smoldering embers from an erotic blase'; 'passion's roaring fire.' See what I mean? I don't mean to be bawdy; I'm just being scientific. This is a decent panel discussion here, we're all respectable, us panelists. No dirty stuff. None of that pornographic smudge. No, we're only trying to convey truth. No sin in *that*?, I hope.

"I presume, colleagues and listeners, that what I just said about thin women for summer and fat for winter, is not just my private eccentric idiosyncrasy, but is held up by the universal weight of consensus as the prevailing phenomenon with men everywhere. I was their spokesman, not just sounding off my *own* views. Scientists will verify and confirm my findings. This is not mere idle data, I'm giving you. It's holy generalised gospel in the multiplicity of its applications, dignifying it as principle, formula, rule. Men are alike, in that respect. Tap them, you'll see. Not that they're automatons, mere machines, creatures of predictability. No. But they're sort of *built* alike. You get me?

"Thin women, in winter, get precious little patronage from the menfolk. Fat women, in summer, likewise. For thin women, winter is a *lean* season. (That's a pun, get it?) But their prospects wax, in summer, with stout vigor, and robust expansion.

"I suggest that fat women hibernate in summer; that thin women hibernate in winter. Why waste their energy, in vain, to no futile avail? Let each thrive at her season.

"For men, the season is *always*. But *who with* is important. Different tools, under different circumstances. We must use our women wisely! But we *do*, anyway; no 'must' about it.

"Of course, women have *their* say, too. They're just as free as we are. *They* can pick and choose, too. In fact, they do.

168

"Folks, this is a very varied world, rich with diversity. Sex is stable, as a year-round activity, for the human race. But seasonal differences have to be observed. To season our stability, with rich variety's yield."

Tom Gervasi was much applauded, as his speech ended. The other panel members gave way to him. It proved not to be a panel discussion, but a one-man lecture. This was accepted; for such a renowned expert was granted his exceptional privilege by colleagues and listeners. *Women* were in the audience, too: some fat, some thin. The season was one *in-between* summer and winter. That allowed for a theoretical, academic approach, at an intellectual remove. Otherwise, it would have applied too closely, to specific cases, then and there, creating practical problems and anxious discomfort.

Tom Gervasi's theory is now the widely accepted one, even definitive, in universities and laboratories. He preaches what he practices. He doesn't just *do*; but imparts such knowledge to the world, as his doing imparted to his own mind. He *shares.* He reaches out. Toward universality. He doesn't blow just hot and cold, just thin and fat; he seasons the whole year with lustful appropriateness, to outstanding conditions.

Himself, he's temperate. He's between extremes. He waxes hot and cold, goes for thin and fat; and from all those parts, compiles the round year.

XLVII. CROSSING THE FICTION-REALITY BORDER LINE: THE DOUBLE LOVE OF TOM GERVASI.

Tom Gervasi was in love with a woman who died two hundred years before he was born. That made his chances very slim. What hope could he possibly have, of prevailing upon her long-dead heart?

To *compound* the difficulty of winning the woman he loved, not only was she already dead, therefore unresponsive to his wooing courtship; but she hadn't even ever actually lived in the real world as a person: she had merely been a fictional heroine, in some British author's novel!

Thus, Tom Gervasi's hopes of courting her successfully, of winning her love, were most discouragingly remote.

If the British author were only living now, Tom Gervasi would ask his permission to somehow "visit" that beloved heroine.

But not only had the heroine died at the end of the British author's novel over two centuries ago according to the dates of events that the author had provided for his mark of fiction; but the author himself, who had once been a real man in the actual world and not a mere created character, had also long, long been since dead. Thus, Tom Gervasi couldn't apply to him for permission to see the beautiful heroine of that old romance written in a mock-detail style of elaborate period realism.

"Give up; you have no chance to win her love," was the advice given by Tom Gervasi's contemporary friends. They were worried that Tom Gervasi's desire was pathetically unrealistic, and severely doomed to failure.

In fact, if he persisted, against those impossible odds, to actively try for a woman who not only had never lived but who, even as a fictional character, was long dead; if he persisted, he might truly become insane. This was the major concern of the poor man's friends.

They must snap him out of it!: Drag him out from the spell of so eerie an infatuation that crept across death's sacred boundary and art's holy division from life.

How? By introducing him to an actual real-life woman of his own contemporary generation, of his own culture, of his own worldly conditions. She should be a few years younger than he, as well as so beautiful as to convert his love from that long-dead woman of fiction to this real-life woman who dwelled within his very world.

Thus, they produced Marge: beautiful, and available.

They turned her loose, on him: Hoping she'd save him from the madness he was dangerously close to.

When Tom saw Marge, he said, "Hey, you know, you remind me of someone."

"Do I? That's unflattering. I'm supposed to be unique. Who is it I remind you of?"

"Someone I've been in love with, but alas, in vain."

"Really?! What a hard heart she must have! Who, then, in the world, is she?"

"She's not in the world."

"Dead?"

"She never even lived, therefore she *can't* be dead."

"Then how could you love her—if she didn't exist?"

"She *did* exist; but as a fictional character, in a novel."

"You must be crazy, then—out of your mind—to have wasted your living heart's love on the mere concoction of some author's brain."

"Come to think of it, it *does* seem crazy."

"Then you're cured, if *you yourself* see your love in retrospect as having been crazy."

"You're right. Should I love you instead? You're real, alive, in my world."

"Why, Tom! This is so sudden! We only just met! Restrain your impetuosity, you rash romantic fiend!"

"But Marge, I'm serious about you. You're quite beautiful, you know."

"Oh, I've been told that all my life. Can't you be a little more original?"

"I'll try, Marge. But I'm not a poet."

"I require, if I'm to be loved at all, that I must be loved with a *poetic* fervor, an artistic vision, which paints me over in glowing colors and transforms me from this ordinary world in which we merely live and breathe, to a world of sheer invention, pure fiction, of magnificent unreality!"

"I'll oblige you, Marge, by rendering you in a novel as a fictional heroine. That will immortalize you. To make sure, I'll arrange the plot so that you never die at the end of the novel; the novel will end with you in a healthy and happy state."

"Yes, but Tom, can you write?"

"I'll try my hand at making the story. Maybe I have a genuine vocation for it. Perhaps I'm a hidden talent."

"I'll be delighted to be your heroine. Describe me as I *am*—because I'm *already* beautiful. Depict me to my every living detail. Render me stunning, gorgeous—which I amply am, as the Marge who's now your model for the heroine I'm to become. What name will you give her?"

"Yours. She'll be named Marge. As a character, she'll have *your* character—including, of course, all your characteristics.

She'll be a marvelous creation! And you're the true original, from whom, happily, I derived her."

"Good. When will the book be finished?"

"It already is."

"So quick? How?"

"It was written over two centuries ago by a British author. I'll plagiarise the book almost entire, except in changing *that* heroine's name to Marge and in updating her description to fit yours."

"But I'll be out of context, anachronistic, if the setting is the world of *that* time, and the events therein. I'm a modern woman, in modern times. Was Britain of two centuries ago the world and time that environed that heroine you'd have modernized in the person of *me*?"

"Yes. But I *loved* that heroine. Then my love for her was transferred to you; you bodily replaced her, intact. She's become you. I *love* you, Marge."

"Thanks. I must read that novel, to see how I compare with my predecessor."

"You're *both* paragons of beauty. You're both perfection, itself!"

"I'm jealous of her: as though she really lived."

"She *does* really live—but in *you*. She's incarnated: as you. You're her fulfillment. You've embodied her. Her spirit is in you. Read the book: behold: thyself!"

"But aren't you going to modernize it, somewhat, and change the setting to mine?"

"You're being too literal; too technical; too irrelevantly material: hence, immaterial. Marge, in *spirit*, she's you!"

"With my shape?"

"To the inch."

"My coloring, of skin and hair?"

"To the precise shade."

"My intonations? Which are modern American?"

"A mere detail! I'll fiddle with the book, and make the suitable alteration. In the book, she loves me: *that*'s essential."

"Oh. So you're in the book too?"

"Yes. A two-hundred-year-ago British version of me."

"Oh. So ours can be a storybook romance?"

"Yes. But that book ended with her death. I'll fix *that*: *you*'ll stay *alive*: as my lovely *bride*!"

"That's how *your* version will end?"

"Yes. Endlessly. It's a true romance."

"Oh, Tom! You *are* poetic!"

"For *you*, I am. Dear Marge."

XLVIII. ALICE, JUDY, AND TOM GERVASI. THEY ADD UP TO JUST TWO PEOPLE, BY LOVE'S WEIRD ARITHMETIC. WHAT FORMULA TOTALLED TO SUCH A SUM? MATHEMATICALLY, HERE'S HOW.

Nothing is so stale as last year's joke—or is it yesterday's newspaper? Tom Gervasi's saturation-threshold is indeed low. He's so brilliantly quick, he needs new stimulation. Not that he's jaded. He's far from decadent. On the contrary, vital freshness is required, releasing vigorous new impulses. He *lives*. He consumes what's past: which he's too alive to repeat. He loves to plunge into the ever-renewed unknown.

Alice is overknown by him. No more does he regard her with romantic bloom—it's worn off, in time's autumnal maturity. She has but one recourse: so to change, as to present a different Alice than before, and thus provoke Tom Gervasi to a fresh impulse, as though, in fact, he were reacting not just to an altered Alice, but to a totally new woman, whom he was meeting for the very first time. This is what Alice knew was required, for her to (as it were) "retain" him. The only way. Otherwise, he'd be with an *actual* different women—one whose body was separate from the one that Alice had to offer. Alice had to make her same (more or less) body do. She had to be different in what she was and did, as she couldn't control *looking* more or less the same. Then, Tom Gervasi would become rapidly unbored. He'd woo her afresh—or give a new her the same great wooing. For *she* didn't want *him* to change. She loved him *just-as-he-was*: except for his attitude to her; which she'd re-ignite to that of loving her with restored ardor, with deep devotion, with pure passion—not the former, but the new Alice: whom he'll meet with the shock of immediacy, the romantic impact of novelty.

Yes, but she had a stable personality, an ongoing character. How could she radically depart from that, without doing harm to "the genuine core of her being"? She could *modify* her behavior. But a drastic change might destroy her integrity as an individual whose development evolved from past slowly to present, in the sure identity of growth.

Herein was certainly a conflict. Was the chance of renewing Tom Gervasi's love worth the possible mangling of her slowly-time-wrought old self just because Tom's familiarity with it had dulled his interest to the halting point? She had to consider. For even if Tom were to fall in love with a *new* Alice, in time wouldn't gradual familiarity with that new self become, by the same cycle pattern, still another indifference at the end? How could Alice really *keep* his interest alive? She couldn't go on changing, indefinitely, like the Greek God Proteus, who had inexhaustible resources of new transformations at hand, like a wardrobe of new clothes to be changing into. No, Alice faced the same sad future waning of Tom's interest as the waning that recently tormented her into the rash necessity of some total change. The problem might remain, in its essential perplexity: how to impart renewed vigor into Tom's love for her? Were the answer to this known, it would be the magic secret of all time, the sacred key to the outworn human heart. Alice would give it a try. Not without a fight, would she give Tom Gervasi up. He alone spurred her ferocious thought, her strenuous continuous probe for this crucial problem solution. She wouldn't rest, till she plunged to ultimate failure, or soared to an unparalleled success. It was a "scientific" pursuit, a relentless search, a pilgrimage, a crusade, a sacred mission, for the Holy Grail of Tom's Eternal Devotion. Fruitless, doomed at the outset to barren despair ultimately? It's worth the chase. Whoever wins his undying love, has won the rare wonder of the western world. No grander glory could there ever be, in all God's sphere. For no greater man ever lived, beneath the saints. Tom Gervasi. The Dream of Dreams. Attainable? If not, it wouldn't be for want of Alice's trying. She'd relocate the universe, to get a nearer clue.

First, Alice changed her name to Judy. That gave her a new outlook on life—nominally, at any rate.

Phoning Tom Gervasi, she cheerfully spun, "Hello, Tom, this is Judy."

"Judy!? I don't—at least *now* I don't—know anyone by that name. Yet from the sound of your voice, you know me well. In fact, you sound just like Alice. Is that you, Alice?"

"I was Alice. The Alice you knew. But I'm Judy now. The Judy you don't know yet."

"Stop being cute. What is this, a gag? You're just 'pulling my leg.' Come out of it, now. You're Alice, and no-one else."

"I *was* Alice—unmistakably. But a woman's got the right to change her name—*and* identity. 'Judy' fits me just fine, now. I *feel* like a real Judy: as though I'd always been born that way. Please, Tom, regard me in this new light. Keep up with me, and treat me anew. Perk up, and take notice. You don't want to fall behind the times, do you?"

"You're really weird, Alice—I mean Judy. Have you turned crazy, as well? After all, most folks who call themselves normal go through their whole life with the same name—or *first* name, anyhow. What's come over you? Were you hypnotized? Were you converted to religion, and rebaptised? Were you psychoanalyzed, heavily? Have you inherited a fortune from some dowager great-aunt named Judy, for whom, in gratitude, you renamed yourself? Or was it all of those? Or for some reason still inexplicable to me? I'm in the dark. Come now, Alice—I mean Judy—enlighten me. Don't keep me guessing. I'm not a mind-reader. I'm just the guy you loved—remember?"

"How can I forget? Tom, I *still* love you."

"As Alice? Or as Judy?"

"As Judy."

"In that case, you don't *still* love me. For as Judy, it's a different you who's loving me. That makes the love itself different. This is really weird. I'm loved for the second time, by someone with the same body. Now I'm *really* confused. Who am I, anyway?"

"You're still my Tom. Shall we marry?"

"Yes, Alice—I mean Judy. To tell you the truth, I must confess I had lost interest in you till your surprising change-of-name phone call just now, which, as you see—or hear, rather—has rekindled my interest and restored my love. You have a revived vivacity in my same heart where recently you had fallen flat. I love you *wildly,* now! I can't control myself! Please, Alice—I mean Judy—marry me immediately! I just can't wait! Oh, I'm reborn."

"So am I, dear Tom. Thanks to my name-change, which has worked such wonders upon your flagging heart. Let's trip on over to the alter this afternoon. How would two o'clock do?"

"Just fine with me, my adored Alice—I mean Judy. It's noon now. That gives us two hours. Let's rent the right clergyman for the job, and notify our two sets of parents, as well as assorted relatives of lesser ranks. Also, our good friends must receive last-minute invitations, or they'd never forgive us. Is there time to have a brief engagement party a little before the wedding ceremony? No, I'm afraid not. Well, let's rent out a hall, and caterers to provide food and drink service, and maybe a band to supply some sentimental music that suits the occasion fine. Oh, all these practical details! All these last-minute arrangements! They're driving me under, I tell you. What a sigh of a relief we'll breathe, when it's all over!"

"It'll be Worth it. We'll be each other's—just you and me. After the ceremony, let's fly away on an intimate honeymoon—just us two, you and I, Tom: as intimate as we ought to be, to fit our married state. It'll be recently behind us, wedding and all. Just us two alone. In complete privacy! Me and my Tom!"

"Oh, I can't believe it, Alice—I mean Judy. Is it really happening to us? Our dreams, coming true, before our very eyes?"

"Of course. By the way, let's contact a travel agency, for plane or train reservations, and to know where our honeymoon will be spent."

"Who cares where!? As long as it's just us!"

"Oh Tom, you're so romantic—you're an *incurable* romantic!"

"With you, Alice—I mean Judy—I can't help but be. You're my dream come true. Alice—I mean Judy—tell me: Is it *really* happening? Is it *really* true?"

"Oh Tom, I can't believe it myself! I'm all basked in wonder. Just you and me. Alone."

"I love you, Alice—I mean Judy. With all my heart, I do."

"Oh Tom, and *you* know how I feel about *you*."

"I *still* can't believe it."

"It's true, Tom. It's true!"

"Is it? Is it?"

"Tom—yes."

"Alice—I mean Judy?"

"Yes, beloved."

"Is it forever?"

"Yes, dear."

"Oh Alice—I mean Judy: It's too good to be true!"

"Oh Tom: it *is* true; and so good!"

"Is it both?"

"Both, dearest."

"Oh; I can't bear it!"

"It'll be over soon, dear. Then we can go away."

"Just us, Alice—I mean Judy? Us alone?"

"Oh, love of my life!"

"Love of mine, yourself!"

"Tom?"

"Yes, Alice—I mean Judy."

"Do you *really* love me, Tom? I mean really? And truly?"

"Oh Alice—I mean Judy—you *know* I do!"

"Well, that's good. I'm so relieved. I once thought I had lost you."

"Oh, really, Alice—I mean Judy! How could you even once have doubted me?"

"Well, I don't now. And you'll never *tire* of me? Promise?"

"Constancy. If you knew your Tom, Alice—I mean Judy— you'll know that Tom is constancy. For you he is. For *you* alone. And this is always, my dearest. And it will never change. So long as I'm your Tom, and you—dear Alice—I mean Judy—are my Alice—I mean Judy." (Pause.) "Say! Which *are* you, anyway!?"

"Both."

"Both! But I want monogamy!"

"You'll get it, Tom. I'm *doubly* certain!"

XLIX. TOM GERVASI TAKES OFF FROM WORK TO GO TO THE BEACH. THE SUN IS OUT, AND HE MEETS GOD. HE RISES TO THE OCCASION.

It was such a beautiful day! It really was. Why not go to the beach? That way, the day can be *really* appreciated. Much more than on city streets, shaded by city buildings, or inside one of the latter.

Tom Gervasi was at the office, but his heart wasn't in it his work. It was summer, anyhow, so there was less business pressure—in *his* firm, anyway. It was midmorning. It was gorgeous sun slanting through the window. The light was dancing with radiance.

Tom Gervasi entered his colleague's office, and said, "Cover up for me, will you? I'm taking off. To the beach."

"Have a good day," he was wished; "enjoy yourself."

As he was passing through the firm's floor space on his way to the elevator, the girl workers eyed him with various reactions: wistful, adoring, intrigued, admiring, pleased for his very existence. Down the elevator, walking the street, in the subway, off at the last station, walking to the beach, on a lovely working day. One sun was playing enchantment off millions of objects. Or was it as many suns as there were objects? Just as, there are as many worlds as there are individual people in it. With his thoughts playing on this metaphysical key, Tom Gervasi neared the beach. It was a summer working day. How deliciously free he was! Alone, in a radiant universe.

He was lying on the sand, with his torso here, his shirt and jacket folded nearby and kept from flapping by the weight of his briefcase lying on its side. The waves lapped up, nearby. A sail dotted the horizon with crazy, jerky white. The ocean was far away, yet so close! The clouds were puffs, of clear white. The blue was blue, straight through. The beach was only moderately crowded, for it was a working day, under a sun that didn't bother to differentiate between a Saturday and a Wednesday, a Sunday and a Monday. God seemed to be present. The day seemed "authorized" by Him. "How divine it is today," would colloquially express it. Or, "What a divine day!" Of that trivial order.

Tom Gervasi was just drinking in the heavens. A subtle din drummed away at his heart's ear. The waves went "splosh." The air was covering his skin. The light and his thoughts were melting together. God seemed about to burst forth into speech. The people seemed to dance in eternity. The beach umbrellas seemed like mushrooms in another world. It was all so strange, that some serene delirium seemed to dull Tom Gervasi's senses to the ordinary plane, while his keyboard was tuned to dimensions for outside these assumed by banal discourse at the social level. He was taking off. He and God were just on the conversational point. Their breaths had already mingled, from separate realms. A visitation was at hand. Revelation, in the simple order of things rather than by tumultuous ordeal or lightning-drenched agony.

Tom Gervasi was taking off. He, God, and the sun, and the land and the sea, were holding a high-level conference. Wisdom was oozing in, at every pore.

Life wasn't explained: it was just "there." There *he* was, in one of its forms. He was blessed with women's love. Each heart that loved him sang its song to him, at different ages of life, making a full chorus. He was loved by women, and God approved. Benediction for earthly love. Sanctity, for squeezing pleasure from flesh tensions between bodies in a bond of conflict. Love as

Grace, as well. Love as grace and dignity. Love, as a secure sense of well-being. Being cared about. Being unalone. These loving women were God's delegates. They showed him that his life mattered—to them, to Him. His life meant something, to beings beyond the self-form his life took. His mother once did care. Now, younger women do—in a special sense. His life had links and extensions, through love-waves, to hearts outside. And to that Total Heart, that was chatting quite casually to him, as man-to-man, under the divine air, near the ocean divinity, on the eternal shore, the beach crowded with souls. The sun was there. It blazed through working day. Through the beach. Through Tom Gervasi. It blazed straight through. It carried God down. It took up Tom Gervasi. Up through love. Up through women. Up so high, he met his own life, on the other side. Looked at, from an opposite blessing. On an air that burned. Sun, love, life, and Tom Gervasi. Bound to the solid world. Where co-souls drifted through.

L. UGLY PRISCILLA, WHO'S A GENIUS, LUSTS FOR TOM GERVASI. ONCE, HER DREAM COMES TRUE. FOR HER, THAT'S ETERNITY.

Unfortunately, Priscilla is plain: if not, in fact, somewhat downright ugly. This injures her chances with men; but by way of compensation, she's developed her dreamlife. As long as she bothers to dream at all, then what's the point of dreaming about merely ugly men, equal to her own ugliness as a woman? That's not what dreams are for! They're for conjuring up true *paragons* of men. She has, therefore, come to pick, of all men, Tom Gervasi, that inaccessible legend, for her dreamboat! What a weight to put on a dream! Can the dream survive?!

Actually, Priscilla looks hideous. Every dream should have *some* little reality-weight, to hold it up. What is it, in Priscilla's case, to drag in justification where none seems possible?

It's this: She's a genius, in intellectual matters. And Tom Gervasi being, more than merely handsome, but brilliant, he'd hold as naught Priscilla's physical ugliness; for what would truly matter to him—transcending the mere surface appearance of any woman and making it perfectly irrelevant—is a woman's mind. Fortunately, Priscilla has a *rare* mind. She's a *certified* genius!

Therefore, Tom Gervasi would excuse her ugliness as being merely external; gallantly, nobly, he'd overlook it. He's too great a man himself to hold it as truly important. It won't be an obstacle, an impediment, to the marriage of true minds. Once that marriage happens, their bodies will get married too. Yes, Priscilla will snare Tom Gervasi's beautiful body! *Real* compensation, for her own ugly one.

She's a virgin, long delayed and preserved that way. She lives a secret life of gnawing lust, like a masochist who mortifies his most poignant appetite in martyrdom to its excruciating pang.

Priscilla craves sex, with the most darling of men. Tom Gervasi is the Hector, Achilles, Don Giovanni, Casanova, Lothario, Tristram, the Romeo of today, the official heartthrob of the city's loftiest intellectual circles. Socially, he's the most sought-after of all men. He's wanted, principally, in bed. That's just where Priscilla wants him. And *permanently* there, too.

She'd *get* him there, via—what else?—her much vaunted brains. The brains that no other—*literally* no other—woman in the social sets could even conceivably hope to match. That's her weapon, to snare Tom Gervasi. For he *appreciates* brains. He puts the top value on them! And that's what *he* has, himself! Brains to spare, brains to burn! Why, Tom Gervasi and Priscilla would go down in social history as the most *authentically* intellectual couple—she could only think of George Sand and the composer Chopin, or Mary McCarthy and Edmund Wilson, as anywhere *nearly* comparable! And even they dim, by comparison. So that's her chance, for Tom Gervasi. She knows what card to play—her *trump card*! Not her face—it's just too hideous for words. *Nor* her body—ugh, it wouldn't tempt a sailor who's just come back from a ten-year voyage with not a woman on deck, not one!

Priscilla would pit her brains, in fair contest, against any other woman's beauty; knowing that Tom Gervasi has a weakness for intellect (it's his own formidable strong point), and is vulnerable to assault from that quarter. Then, his physical beauty, by being Priscilla's directly acquired possession, would be *her* beauty, by proxy. He'd be her representative, in that department she's so notoriously deficient in! Indirectly, she'll be beautiful—in form and physique, and in divine face—through her dear husband. She'll own all his properties. His attributes become hers, in the wedding trade. It's all their property in common. His endearing charms, his superb qualities—turned over, fully, to Priscilla's keeping. Her life's principal adornment. The crowning achievement, for the gift of brains.

The acquisition of Tom Gervasi's beautiful person into Priscilla's safekeeping as her own added second nature would be, of course, no easy matter. Would Tom Gervasi relinquish his freedom? Didn't *he* value a face divine, and a lovely body, for his chosen own, as fitting his proper mate? If so, Priscilla wouldn't do. It's a ticklish matter. She'll plan her strategy with the utmost care. She'd use her full genius for it. For such a goal, she'd deploy every resource she had, mobilize her full capacities, and recruit outstanding reserves from her as-yet-untapped mountains of talent. Every God-given aptitude she could scrap together from the vast wealth of her nature, her prodigious endowments, will be tossed into action, but co-ordinated in perfect harness beforehand. She'll spare no weapon, from her considerable arsenal.

Her cunning is at work. Currently, Tom Gervasi is key editor in a publishing company. His job is to find great books, and publish them. But great books, because great, are rare. Priscilla phoned him at his office. "Tom Gervasi, drop everything. I have a *great* book for you!"

He did drop everything. He said, "Let's meet, anywhere, now. That's great news, your having a great book. Is it an *idea* for one, or did you already write it? Or have you a lead to someone *else*'s great book? I'm avid to discuss it. Can you come to the office?"

"No, get out of your office, and come to my apartment. It's near the end of the employment day, anyhow, the time when offices will soon close. Here's my address." (She gives it.) "Come here at once, by taxi. Use your expense account to pay for the taxi, since this is a *purely* business matter, I assure you. It's *lethally* business. If it were a private matter, you should pay for the taxi yourself. But no. Prepare for a *working evening*. You'll get paid overtime, I assure you."

"But I receive a flat salary, independent of what hours I put in."

"Well, so be it. But arrive. Goodbye."

His office is on the other side of town from her apartment. And the taxi will have to dodge through rush-hour traffic, and often be stalled, at the time when all the offices close. So Priscilla has time to prepare. She has no book at all for him. But she'll use her wits. She'll seduce him, this very evening. He'll devirginize her, and she's already in her thirties, so what a belated baptism that'll be! He'll find that she's his true soulmate, that intellectually they have a marriage made in heaven. That'll clinch it, and soon they'll marry.

She liberally perfumed herself, especially in the genital crotch area and straight between her breasts, where the "cleavage" is supposed to be, according to anatomy standards. She'll prove irresistible! She'll dangle a book before him, as bait. He'll fall—hook, line, and sinker—for *her*, not the book. *She*'ll be the book! He'll publish her—not a manuscript of words. He'll publish her on the printing press of bed and marriage. As for binding, they'll be between the covers. And they'll read proofs, together.

She's hushed with romantic expectation. He's coming for a book—a *great* one, it's supposed to be, otherwise he'd never bother. But she won't disappoint him. "*I'm* your book!" she'll say. "Turn my pages, as you will. Read me, with your burning eyes. It's an illuminating text. It will change your life. You'll be never the same, ever after. I'll go to your head. You'll see."

Oh, she ached with romance! She's starved for sex. Her first time! With him!

But not so fast!—She won't give in, till he promises to marry her! Only then, will it be aboveboard, and honorable!

She's not just going to *throw* her virginity away! Hardly! She'll barter it, for a wedding ring. For the matrimonial vow. From a man as good as his word. From the man of all men. From the stuff that dreams are made on. From Tom Gervasi—no less.

The moment is at hand. The buzzer is ringing. He's arrived!

She opened her door, and he came in with a smile. His teeth flashed, his eyes gleaned, his handsomeness was sinfully outrageous. (As her own ugliness was.) In fact, she near-fainted. She barely recovered, in time, before falling flat. Her wits went numb. She lost her nerve. She couldn't go through with it. Immediately, she confessed:

"It was all a ruse. To lure you here. I want to devour you, amorously. But so do hundreds of other women. But I alone deserve you, whereas they don't."

"On what grounds, is *your* deserving so exclusive?"

"Darling, I'm a genius. We've never known each other, we've only met here or there at social occasions, superficially, in passing. This is our first real talk together. You're *real* now, you're not just your reputation."

"Which is what?"

"Ladykiller. The notorious Casanova of our times. Well, I love you for your*self*: not your reputation."

"My*self*?! I'm many facets. To which are you referring?"

"To your love of truth. To your mind. To your inquiry into the nature of the human universe, to understand life itself, in every motive and manifestation. Admittedly, that's a tall order. Well, I, with my great brains, propose to help. How's that?"

"Not a bad proposition. But you wouldn't do for a *girlfriend,* if that's your game. You just don't attract me, that way. I have real beauties, for girlfriends. I don't need you."

"Oh, stop dividing the mind from the body, spiritual pursuits from sensual delights. I'm one gestalt incorporated whole. Accept me, accept my body too. Love me, love my dog. If you make a mental bed with me, then lie in it physically as well. Take me, for all that I am, for better and worse. I'm the rarest mind of our generation, among women at least. Avail yourself of it, by accepting its possessor as well. And anyway, your beautiful women aren't the *only* ones to have a vagina. May I tempt you with mine?"

They had been drinking, but he spilled his in amazement when Priscilla lifted her skirt up, revealing just tight shorts beneath. In spite of his fastidious taste about women's beauty, he was stirred with excitement, partly owing, of course, to the audacious shock of her brazen move. He burst with lust, as hardly ever before. They went to bed, which rumbled like a tank over rocky land. He literally walloped love into her. This officially ended her virginity. Now her new life would begin.

"Boy, that was great!" he said.

"But Tom Gervasi, you're supposed to be so sophisticated! You really liked it, huh?"

"Boy, I sure did! Let me tell *you!*" He smacked his lips, with emphasis.

"And you didn't mind my face or body? Was your pleasure that keen?"

"I took the precautions, Priscilla, in advance, you might remember, of extinguishing the lamps and other artificial lights,
despite my frenzy of wild, bellowing lust that you had inge-
niously, somehow, inspired in me, partly due to the circum-
stance of your teasing me with the offer of a great book—which
hugely excited me—and then, demurely, with coy bluntness,
sputtering out the confession that it was only a ruse to lure me
into this erotic trap. What a device! You're brilliant! Why, I worship you! *Please* be my mistress."

"Tom Gervasi, I already compromised myself by submitting
to your bestiality before you even proposed marriage, in spite of
my firm principles on that righteous score. I was quite carried
away, just like you. Well, now do the honorable thing by me. I'm
seduced, I find, much to the loss of my longstanding maiden-
head. I was deflowered. I'm a fallen woman. Tom Gervasi, raise
me up again! I beseech you, to do the honorable thing! Give me
back my self-respect! Which is retained only were I to become
your bride."

"But Priscilla, *you* seduced *me*! *You* lured *me* here!"

"Oh, that's right, Tom Gervasi. I slightly twisted things to
serve my own fallen pride, and to appeal to your manly code
of honor. But my inaccuracies may be pardoned. We're in bed,
now."

"We sure are, Priscilla. Under the covers together. Intimate
with hardly a prelude. But it was a false pretext that brought me
here first. I'm interested in great books. Could you write one,
please?"

"Tom Gervasi, the lights are out, so you can't see my face or
body, except dimly, from street-light outside my window. But
we're in bed together, you and I. I can write *many* great books,
Tom Gervasi. And I could let you publish every one of them.

My literary fame and your publishing career could skyrocket together. Wouldn't that be nice?"

"Of course, Priscilla."

"It's a bribe. You must marry me first."

"Sorry. Not interested. I value my freedom. I like my other women. And anyway, I don't really love you."

"But your *career*, Tom Gervasi—think of that!"

"I'm a man of honor. My career can get along *without* your bribe. And I wasn't dishonorable in seducing you, either: *you* enticed *me*. I value my integrity. I'll marry only for love. Let your great mind thrive in loneliness, if it must. I dearly esteem intellect: But I won't *marry* it."

"Such are your principles? You stand by them?"

"Not principles. Impulse. Now I'll grope in the dark, and regather my clothes. Leave the lights out. Sorry, you can't have me. Except, I'm afraid, as only a dream. Dream deeply of me, Priscilla. I've found my clothes. Stay in bed, don't get out. I'll find my way to the door, and leave by myself. I arrived here expecting a great book. Instead, I got a great lay, partly stirred up by circumstantial excitement. You *are* a genius, Priscilla. Fulfill it. Write great books. Publish than elsewhere, not with my firm. You "possessed" me once. I fell for the trap. But I'm free. I won't be possessed forever. I'll be your dreamstuff, my lonely nonbride. Sublimate, and create great works. You have it in you, I can tell. I *know* talent when I see it—even at its genius extremity. Priscilla, goodbye. Our little romance is ended. It was quite an erotic intrigue. It pumped me up to the gills with lust. Well, that's over now, for both of us. Our little episode. Our big city adventure. With my gleaming reputation from high circles. With your repulsive appearance, but brilliant mind. We were charged with the novelty of all these ingredients that achieved a unique compound of unlikely collisions. It happened once, Priscilla. Dream on, poor dear. With your lonely genius. And newly released from your infant girlhood virginity. In new circumstances, we'll meet again. Behind sophisticated trappings, socially masked with dinner party repartee, cocktail party superficiality, afterdinner party inebriation urbanely moderated. Now, I resume in dream form, my dear Priscilla. Our bodies will never touch."

He gently closed the door behind him, the door dividing her apartment from the world outside, and was gone, his presence removed. No further dialogue.

She's still consumed with lust, and it's fifteen years later. She hasn't vindicated her "genius" promise. And she never "repeated" the sexual act with anyone else. She's still intact, for him. She's virtually as he left her, though older and more ugly. She hasn't written any book, at all. Just a few obscure articles, here and there.

Tom Gervasi has gone on. His legend stands higher yet. He incarnates his legend with great dashing presence. He's all there, as Tom Gervasi.

After her memorable evening, Priscilla occasionally would meet Tom Gervasi at social events, parties, here and there. Neither alluded to that memorable evening, nor will they ever, as things are turning out. They keep civil decorum in their nods, no warm outburst of familiar recollection of their astounding intimacy sequence. It lives on, in great dreams of lust, by Priscilla. In them, she captures him, for permanent possession, for a well-celebrated marriage. She doesn't indicate it, or betray a sign, when they meet at parties or other gatherings of the social variety mixed delicately with business interests. She keeps a cool aplomb, with him.

But he's not fooled. She's seething inside: Dreams of a genius beast that rapingly ravishes the world's most beautiful man, who's also her mental soulmate for scaling heights together on truth's difficult mountain.

"I love Tom Gervasi. He *was* mine, once, with rapture. My only sexual encounter was a supreme triumph. It's become immortal, preserved. Tom Gervasi is my own, with all his beauty. It's my beauty too. It's both our beauty. He's my Muse. Great books are inside me, like children. He impregnates me with their conception. Now, I must labor. I'm worthy of you, Tom Gervasi. Your rejection of me was incidental, accidental. We're each other's very own. *I* know it, even if you're too busy philandering to take notice. I'm your ugly beast. We climb to intellectual heights, in truth's relentless pursuit. We're a husband-wife team. By way of one evening, we are. I merely project that evening—its exquisite aspects—to its infinite extensions. With eternity, we're married. I guard our eternity, till you tire, Tom Gervasi, of pursuing more trivial things, like a glamorous social life and the loveliest woman. I'm keeping our eternity on ice for us, Tom Gervasi. It's *our* eternity. Come help me claim it, redeem it. I need *your* endorsement, too. Then, it'll open up. There, beauty and the beast shall mate surrounded by truth and ideals. I'm consumed, by that immortal lust. My loins are ablaze with it. Dear Husband, together we're divine. Apart, I'm only me. You have your glory, apart from me. I grant you that. But not the *divine* glory, that's ours together. Come from out of your secular cosmopolitanism, Tom Gervasi. Let lust join us, in Universal Paradise."

LI. WOMEN, NUMBERS, AND TOM GERVASI.

Asked how many women had ever loved him, Tum Gervasi lost count. When he had been an early post-infant, he had used his fingers (thumbs included) for doing simple sums. When the world got a little more complicated, he added his toes as well. By then, it was time to start school. He had less aptitude for subtracting than for adding. In addition, he had more capacity for multiplying than for division. His world kept growing, numerically, in experience events. Higher mathematics, as a study, was concurrent with fascination by women. Geometry, trigonometry, and algebra had to be pressed into service. He had come a long way, from adding with his little fingers. It had served him, as a handy way of counting. Then other methods came to hand. This helped him to grow handsome. It all added up, to more women.

Yes, but that's quantity. Quality? Whom he values, how, with what feeling. Whom else he values, how, with what feeling. Quality can't be measured. There's no reckoning it. You can't computerize it. It's intangible, and within the province of poets, writers of stories. So Tom Gervasi reads a lot of fiction, poetry, about love, about men and women together. He reads it, thinks it, and lives it. Numbers are irrelevant. Women who've loved him. Women he's been with. Women he felt *this* for, women he felt *that* for. It all adds up, in varied categories. But it's outside measure. Feelings for women, feelings from women. For or from *this* woman, at this stage of knowing her, at *that* stage. *That* woman, at stages. Outside numbers. Numb. Dumb. The poets and story tellers say what he's felt. It's closer to truth, to reality's universal soul in life, than all of mathematics can be. Counting on the fingers was useful. But now, it's better to read and be

with women. Better? It's what he *does,* now. "Better" justifies it.
he knows the women, and reads poetry and fiction. Love is at
the mystery of life. It blazes with qualities. This women, now,
or later, or that woman. The heart of mystery. Between people,
qualities arise. They're Tom Gervasi's study, while his slow aging eats a path through his life of thought.

LII. LOSING TOM GERVASI AND GETTING HIT WITH A LEAD PIPE: VARIATIONS ON PAIN.

Some women got into an absolute tizzy over Tom Gervasi. They began throwing lead pipes at each other. Things were getting out of hand—especially the lead pipes.

Then they said, "Let's throw these things at *him*: he caused us to be like this."

"But if we love him, we don't want to vent belligerent harm at him. That's not love, is it?"

Thus they debated. While so debating, they had stopped throwing things at each other. Their angry rivalry calmed down. They loved him in common. No violence at each other or him. Let one win him. That's damage enough, for those who don't. That's hurting them. Throwing lead pipes can hurt them. But so can they hurt themselves, by not gaining Tom Gervasi. Why inflict *more* pain? Not gaining Tom Gervasi, or losing him, is pain enough. So they became passivists. Or pacifists. Quiet. Waiting to see who wouldn't get Tom Gervasi. And who would, if any.

LIII. WHAT MAKES TOM GERVASI SO ATTRACTIVE TO WOMEN? A CLEAR NON-EXPLANATION FOLLOWS.

What makes Tom Gervasi so attractive to women? This question is asked by men whose envy can change to emulation—if they knew what to emulate, in the man they envy.

Tom Gervasi has certain intangibles—but he also has tangibles. Charm, suavité, poise, sweetness, brilliance, perception, compassion, generosity, fairness, reasonableness, humor, a handsome face, a splendid body. So what's intangible?

Everything. The women don't know what makes him so attractive. Nor does he know why they're so attracted. It just happens. And goes on, mysteriously.

LIV. THE GUILT SUCTION.

Tom Gervasi was getting tired of Sandra. But how was he to tell her? He had to be delicate. She wouldn't take no for an answer. She'd only take *him*—for *all* answers.

He couldn't quite "break" it to her. Every time he would open his mouth, he had to snap it shut again when he saw her dog's-devotion dribbling from her all-Tom-Gervasi-seeing eyes.

Could he write her a letter? Should he inform her by phone? Or get a mutual friend to tell her? Reproach was about to burst forth, held in readiness, from her already cringing face. The guilt she had in store for Tom Gervasi! Guilt would replace her. It would make her immortal, in that man's shaking heart. She'll cling forever, from his guilt. She'll become the guilt. And live fastened upon him. Sucking milkguilt, from his open breast, through a slurping straw. Sucking her own life back up again, her life as fastened to him, through guilt's pang of permanence. She's latched on. She sucks Tom Gervasi back, through the straw of guilt. He's stuck in there, somewhere. And the wind pressure carves a vacuum, of permanence.

LV. TWO FIGHTING WOMEN, A PEACEMAKING PO-LICEMAN, AND TOM GERVASI.

There was a terrible uproar. Women were fighting. In the street, of all places. A policeman, keeper of the peace, strolled over. "Stop it ladies. You can *hurt* each other, that way."

"But we want to. Or at least, *I* want to hurt *her.*"

"And *I,*" the other woman said, "want to hurt *her.*"

"Well, it's *bad* to want to; you might *do* it," the policeman cautioned.

"But we *want* to do it."

"But you might get hurt," tried to reason the policemen, but gave up, and decided to approach the problem from a new angle: "*Why* were you fighting?"

"We both love Tom Gervasi."

"Why don't you let him choose one of you? That's a more reasonable solution."

"But he's already rejected us."

"Both?"

"*Both* of us, he rejected."

"Then why is the fighting necessary? It wouldn't do you any good, so far as *getting* him is concerned."

"To relieve our frustrations, officer. To take out our miserable grief, upon each other."

"Well, it's against the law to disturb the peace by fighting in public. Tom Gervasi or *no* Tom Gervasi. Therefore, cease and desist. Say—I'm not married. Could *I* have one of you, since Tom Gervasi wants neither?"

"No, officer. You don't compare with Tom Gervasi. So stop disturbing *us.*"

LVI. WHY ARE TOM GERVASI'S CLOTHES AND SHOES GETTING SO TIGHT, JUST SQUEEZING AND SUFFOCATING HIM? A HABERDASHERY SHOPKEEPER INVESTIGATES. HIS DISCOVERY IS AMAZING, BUT TRUE.

Tom Gervasi was wondering why his clothes were getting so tight on him, and why his shoes had begun to pinch. "I took my clothes to a good laundry that guaranteed non-shrinkage. And these shoes *used* to be roomy and comfortable—why *recently* have they gotten so tight? It's all too peculiar. What could be the reasons for the clothes and shoes apparently converging on my person, closer and closer, till I'm all but smothered by then now?

"For answer, I'll go to a haberdashery shop where male shoes and clothing are sold. I'll speak to the top expert there— the head executive salesman. By and by, he'll tell me why."

The shopkeeper examined these clothes and shoes under a microscope, picked apart the fibers, even smelled the material, with intense scientific concentration, as though he weren't in a commercial business but rather in an occupation of academic truth-for-truth's sake, seeking knowledge with *pure* disinterest.

"What's your finding?" Tom Gervasi gently asked. The investigation had become elaborate, thorough, without discovery yet.

The shopkeeper was so absentmindedly absorbed in his work, that he didn't hear Tom Gervasi, who then shouted, "Any luck yet?"

At that very instant, the shopkeeper was rewarded for his efforts by the dawning of the truth upon him.

The truth was hard to believe, but it was the truth; so belief somehow had to accommodate it, as best it could, and suspend its incredulity to oblige the imperative insistence of the truth urging itself upon the unwilling ear of disbelief.

"It's amazing," the shopkeeper said. "You might not believe it."

"If it's true, and only if it's true, then I'll believe it," Tom Gervasi promised. His regard for truth was so high, he'd believe it at all obstacles, if only it were credible. It *must* be true: upon that condition, Tom Gervasi will generously donate his belief.

"You know why your clothes were getting tighter and tighter, hugging your torso and limbs, and your shoes were contracting to squeeze your feet to pain?"

"That's why I *came* here: to find out why."

"Well, I've discovered why."

"Don't keep it to yourself: *Tell* me, at once."

"Are you sure you want to know?"

"*Oedipus* wanted to know the truth, too. But it turned out bad for him. Well, at all costs, I *must* know. Whatever the consequences."

"Sir, are you ready?"

"I've *been* ready. I'm waiting. Too patiently. I'll burst, unless you presently relieve me, on the instant."

"Your clothes and shoes are in love with you. So, in magnetic gravitational tropism, they converge on your adored body, from feet on up, to hug you, embrace you, clutch you, cling to you, kiss you, neck with you, dearly smother you with love; to whisper sweet nothings, all day long. For they love every inch of you."

"But they're inanimate! They're textiles, cloth, linen, leather, cotton, rayon, wool, nylon, whatever. They're sheer fabric! They're nothing but minerals! How can minerals love a human being?! How!?"

"Sir, that's metaphysical, it's beyond my reach."

"What do you advise?"

"Buy clothing and shoes many sizes too large for you. Then it'll take them a slower, longer time to bear down tight on you."

"You mean *new* clothing and shoes will love me just as well?"

"Yes. You *inspire* it, sir."

"I only welcome love from human women. Clothes and shoes are supposed to be genderless."

"Well, you can't control *everything,* in the outside world."

"I'm afraid not. I'm being choked."

"In our back room, remove all those clothes and shoes. I'll get you a new set, the largest articles our racks have. *That*'ll hold you, for a while."

"Not *tightly,* I hope."

"No; *loosely,* at first."

"Thanks for your research."

"Thanks for your patronage. Sir?"

"Yes?"

"What's your secret?"

"For what?"

"For inspiring love."

"But *you* don't want to be *similarly* afflicted!?"

"Not by clothes and shoes. But by women."

"There's no proven formula. I just act natural. I'm just me, that's all."

"Will that work, in my case, on the women, sir?"

"No."

"Why not?"

"You're not me."

"Oh, so *that*'s the secret: to be *you.*"

"It's rather an *open* secret, I'm afraid."

"It's very difficult to follow. Only *you* can be you; no-one else can."

"So my 'secret' is limited to my own application."

"I wish it could be more generally applied, sir."

"No. It'll die with me. *Ow!* My shoes and clothes are getting *unbearable!* I'm in their amorous clinch!"

"To the back room, sir! Off with everything!"

"What a great relief, *that*'ll be! Ah, love can get out of hand. It must be restrained, at times."

LVII. JUNE THE IMMUNE. TILL WHOM DID SHE MEET? TOM GERVASI, TO UPSET THAT. TO THE TUNE OF GRAVE REPERCUSSIONS. TO THE SETTING OF JUNE'S MOON.

June's friends wondered when she was *ever* going to fall in love. She was already in her middle thirties and had never been stricken by that glorious dream-disease. Was she immune to it? She had been the despair of the woeful men who had loved her. All they craved was her requital. That's all she didn't give them.

She didn't *seem* cold. On the contrary, she seemed warm, affectionate, generous with her feelings, expansive, protective, compassionate—quite loving. Yet, she was never *in* love, passionately. She never throbbed with quickened pulse to the approach of any special man. She never dwelled in reverie, on gorgeous clouds of fantasy, upon a particular man. She *inspired* that sort of thing in *men's* bosoms. But her own was devoid of any enshrined image.

Her girl friends described the ecstasy, the bliss, the radiant hope, that highlit the "in-love" experience. June listened, was glad for them, but was content to have missed it all herself. Her life was full enough, thank you. She had identified with movie heroines, and those in novels, and of course with her girl friends in actual life, in the matter of "feeling love." Such sympathetic empathy was the extent of it, in her own personal life. No matter. When she dies, she will never have felt it. But really, she's lived life to the hilt. She'll carry no regret, no "missed-out" feeling, to her final resting place. It's been fine. And lots of fun ahead.

Still, her friends wouldn't give up. They introduced her to some irresistible men: whom June resisted. But often *they* didn't resist *her*. Some men were devastatingly attractive. But June devastated *them*. They couldn't dent her heart. It remained impervious; poised; exempt from passion's risky poison.

"June the Immune," they called her, her friends did. She smiled, and didn't care.

Her calm reserve, her cheerful indifference, her even-tempered life, collapsed, all at once. It so happened that she met Tom Gervasi. That did it.

She was transformed. All the love she had never felt, got its revenge on her, with merciless insistence. She worshipped every last hair in Tom Gervasi's skin. Never was man so loved, as he by her.

Her friends at first worried, then grew alarmed, to find June perfectly unloved, herself, by Tom Gervasi. Would she survive this raging passion, this furious outburst of all her soul, that dashed itself, to no avail, all unrequited, upon an unperturbed man? Tom Gervasi *slept* with her; was sweet and courteous to her; but shared nothing of the tumult she felt toward him. June was expending all her forces, her final reserves, all in vain, upon the idol of her life. She was in for unmatched sorrow. Her agony could not be wished upon a sadistic murderer, so keen it must be.

Her friends signed a petition, which they presented to Tom Gervasi, imploring him, for June's poor sanity, to *somehow* love her in return. "I can't fake it," he replied. "Either it's there, or not. In her case, alas, I quite like her a lot: But love? No, I'm afraid."

June's heart broke. Tom Gervasi was genuinely sorry. He brought a wreath to her funeral. He wept. In pity, not in love.

June's friends detested him. But he was within his rights. It's legal to feel no love, however gratifying that would be to an afflicted soul. They had no case against Tom Gervasi. They mourned June. If only she could have *remained* exempt, for her dear sake! June was *not* immune. The epithet lost its humor. And June, her life.

LVIII. THE BENIGN VISION OF TOM GERVASI: A USEFUL IDEAL TO HAVE.

Tom Gervasi had a benign vision of the world: people wouldn't threaten other people; people would be good to other people; no-one would harm anyone else.

The world was to be safe and secure; walking in a tough neighborhood, late at night, would be anxiety-free. There'd be no worry and suspicion about what other people are up to.

This was only a benign vision; not the actual state of things.

Still, to *conceive* of the benign vision seemed grounds for hopefulness.

Well, the world is often hazardous. You could be beaten in the street or in your building; your briefcase, with things important to you in it, could be yanked away; *very* bad things could happen to you: by the agency of other people, over whose behavior we might have such terrifyingly little control, in securing safety and predictable peace in our own movements.

Against this insecurity, Tom Gervasi had a benign vision: the *hoped-for* state of affairs. Not much guarantee in it.

More an ideal than a possibility, that benign vision.

Well, ideals can do *some* good. Just conceiving them can afford some relief, while bolstering fortitude.

So he *valued* his benign visions. And tempered his realism, his worldly wariness, with that sweet release: ideals—their conception.

Ideals happen in the world—they're conceived by real people.

Ideals, then, take their place in reality.

Otherwise, experience grows too pessimistic. Tom Gervasi wanted to sing what would sound somewhat joyful. Ideals helped to promote this.

He's happy. He has his ideals. The world can't rip them away. Let people do their worst, and be a threat; Tom Gervasi can counter them, and not be trampled or submerged by fear, morbid fear.

Ideals did dare to hope. They spared him from fear. He needed them. To sweeten things. To sprinkle some hope on the path ahead; letting him tread lighter, with some gaiety, some trust and confidence, that he might get by.

And he *does* get by. He's buoyed up, to the occasional bounce, by taking ideals along. They have *some* magic effect, on what others might do. The ideals are talking to others, saying, "Be good, don't worry. Let's all get along. For all our sakes. Spare me, please. Don't harm me. I'll be good to you. Don't *force* goodness from me. Trust me. Let me trust you. Let's live, together."

LIX. WOMEN, AND TOM GERVASI.

Tom Gervasi was deep down (or up) Angela, and they were flapping like seals sending frantic signals via the eddying of cross-tides across a strait so narrow that the flip of one seal's gills flapped with the flop of the other's, in a slippery slide of forth-and-back messages, dripping-drop, in aqueous conduct.

Waves poured splash. Splish-and-fro, all in a spray.

When Angela and Tom dried up, Tom was bored. He yearned for Janet. Angela intercepted this yearning, and accused him (rightfully so) of mental infidelity. "I'm so attuned to you," she snapped, "that even your thought-waves leak through the privacy you intend for them. We're so familiar, you and I, that I know your least pulsation, and trap you into my net of insight. I know you *too* well. It's a danger-sign, that our love-affair has worn thin and lost its fresh edge, its keen turns of surprise."

"I agree, as usual," Tom replied. "You're never wrong, about me. That's a danger-sign. We don't charge into romantic blunders, any more. We don't quicken to the delight of mutual error. Instead, we're right, about each other. That's wrong, for love. Dead wrong, for we're too dull. A dreary yawn of decadence is our hum-drum tune, now. We're through, Angela. You're opaque, to me, through and through. And I'm an open book, to you. But Janet is another story. Unread, romantic, up in the air, charged with the little spice of intrigue which, in our case, alas, we've both used up. You're a faded, former mystery. But Janet's an untasted one yet. I'm enchanted by how little I yet know her. It spins me in suspense. I'm drawn to her. She's yet to be. I long to prong. To probe. But never to find. For that's been *our* failure. We're doubly found by each other, and have no more to seek.

For where 'find' occurs, 'seek' stops. We're exhausted, by attainment. I was *so* fond of you. I still am. But I'm bored. I have you. I lack Janet. I'll discard you. I'll get Janet. To get her, to find her. And in finding, lose."

"You'll repeat the cycle—our cycle, worn to fulfillment—with Janet? But *that's* self-defeating, too. But it's a new chase, for you. Oh, I hate you. Because I'm *not* tired of you. There's more of you, yet. You're not finite. Not to me. But I am to you. So I'm dropped by you. I'm so miserable. Oh, Janet is so fortunate, to be my successor, in your arms and heart. And my loss is great. I'll love you, forever."

She wept, with self-pity. Tom held her, to console her. But he was Janet-minded, even then. Angela saw through this, in her tears. All that he willed, by private mental process, she could lovingly translate, and decipher its code. She knew him, and loved on. He knew her, in love's cessation. Such contrary knowings! So killing to her. So dull to him. For she became an indifference to him. Someone to leave. To her, he was being lovingly lost. She loved on, in terror. In plight of disaster. He grew intensely real, in her despairing imagination. Who was Janet? Angela only knew *of* a Janet—but not filled in. Janet didn't *take* Tom away. Tom was first fading to Angela, *anyway. Any* woman could be next. From that general "any," Janet looms to be the lucky particular. So Angela doesn't *hate* Janet. She hates Tom. With love.

Janet is thinking of Tom. They only met recently. They have a date tonight. He told her when they met, that he had been growing tired of someone named Angela. What a confiding to make to a stranger! was he unreliable, fickle, treacherous? To this "Angela," he obviously was. Taking up her name in vain, to a perfect stranger upon meeting! Janet feared that in time, Tom would treat *her* that way, too. Angela betrayed, to new-found Janet. When would it be Janet's turn? What a way to treat a loved one, with her back turned! Admittedly, however, it was a *formerly* loved one: about to be dropped, anyway. Still, where's his loyalty? Was he a ruthless, amoral rake? Janet longed to know. Already, she was his. She'd fall for him, this very evening! He'd cuddle her: and breathe the word, "Forever."

In jealousy Angela followed Tom about, on the evening of his date with Janet. She stood outside his office building before the time his work usually closed for the day. When he emerged, she followed him to a bus stop, keeping a few people behind him. He got on, she got on, but he never suspected, so he never looked back and saw her, as he stood in the middle and she kept inconspicuously to the front. He got off, and stealthily she got off. He headed to an apartment building, and so did she. He entered it, but she stopped outside the entrance. So here was where Janet lived! Her successor-to-be. Her successor already. He must already be entering her apartment. Janet would offer him a drink, and then Tom would take her out? Angela assumed so, and waited downstairs, outside. Maybe Janet lived on the ground floor, so Tom didn't take any elevator? Maybe he's on the same street level with waiting Angela now? But that technicality hardly made much difference. Angela had sacrificed dignity to jealous curiosity. She was following her former man about. A morbid, self-pitying act. Instead of guessing, in pain, she's sleuthing: a more active, involved pain path. She's lost him, in either case. Tom Gervasi. The man who was hers. The man who's not now. Two foreignly apart men. Two Angelas. The happy, Tom-having one. The abject one, scouting her successor's residence area, to relieve and intensify the excruciation of a jealous loss.

Already, hours have passed. No Tom with his new Janet spied upon. He must still be in her apartment. Unless this building has a side or back exit, which they took while Angela waited in front? At any rate, Angela will abandon her forlorn post. For the antiromantic, pressing need to decently pass urine from a bursting bladder. She's debased. She's stooped to follow. It proved in vain. She gives up, to go to some public or private bathroom somewhere. Nearby is an elegant bar, where they'll let a lady relieve herself. Tom might still be in Janet's apartment. She's fed him there, maybe, and they're in an embrace. Or else, they left the building via a non-front exit, and he's taken her to dinner somewhere. Oh Tom, you were so *recently* mine! Just last night, we made love! Now, your heart is elsewhere. Who *is* this Janet? You got tired of me *before* you met this new person. I can't blame her. She didn't willingly hurt me. No intentional malice, on her part.

Oh Tom, I love you. Can't you hear me? Where are you?

I knew him through and through. *When* his mood would change, *what* he's thinking. I could detect it, on the spot. I was losing him. He was falling out of love. I saw this, helplessly. I "watched" it happen. He was my expert study, my devoted pastime, as I refined my aptitude to know his least whim, to anticipate a new mood. I developed a knowing mastery over my adored subject. Of what use is that to me now? The subject has bolted. My talent falls back, on its barren self.

That monologue of Angela was back in her apartment. She's not out chasing him any more. She lost her lead, and it was no chase anyhow. Would she have *confronted* them, if her detection had worked? What an embarrassment. Tom was free, to go his own way. He was in no way obligated, to remain steadfast. Janet was his prerogative. It was out of Angela's control. Her private research was impractical, academic. Tom was released. By his own decision. By the weakening of his love for her. Hers for him has strengthened. Perversely, and too late.

Not "too late": at no avail, *any* time. Strong love for him was no means of keeping him. What mattered was his for her. It weakened, and he want.

It's still the night of Janet's date with Tom. But it's very late. It's past midnight. He's asleep, by her side, on her dearly rumpled bed. But she's awake, and in love. She's sitting up against the headpost. Her first time "out" with this man, and already they're "deep." She had asked him of Angela. Tom was sad to disappoint Angela. He was afraid Angela was jealous and in grief for him—as though he were dead. And he *is* dead: to that poor girl.

Janet worried. In time, would *she* be treated this way? Was he prone to that sort of thing? To get out while the other was plunging further in?

It was her risk. She loved him. So had Angela. Could Janet keep him? If so, how long? She wanted marriage. Presumably, so had Angela. Well, Janet was *determined*. *Not* to share Angela's fate. To win Tom forever. To have him, always. *Never* to be in a jealous position. Never to be—another Angela.

As usual, time went by. (It's got to go *some*where; so why not "by"?)

Tom was exclusively seeing Janet, they were close and thick. But they kept separate apartments. Janet said, "Live with me: either in your apartment, or in mine, or in a new one. Please."

He answered, "I love you, but I still want to live apart from you. We can be together every night, in your place or in my place. But I insist on separate residences."

"How is Angela?"

"She phones me periodically—in fact, regularly, at the office mainly, to beg me back. She knows I love you. It hurts her to keep on, to beg me. It hurts me always to answer no. When will she ever 'get over' me? She's attractive, why doesn't she get a new man? Maybe she *has* gotten a new man. But goes on loving me, still the same."

"Tom?"

"Yes, my love."

"I'm Janet, you know."

"What are you getting at?"

"I don't wish to become another Angela. To be loved and left by you. Before Angela, were other women victims like she was? Is that a habit of yours? Am I doomed next? I refuse to be a repetition stage. I want to break you, of brief love affairs, in rapid succession, with women who become interchangeable, or cheaply replaceable. I want *special* status with you: *durable* status. Reform. Love me alone, and forever."

"I love you forever—*now* I do. But tomorrow—who knows? I *might* change. I might not. You *are* special to me—*now*. Now, is all I know. Beyond that, who can tell? I don't promise. I won't commit myself. It's all unpredictable. I like it that way. I'm ir-resistible, I can get any woman I want. That's why I won't tie myself down. There's variety ahead, just like behind. Younger girls than you are growing up. You'll age. I'll *still* be attractive. You'll be replaced. By a *lovely* young girl. And she, in turn, by a still younger one. I love *women*. I love your gender. You're its rep-resentative, just now. You're the particular she, of the general tribe. Of course, you're Janet. I love you for it. But I loved Angela, once. And left her. She still mopes and pines for me. Prepare yourself. You might, too. She's your sister."

Tom had said exactly what Janet craved not to hear. It plunged her into insecurity. She couldn't bear inheriting Angela's outcast state. So she said,

"Tom, we're through. Right in mid-love. *I* terminate this. I won't wait, for you to do so. I won't be passive, resigned, helpless. I actively take the step. I choose to end it, now."

Tom was shocked. It was a slap on his hurt face—a hard one, and he recoiled. *He* was used to rule. Janet was no Angela. He admired her. His pride hurt. But he accepted it. He agreed, too readily. He put on clothes, and left her apartment. She never phoned him, nor he her. Angela kept phoning. He told her what happened with Janet. Angela admired Janet—but pitied her, too. Janet wouldn't wait. She jumped up to reject first. In her love's very height. In her love's sacred prime. That *was* pride.

Tom was hurt, too. But Christine has crossed his path. He's working on her, and she's smitten. She thinks, "At last! My true love!" They go to bed immediately. She dreams of marrying him. But he tells her of Angela, and of Janet. That scares her. And *before* Angela? The same pattern, just about.

Christine is determined: *she'll* be the exception! She *will* be! It will be. It will. It will.

Oh, her hope! Oh, how she hopes.

LX. SARAH AND SHEILA COULD *DIE* FOR TOM GERVASI. THAT WORRIES HIM. BUT THEN, THERE'S NORA.

Sarah and Sheila were supposed to be loyal buddies. Their friendship was beyond any vow or pact. Their bond grew up practically from infancy. They helped each other through a progressively higher system of schools. They assisted each other through the rites of adolescent puberty, surviving those years of conformity initiation. They loaned each other class notes, and nursed each other through examination study. They confided in each other on boyfriends, and traded sympathetic advice. They defended each other against others. But this all blew apart, when their sturdy friendship couldn't withstand being rivals in love with the same man. This fundamental clash cracked their tradition of lifelong devotion to each other. So frail, so unsound, could true friendship be at its core? The tester of this soundness, but not on purpose, turned out to be Tom Gervasi. "I didn't mean to drive you apart," he told them both, when he summoned them to a hoped-for reconciliation conference over which he presided in the role of peacemaking arbiter. "Shake hands. I'm really not worth it, girls. Kiss and make up. You've gone through so much together. I hate to be responsible. It's heavy on my conscience. Should I decisively choose between you? And will the loser, in good faith, with brave grace, abide by my decision without bitter hatred for the winner? Will you swear to patch it all up between you, once my decision, for better or worse, should determine the course and fate of your young careers in the risky stakes of love? I'll marry the winner, but the loser must agree to be the wedding bridesmaid and remain best friend to the family. Do I have your word, on this?"

Sarah and Sheila looked at each other, with blushing conflict, loyal rivals split by love's grim divider. Sarah first spoke out: "Dear Tom, to lose you would kill me. Rather than be bridesmaid at your wedding to Sheila if she's your choice, let me be co-featured at the ceremony by combining the wedding celebration with my own wake. For your wedding *would*, literally, be my funeral. My farewell and my congratulations would be delivered all in one."

Not to be outdone, Sheila next spoke: "My competitor's sentiments echo my own. Should Sarah win you, Tom, my contribution to your marriage festivities would be my departure from this sad old earth of ours, which we cannot share in full amity. I'd get out of the way, and leave the blessings of life to you uncontested. My leavetaking, in its solemn note of finality, would signal that now your glee would be undisturbed. Life without Tom Gervasi, Sarah and I have come to agree, would be a life too bleak to abide. So decide, Tom. The loser will lose, indeed."

This alarmed Tom. He had called this conference to mend their friendship. Now, the voluntary death of the loser compounds this triangular horror. Humanely, he must prevent this. "In *that* case, I choose *neither* of you. May you *both* live: and share your double loss, of me."

But *that* wouldn't do, either. Sarah and Sheila, in a united front, threatened to *both* die, to mourn their equal loss of their true idol. "You'll have *two* deaths' guilt on your hands," they warned their shocked appeaser, "if you choose neither. Choose one, and slice it in half." What an ultimatum! They forced Tom's hand. He had no choice, but to choose. His choice would be a killer. But *not* to choose would double the atrocity. He was an innocent villain. *He* would lose. His would be a fatal preference, with these sworn rivals. Their love for him was so vast, that death alone had the weight to measure compensation on so grand a scale. This honor humbled him. To inspire Death, as equality with Love! He felt weak. How noble Sarah was, how noble Sheila! He felt dwarfed, by such heroism. For surely, they've decided heroically how to greet his *own* decision. But choice was paralyzed now. He would delay it. Delay meant longer life, for either Sarah or Sheila. Which?

Who will die? He felt like God, or Mephistopheles. He's the Grim Reaper, himself. Such unequal apportionment, he's to dole out! One gets his love and a happy life. The other—as aforesaid. The conference had been declared over by Sarah and Sheila. But they had scheduled the next one, at his same apartment, for the following night. Their fates would then become known.

As yet, their fates were unknown to Tom. They wouldn't permit him to delay tomorrow night. Right on the spot, they'd get it over with. They might even bring a knife or gun to do the trick, or some poison acid, or a pill overdose supply. A gun might make noise, to be heard perhaps in neighboring apartments and to cause suspicion. But all death is ugly; the "how," the means, are trivial compared to the result. The result ends every little hope that ever leaps with potential joy. "I love Sarah. I love Sheila. I want them to live. I'll die, instead."

But that wouldn't work, either. If he kills himself, the women would follow, and all three would have an underworld reunion, of sorts. Even at that underworld reunion, they might *still* demand he choose between them. Better to solve the issue aboveground, then, where a less lugubrious choice, in less morbid circumstances, would be tragically permitted. "I love Sarah. I love Sheila. One not more than the other. One not less than the other. Oh God, come to my rescue. Tomorrow night will soon be here. The women will arrive, with pathetic promptness. For my life-or-death decision. Oh, it's so unfair, to me! What a pitiful predicament I'm in! *I'm* to be pitied, too. Greed in love will get stern revenge. I loved *one* of these women to death. *Which* one? I can't choose! I'm stifled; mortified; frozen. It's too much!"

Tom Gervasi fainted away. The pressure was getting to him. The toll of mounting tension drove his nerves crazy. He's crumbled out. Blackness crackles, in his skull-like heart.

He's wakened by a phone ring. "Hello, it's your former love, Nora. Do you still love me?"

"I love you immortally. However, at the moment I'm taken up by Sarah and Sheila. Do you wish to claim me back? I've never been asundered from you. Sarah and Sheila are making it hot for me—and on themselves. The complications would amaze you. But Nora, why should I talk about *them,* when *you're* on the phone? You were ever my only true love. I took on Sarah and Sheila just to forget you. But by phoning me, you've stopped my forgetting. Is your love still alive for me?"

"It blazes higher than ever. I phoned, in fact, to ask if you wouldn't like to marry me. I'm in the mood—for you especially. For you *only.* Dear Tom Gervasi. Let's light up our sacred past, and consecrate it. Let's bring our past forward, to our very present. By holy matrimony. Does that sound all right, by you?"

"It's just what the doctor ordered. It couldn't come at a better time."

"But will it make Sarah and Sheila unhappy?"

"Yes. But they'll recover. They'll get over it."

"Is that so? Then their love for you must be finite."

"It is. It's just a passing love. When they see that I've taken *you* instead, it won't be the end of them."

"Of *course* not. They'll live."

"Thank God, that the human heart is resilient. It can bounce back. It's elastic, rubbery. For Sarah's and Sheila's sakes, I *hope* so. I'm glad you phoned, Nora. I was thinking of phoning *you* some day soon. You've spared me the trouble. I feel lighter, already."

LXI. THE REJECTED BOYFRIENDS OF EMILY AND LUCY WILL PUNISH TOM GERVASI, BY BEATING HIM UP VERY BADLY, FOR HAVING "STOLEN" EMILY AND LUCY FROM THEM. BUT TOM GERVASI IS INNOCENT. HE DIDN'T *ASK* EMILY AND LUCY TO LOVE HIM. THEY *VOLUNTEERED* THEIR LOVES. NOW, HOW CAN THEY SAVE HIM FROM THEIR BOYFRIENDS, FROM A BEATING THAT WILL DIVIDE HIM FROM HIS WITS AS A PERMANENT INFIRMITY? ONLY BY RETURNING TO THEIR BOYFRIENDS, THUS TURNING MARTYRS TO THEIR LOVE WITH HEROIC RENUNCIATION, CAN EMILY AND LUCY INSURE THAT TOM GERVASI WILL BE SPARED? YET THEY WILL *NOT* GIVE UP TOM GERVASI. YET THEY WANT HIM IN GOOD HEALTH. BUT THE BOYFRIENDS ARE SINCERE IN THEIR THREAT. WHAT SOLUTION IS POSSIBLE, FOR A GOOD END-ING? WHAT?

Emily and Lucy each had a steady boyfriend. All was well. Suddenly, the boyfriends meant nothing to those women any more, because they were eclipsed, in total, by the advent of Tom Gervasi into the lives of Emily and Lucy, due to business connections between the firm Tom Gervasi worked for and the firm Emily and Lucy were employed by. Tom Gervasi caught both girls' fancy. Somehow, their boyfriends became irrelevant. Completely. Put in the lost shade of oblivion. By Tom Gervasi's blaze. Tom Gervasi didn't *mean* to have that devastating effect. It just *caught* the girls, unaware. They were stung by it. In the sting, some amorous poison spread. He replaced their souls.

Not their boyfriends merely, but their own private souls. They moved, to his rhythm.

Emily's and Lucy's boyfriends grew from grief at their loss to anger at the man who caused it. "Let's beat him up," they decided. "He won't look so pretty anymore, once we give him a going-over, lightly, just a few rough reminders. Emily and Lucy will take one look at him, and come crawling back to us, begging to be forgiven. We'll be slow in deciding, so as to eke out a few more apologies from them. Then, we'll show compassion; and out of the goodness of our hearts, with the admonishment, 'Don't let that ever happen again,' we'll let them kiss us and take us back, letting them play with our bodies as a way of showing that we've allowed ourselves to be *ex*-former boyfriends, now reinstated in full, but being owed reparation to cover damages to our collective prides."

Thus these bruisers conferred. They were big and strong, athletic in build, and amateur weightlifters on the side. They had been local boxing champs, as well, and were in addition versed in karate, ju-jitsu, wrestling, and other "defensive" sciences. They were well motivated not to spare Tom Gervasi hardly an inch. He'd be in for it, all right. He'd better watch out.

But in all fairness, those deposed boyfriends thought they'd first warn Emily and Lucy about their belligerent intentions. Then, Emily and Lucy could reconsider their rash rejections of their brutal ex-swains. To spare their new idol the beating of his lifetime, perhaps in martyrdom they'll return to the fold, and resume with their boyfriends. That would be *true* devotion, to Tom Gervasi. To shield him, from an awful threat. And for *his* sake, heroically to renounce him. Like two saints who sacrifice love for the peaceful safety of the idol they protect and forsake in an agony of devotion.

"We're warning you, Emily and Lucy. If you don't take us back, Tom Gervasi won't be worth even remembering, once we get through with him. Not even his own mother would recognize him, after the tattoo job we do on him. You want your hero safe and sound? You want to *be* heroines and save him? Just reinstate us, then, and forget him. If you don't, we'll frankly abandon all mercy, in our treatment of him. Choose now, Emily and Lucy. What's it to be?"

The girls were scared. These thugs really meant it. It was no bluff. But Tom Gervasi had encouraged Emily and Lucy in their worship and ardor. He was about to choose which of them would be his girlfriend, and had hinted that, as choice was difficult, they might *both* become his girlfriends. Thus, *neither* would lose him. But now, this awful threat. They were up against it. To forgo the one they loved and save him? Or by holding on to him, be responsible indirectly for his permanent crippling, his being organically battered to the extent of loss of functions, marring of good looks, severe curtailment of vital movements, extending even to the knowing organ, which perceives and discriminates? It's only humane to spare that dear rare one, in all his loving innocence. Yet Emily and Lucy want to retain him: for their very own, or for the one lucky one if he narrows his field of choice from them both. They wanted him intact. All of a piece. Still held together, in life and limb.

They looked into the commercial yellow pages of the telephone directory, till their eyes stopped at this listing: "We Beat Up People For You Syndicate." They phoned the number, said they had two brutes in mind for treatment, and were quoted quite a steep price. But Emily and Lucy had sizable savings in the bank. They withdrew most of it, and went to the "We Beat Up People For You Syndicate" office, with trembling hearts. What monsters worked for that firm! They looked like fat football players.

Specific instructions were left: to be carried out next day. Not only the *instructions* were carried out: the ex-boyfriends as well. Mangled for life. Reduced to squash.

Emily and Lucy had done an enormous service to Tom Gervasi. It had cost them most of their life savings. Of course, they were responsible for his life having first been placed in danger. Now, they were responsible for the destruction of that danger.

They didn't tell him about the danger. Later, some day, maybe, in intimacy.

They had an appointment to see Tom Gervasi and hear whether both would be his girlfriends or just the one lucky one. With trembling hearts, they entered his apartment.

"Emily and Lucy, I've changed my mind. I don't want both of you for girlfriends; but neither do I want either of you for a girlfriend. In short, I reject you both. This is our final interview. I'm busy."

"But Tom Gervasi: We demand an explanation. You've ruined our lives. Why?"

"Recently, some lovely new girls fell in love with me. Frankly, I prefer them to you. Sorry."

They wept. They both wept.

Tom Gervasi *was* sorry. Too bad. He destroyed their hopes. They offered him pure love. He felt like a scoundrel, for turning them both down. An out-and-out cad. A real rat. "I hate myself," he said. "I spoiled all their dreams. They're sobbing, now, in front of me. Well, I'm not the *only* man in the world. Others will be willing to be boyfriends to them. But Emily and Lucy may not *value* those others. Well, they can't have me. And that's final."

Emily and Lucy weep. They weep out their lives, practically. They were so close, in hope. So *very* close! Now, all taken away.

Still weeping, they leave his apartment. Tom Gervasi feels lonely. So much love for him has just left! All that love, gone to waste.

Quickly, he phones the new women in his life. He summons them to visit him, fast. They quickly respond. They dash there, in no time. They fill the vacuum, left by Emily and Lucy. They bring in fresh love.

LXII. GERTRUDE'S LIFESTYLE IS CHANGED, BE-CAUSE TOM GERVASI MISSED AN APPOINTMENT (STOOD HER UP). SHE SEES THE HIDDEN MESSAGE, IN HIS INSPIRED, FORGETFUL ACT. IT TRANS-FORMS HER. SHE SEES THE LIGHT. AND LIVES, BY IT.

Gertrude has just been "stood up" by Tom Gervasi. They had clearly made a date appointment for a definite time, a definite place. The when and where had been unmistakably gone over, eliminating any ambivalent misunderstanding. Therefore, the failure of Tom Gervasi to show up was inexcusable, as sorrow spread over Gertrude. To say that she had "looked forward" to their appointment would be a careless lesson in understate-ment. This was to be the most important event of her life! It was to be the dividing mark between the "just treading water," the "marking time," of her previous years, and "the true begin-ning of her whole life and soul in the world of the real universe, as herself." Tom Gervasi was to lead the way, as Virgil did for Dante in the other world. He was to be her guide. She was to fol-low, and find—everything: not a bit less. She thought that he had shared the sacred nature of this mission. But lightheartedly, he just hadn't shown up. Love fled. Life was back where it started. Without, this time, hope.

She went home, and stayed home, waiting for his explana-tory phone call. Maybe something *had* prevented him, which he was powerless to prevent happening. Something not his fault at all. Something outside the power of his circumvential will; be-yond the reasonable measure of his control. Some accident? An act of God? A friend dying? A sudden emergency? A matter of life or death? Something that begged for her pardon? She died for the opportunity to forgive; how sweet her mercy would fall!, like light rain upon the parched traveler.

Still no phone call. Gertrude, of course, could call *him*; But it wasn't her place to. Dignity and pride required that she wait. Not eagerly. But with dignity. Proudly. Gently, with forgiveness in her heart.

A week went by. She knew he was in town, she knew he was safe and about. Gossip had delivered her these comforting facts. Nothing "had happened" to him, of a major order. He couldn't have *forgotten*. Her life wasn't *that* slight to him.

Wasn't it? Maybe it was. What was Gertrude to Tom Gervasi? Yes, what?

One of countless women? Just another woman? Not singled out for herself, but numbered in an amorphous group in a "gender" category of available tools for Tom Gervasi's amusement "in passing," on the run, going off elsewhere?

Gertrude was demeaned. Debased. Lowered. Insulted.

Could Tom Gervasi actually take so little trouble over someone he had promised so much to? Could there *be* such a man, with such a character, which in old-fashioned fiction went by "scoundrel"? And had he come into Gertrude's life? Had her inexperience been caught off guard? Had her simple, trusting innocence been so knavishly used? Could morality be given such off-hand dismissal? Was human decency the flagrant fodder for cavalier disrespect? Or were these scruples just instances of Gertrude's puritanical bent, her prim prissiness, her premature old maidenliness? She *did* feel stuffy. Tom Gervasi was just a breeze, wafting through her antiquated stuffiness. Yes, *that* was the lesson he wanted to teach her! Of course! Finally, the message seeped through. Was she so thick? It was a *subtle* lesson, he taught her. By not turning up as scheduled, he was trying to drive home to her the essential modern virtues of easy-going casualness. Well, she'd *heed* that lesson! And how!

Gertrude became totally transformed. Her whole way of life became something else. Altogether.

She became loose, even promiscuous. She "slept around," casually. She had lived in such tight rectitude, before! She had been a precocious virgin spinster at the time of being "stood up" on her appointment with Tom Gervasi. Now, she was a wild thing. The whim of the wind. Open to all caprices, especially with men.

"Gertrude is game! You can have a ball with her!" So, word got round, in the world of men. All due to a mistake. Tom Gervasi *hadn't* intended to teach her the value of easy casual life, of loose readiness for anything, of cheaply floating into men's beds. He hadn't had *any* lesson to teach her. He had no point at all, in forgetting their appointment. He just plumb forgot! It just slipped his mind. And it hasn't returned: he's *still* forgotten.

Gertrude thinks that her "easy living" is preparing her for his approval, his rewarding of her for being such a splendid pupil. So she thinks, and so she goes on. The way she's going, Tom Gervasi is bound to admire her, even venerate her, as equal only to himself. So she thinks, and goes on. It's all for him. As a teacher, he's enlightened her. The greatest homage the student can pay the master is to adapt her whole lifestyle to the master precepts. Thus she does, and lives in hope. He'll see the change. He'll approve, by changing the change—to a conventional wedding. To an old-fashioned lifestyle, in their married state.

However, Tom Gervasi himself is not thinking of marrying her. He's not thinking at all, of anything, of her. He's forgotten her, altogether. He knows no Gertrude. He never *did* miss that appointment: he forgot he ever had it.

Did he ever have it? Once, yes, maybe. But if so, it's a total loss. To Gertrude, he has pure oblivion.

Gertrude, meanwhile, is living a lifestyle in his honor. All due to him. And *for* him.

She expects to be Mrs. Tom Gervasi, in reward. But she's not on *his* mind. He knows no "Gertrude."

What's Gertrude to him? Nothing at all. And he to Gertrude? Her guru, Saviour, her saint, her deliverer, emancipator, her God, her All. Not a bit less. Her least act has as its goal: "Is it *worthy* of Tom Gervasi? Would he approve?"

Even her promiscuous slipping into men's beds. She's in one now, with a total stranger. She's thinking, "He'd be *proud* of me, if only he could see! I'm his faithful disciple, to the end."

The end being, marriage. She's building up her worthiness, for that holy event.

LXIII. LAURA AND ADELE HATE EACH OTHER IN LOVE FOR TOM GERVASI, WHO'S POSSESSED BY DOLORES, WHOM LAURA AND ADELE HATE EVEN WORSE THAN EACH OTHER. ALL THAT HATE! IN LOVE'S NAME.

Laura and Adele were best friends; or at any rate, they *used* to be. Certainly not now, by any means. They're raging enemies, thanks to the coincidence that they're both in love with the same Tom Gervasi. However, the latter is now in the possession of Dolores. Or so Dolores thinks. She loves him too. But she doesn't know either Laura or Adele, who are both about to become her ferocious rivals, eager to displace her as the exclusive captor of the much-fought-over heart of Tom Gervasi, God's prize to women.

What do they see in him—Laura, Adele, Dolores, and his other adorers? He has a peculiar effect upon women. *They* don't know what it is; *he* doesn't know what it is. But it works, all right. It works all around.

Laura and Adele aren't speaking now. Each is trying her darndest to extricate away Tom Gervasi from the wicked clutches of Dolores, who has somehow cast over him a magic spell, the formula of an alchemy witch who's had him sniff a lotion of love potion to give him notions that she's someone special, which of course both Laura and Adele know that she's not, but only a pretender to the royal throne of the great kingdom of the far-flung empire of Tom Gervasi's heart, that Dolores wants to colonize, but Laura and Adele know that she—as well as each other—are not so nearly worthy of such magnificent eminence. The supreme glory of any woman's aspiration is Tom Gervasi's hand in wedlock. Hysterical, combative candidates are rife and quick to screech, for such holy sweepstakes in all-out contest

230

and immoral competitive ruthlessness. *Any* means are justified. Tom Gervasi blinds his followers. He's their royal sun. They gaze, and are lost.

What did *Tom Gervasi* think, about all this? Surely, he has a voice in the matter? After all, it's he who's being loved. That confers upon him *some* privilege, doesn't it? He's not just a passive chattel, in meek helpless docility to Dolores, his self-imposed Guardian? Nor is he pliantly submissive to Laura and Adele owing to their imperious claim, by elective divinity, by ordained autonomy, on passion's all-purpose passport? No, he's his own free man. "*Let* them fight over me. They're boosting my value, that way. I'll do as I damn well please. I'll shake loose from Dolores, who's too bossy by far. Laura and Adele act like potential Doloreses. Well, I won't be taken over by either. They're making a strong play. Former friends, they're now hostile rivals for me in cutthroat hate for whoever stands in the way. Am I a man or a goal? I'm both together, for all those eager women. Well, *no-one* can have me. I'm free, I'm my own."

Laura and Adele had *other* ideas: similar to each other's, but independently derived from separate cells of their mutual hatred. But first, to depose Dolores: that's step number one. With Dolores out of the way, the *true* bitchfight can come to a direct result. Should Laura and Adele momentarily ally, since their unity could better thrust Dolores from that tournament turf? It would improve their chances, were Dolores to be ousted. Their threat became known to Dolores, who braced herself for any showdown challenge. Tom Gervasi was growing uneasy, restless, and was chafing to ease the unsteady grip, and even shake it off, by which Dolores kept tenuous hold over him. Thus, imperiled by two new rivals, and threatened by her captive's revolt, Dolores faced trouble from outside and in. Should she attend to the domestic dissent first, and quell an interior riot? Or first ward off the imminent invasion by Laura and Adele? She gathered her resources together, and braced for the fight, from both ends; mobilizing her reserves, and steeling her resolve, in grim opposition to the brewing unrest from two ominous fronts. She'll defend her property—from himself and them. She brooded her counter-strategies to any anticipated move on her precarious perch. From tentative insecurity, she plots a brutal rule, should she ever see the day through. She'll not be caught weak again.

Laura and Adele united for the temporary expedience of eliminating Dolores as superfluous third rival, redundant though the incumbent, for possession of Tom Gervasi. "Drop your claim to him," they threatened, having waylaid her on the street, outside her residential building, after a tedious cloak-and-dagger wait for her emergence.

"Don't molest me. I have enough trouble keeping him myself, without your outside interference. Have you brought your strongarm tactics, like racketeer enforcers extorting a small shopkeeper for protection money, with persuasive enforcement to brutally bend him to their will? You can't muscle me off my territory. You can't intimidate me. I'll scream. Police patrol this area. They'll jail you, on a harassment charge. I know that *you*'re Laura and *you*'re Adele. You're temporarily reconciled for expedient power to uncontrol me of Tom Gervasi, planning a takeover to reduce the field to just yourselves, in surviving infight for the closed-in-on prize. But first to yank him loose from my grip. Nice strategy, but I dispermit it. I'll let him go no more than I'll let you *make* me do so. Possession is the law. And you're outside it. I have squatter's rights over him. That's a vulgar image. But I won't be delicate with such hoodlums as you. Your hatred for each other is suspended on ice, while you animate a joint one for me. I'm honored to have so earned it. Go away, or I'll scream. See that policeman there? He patrols the area, for such as you. *He*'ll know who Tom Gervasi belongs to. I'll inform him. Officer!"

Laura and Adele duck away, before the policeman reacts to Dolores' summons. They feel thwarted. Dolores had exerted herself, with stubborn self-assertion. "It's *your* fault!" Laura accused Adele. "Yours, you monkey," Adele answers back. They kick and scream and screech. They pull hair, and use their teeth. The policeman Dolores had called hears them. A crowd gathers round. The policeman keeps the peace by placing them under arrest. It's a disgraceful display. Let Tom Gervasi hear about this! He'll be disgusted with their exhibition. It plays well, into Dolores' hands. She's the winner. As of now.

The fracas made the newspaper. Tom Gervasi reads it, in disgust. Dolores glouts and crows. She raises her skirt in triumph, pouring lust over Tom Gervasi's disgust. He hates her too, but they fornicate. Angrily, on his part. "It's the last time," he vows, "with *this* sweet wench. I'll wrench myself away. To hell with Laura, with Adele. They'll *never* get me, if I preserve my will. And Dolores will lose me. This is her last lay. I'm done, now."

Then he walked out on her. However, it was in his apartment. She ruled the roost there, yet. He returns, with a locksmith, who's changing the lock. "Your key is soon obsolete," he duly informs Dolores. She's undaunted. She's fought this long. And now, the apartment buzzer rings. Laura and Adele have come visiting. They're released from custody. They hate each other, but are banded together. Against Dolores. For Tom Gervasi. The latter feels he's besieged. Momentarily, he regrets his power over women. It's cost him peace. It's raised such disturbance. But he's honored. The locksmith smiles. He's finished changing the lock. He hands Tom Gervasi the new key, with three duplicate keys. Laura, Adele, and Dolores intercept the exchange, slap the hands away, knock the duplicate keys down, and scramble, each to confiscate her own, in the amoral proceedings. Who owns what?

The women are all keyed up. From on their knees, they rise again. Hostility flares from their six eyes. White heat, true lust.

Then they proceed to fight against each other, all three. The locksmith pockets his fee, and flees. Tom Gervasi is left. Being fought over. A signal honor. What a fuss is raised! How three women can right! Well, he's worth it. The measure of his worth is being displayed. But he merits an *intrinsic* value. He doesn't need this clashing proof.

They're still fighting, over him. "They must love me dearly. The dear dears. My mother loved me dearly. I was her dear. Now I'm dear to these three. They endear themselves, to me."

It was really about love. Love is strong. But the numbers were wrong. Three women and only one man. That's not the going rate. Hence, the fight. Aggression, from love. Well, love exists. Laura, Adele, and Dolores are showing it. With bruises. Licking honorable wounds. Limping from the warfield. To cover him with kisses. All that hate, from loving one man! Love started it all. Love was the source. The origin. War and hate were derived. But love was primary. For love, conflicts arise. This gladdened Tom Gervasi. He's being kissed, from three sides. Love asserts its tides. Love wildly flows over him. In waves, from the deep.

The ocean of love. Love's swell. Love erupts. It comes ashore. It splashes him. Three heavy waves. Washing him over. In kissing foam. Love, from the sea. The first mother. Rolling to the land.

LXIV. TOM GERVASI AND MARY. HE'S STOPPED LOVING HER. BUT SHE WON'T LET HIM GO. SHE TAKES OVER. IN TOTAL CONTROL.

Mary didn't appeal to Tom Gervasi any more. But he wasn't callous. He had to break it to her softly, so as not to upset her. He wanted to ease her out, with minimum pain. Even to contrive such a way of putting it, as—paradoxically—to make her glad, relieved, happy, unburdened, to be losing him. He needed a diplomatic touch, for that, or a greasy sales executive's palaver, or an oily merchant's tongue, adroit in hypocrisy's witchcraft, the insincere poet's stylish wind of rhetoric.

Mary was sensitive, and she loved him. He had to exercise as much care as the superstitious farmer in handling a new-laid egg from a clucking hen after having been told by a great wizard that in this egg there was a pure kernel of gold, which would evaporate to nothing were the farmer to drop and crack thc egg in his clumsy trembling. That's how tender, how delicatc, Tom Gcrvasi must be, in handling how poor Mary gets the news: which, if bluntly stated, would be: "You don't interest me any more. It's all over between us. Don't bother to appeal. My mind is settled, and that's it."

"Mary, I have something to say."

"Tom Gervasi, how glad I am of that! I love your melodic voice, and your way of putting words together. I love *everything* of you. I love you to pure heaven. I love you beyond life itself. I love you beyond love itself. You *are* love, yet you transcend it, and are much greater. What have you to say, Tom Gervasi?"

"It'll make you very happy."

"Of *course* it will: because *you*'re saying it. You bring all my happiness to me. Now, what's your latest bit?"

"Mary, let me put it this way. I'm going to freeze, arrest, ossify, make permanent, our love: to eternalize it. We'll not see each other any more. Our knowing each other will stop at its highest, absolute state. The stars, sun, and moon will claim it. It's already at its immortal zenith. Let's not tamper with it *any more*. Let's abandon it, just as it is. We'll never lay eyes on each other again. Kiss me our last kiss, dear Mary. Then, let's surrender our love, to its infinity."

"That's a lousy idea, Tom Gervasi. I definitely turn it down. You're not getting rid of me! We're not breaking up! A thousand times, never! So you've tired of me, eh? You don't love me any more, is that it? Well, it's not acceptable to me! We remain together, always! I'll *never* let you go!

"You gave me a lot of hokum, with that idealism, using sacred words like 'infinite,' 'eternal,' 'heaven,' 'immortal,' 'pure,' 'absolute,' and all that baloney! Well, *stop* that drivel. You're *mine*! I won't let you go!"

"Mary, you're being too possessive."

"Not *too* possessive. I *do* possess you. You *are* my possession. And I'm not about to relinquish it. You're stuck. You can't unload me, in a million years. I'll shadow you every inch of your motion; you'll go nowhere without my already anticipating it and being there already, waiting. I'll stalk you, I'll dog you, I'll echo your least cough or sneeze. I'm there with you. To be released, you'll have to kill me first. And you wouldn't *dare* do that, Tom Gervasi! Not even for your personal freedom, your right to a private life and liberty of choice. You're bound, head and foot, to me. You remain, as my prisoner, in involuntary servitude. I *own* you, Tom Gervasi.

"Don't tell me about eternity, immortal, heaven, infinite, and such 'absolute' rubbish. The plain fact is this: You and I, till your life ends, keep step. I won't let you out of my sight. If you've stopped loving me, then suffer instead of enjoy my presence. My presence goes on, like it or not, as an *omni*presence that binds us continually. Every crevice of your hour I'll fill with ubiquity: as a burden, not a joy, for you, as a relentless punishment for the failure of your heart to keep loving me. I'll make you *re*love me. I'll force my love-sustaining upon your love-insufficiency, and do a takeover of your mind and heart. You'll be under my spell, in total domination. You'll be my subject, and do my bidding. And you'll never be released. My authority will clamp down, and tyrannize you thoroughly. You're my prisoner of love. Emergency regulations are in effect. Bow down in every respect. Hand in your will: it's invalid, as of now, as defunct as the dodo. For not loving me, you'll be reduced to submission without alternative. Be ruled, Tom Gervasi. Don't speak. This is Mary talking to you. Mary is telling you to take your clothing off. Now, 'make love' to me. Now. Good. I approve of your obedience. I'm a *benevolent* despot. I'll reward you, Tom Gervasi. With love, full-scale love. All-out love. Love, at every level. Love, and more love. Love, unending. Love, upon its absolute. Undying. Eternal. Infinite. Immortal. On earth, for heaven. Limitless. Boundless. To hell, and back. *In* hell. As your Mary. Your *always* Mary. Your *only* Mary.

"Well, I've had enough 'lovemaking,' for this physical instance. Withdraw from me. Fall asleep. I'll survey you, under my rapt gaze. And keep you well covered. And looked after. You needn't want. Or will, or hope.

"That'll be my concern. I'll take the trouble. Fall soft. Be my object. Don't object. Be still. Be 'dead,' in a way. *I'll* take over *our* vitality. Let *me* worry. My passive one. My infant, all asleep."

LXV. WHAT'S SO SPECIAL ABOUT HARRIET ROSE, THAT SHE COULD TAKE TOM GERVASI AWAY FROM ALL HIS WOMEN FOR HER SAKE ALONE? IF ONLY SHE KNEW!

Population all over the world has been increasing at a staggering rate. Will food growth and supply hold out, keep pace? Nutrition experts are puzzling this. Meanwhile, people multiply. Of women alone, for example, the numbers have already reached billions. In spite of this, Harriet Rose still feels compelled to inform Tom Gervasi that, as far as he's concerned, the world contains but one woman: herself, alone. "Is *that* all!?" Tom suavely replied.

"The others are just background props, fillers, extras, chorus, superfluities, atmosphere décor," Harriet amply explained, with possessive persistence, to, for her, the world's sole male representative. Tom dominated her whole stage. Supernumeraries crept behind, in his overwhelming shadow. Outproportioning a monster scale, her passion for him bulged in the brute bombast of powerful purity. "I possess you," she added.

Tom ducked away. "Not really," he illustrated with escaping. To complete the act, he had now disappeared.

"He's in my *head*," Harriet pondered. "He's all mine, in there."

This didn't long satisfy her. She wanted her prize in concrete object form, to clutch, to possess. Within her grasp. To hold, to have.

"How can I stop his philandering?" she wondered. "He spreads himself like mountains of butter over endless slices of the longest bread loaf. This has got to stop. I must prove that I merit his exclusive time, reducing other women to dross, degrading my whole sister tribe, eliminating comparison altogether, via perfection's absolute, in unparalleled standard. I won't *compete*. I'll *outshine*. But by what means, unique to me alone, above all other women?"

She pursued this problem of establishing a foremost claim in a sweeping superiority. In *what* was she superior? And how make Tom prize this value? How provoke him to crave, to need it? Should she consult a private advertising agency, a public relations firm, a publicity outfit, experienced in promoting diverse commodities with appropriate campaigns? No, this is purely personal. The sublime object is to build up Harriet Rose as Tom Gervasi's prime object. What, that other women lacked, had she uniquely to give?

Sex is the common property of all women, as men-pleasers. Harriet certainly had no monopoly on it. If only she could close op all women's holes the whole world over! Besides being impossible to do, this would be an atrocious act of inhumanity. It would win for Harriet only a Hitler's popularity.

So what had she to offer, of value to Tom—in fact, *essential* to him—which he could obtain nowhere else? That posed the problem. Insoluble? Harriet was desperate. She *willed* a solution. Her love was complete, but not its attainment. The process stood before her. It would culminate in product. Tom should want her forever. With that simple object, she probes possibilities.

Tom was "too busy" to see her for a week. "Too busy" probably meant "other women": a putrid euphemism. Thinking continuously, pondering furiously, Harriet had come up blank. Whatever Tom wanted, *other* women amply supplied. Harriet merely *shared* that with them. What market could she prompt a monopoly from, to eclipse her competitors?

All the women in Tom's life! In his *current* life alone, the sum positively seemed obscene. Of so many, Harriet Rose found herself so lightly included, with a vast interchangeability of component female units in easy replaceability on a multiple field of quality-nullified numerability. She took her place, among them. Tom Gervasi played no favorites. They could *all* be Harriet Roses. *Or* they could all *not* be. A negligible difference, in Tom's all-devouring greed for women alone, not *the* woman. He loved the species: the genre: the gender: for what was *in common*, Harriet's minimal belonging with them, reduced to the sexual denominator. Tom was a casual stud. On what basis could Harriet teach him discrimination? Under what rule, or principle? To what goal's glowing reward?

She kept phoning him. But he was always "busy." Women came too easy, for him. He didn't have to sweat. It was a cheap market. He cheapened them all. It degraded them. They were debased. They came back for more. They just loved it. Why be important? Tom is *so* much more fun.

Harriet would reform him. By dangling what before him? What could tempt him? He had freedom and innumerable women. What could be better than that? The answer to this, if carefully exploited, could take Tom from all the rest, and repose him, contentedly, under Harriet's breasts, from where he'd never stray, having found a permanent haven, free from such promiscuous wandering as kept him—too long—from his own true nest.

Tom had more women than he could deal with. To economize, he'd release a stale batch, but their place would soon be filled by a new influx. This dynamically kept up a stable flow of full numbers, or even increased it slightly. He attracted more than he could let go. Some released ones, from time to time, made comebacks. His hands were full. Women grew under his feet, and fell from trees. Nature was lavish. Prodigal abundance bloomed from her bounteous lap. And Tom would just lap it up. He could handle it. He rose well, to his spreading challenge, that hemmed him deliciously in. While being thus occupied, he plumb forgot Harriet Rose. Oh yes—the one who persisted. The dreaming one. The one who proclaims herself "different." Who professes herself "the only one" for him. Who claims she could prove it. Well, he'll test her. He'll call her bluff. Just for the fun. To disabuse her, of such fantastic delusions. To end her dream. To loosen her "hold." To pull her up, cold. To teach her more modest notions. To quell her pretense as sole Queen to his solitary bachelor Kingship, in his harem's replenished plenty.

"*Please* visit me. Take a rest from the rest. Come *home*." (This was on the telephone.)

"Home! I'm at home with all women. What makes *you* so special?"

"Come, honey, and see."

"Well, *that*'s hard to resist. I'll be there tonight."

"When?"

"At my own sweet time. If I'm worth waiting for, wait."

"All right. And I'll show you what *you*'ll want to wait for, come the future."

"Is that so!? Well, I can't wait."

※

He arrived late, sexually exhausted. Next day was a non-employment Saturday, so no need to worry about any alarm clock: they could rise late. Tom was in his prime. He had lipstick marks all over him, and several brands of perfume issuing from his clothéd person, that were deposited there by adorers. Here he was, condescending to pay a state visit to—what's her name?—Harriet Rose. Her inducement, her come-on, had been to tempt him with what no other woman had. What secret allurement was this? What subtle enticement, worth his paying a special visit? What had she to offer? It had better be good. Tom could be in the beds of much more beautiful women, had he only chosen. Instead, he was here. Well, where was it?

"What makes *you* the one?" he asked. "Come on, show it, at once."

Harriet kept stalling. She still hadn't come up with the clincher. She said,

"You're exhausted. You've been through too many women. First you need sleep. That will freshen you up. In the morning, I'll make my demonstration. You couldn't appreciate it now. You're too fatigued. Remove your clothes, come under the covers, and slumber your fullest. Dream away all the other women. And dream in me, who's known you on and off, but now I stay, and they leave, as your wide choice closes in on me. Good. I tuck you in. The pillow's soft. You're dropping off. You're parting from the old life of a rake. Your new life will dawn, of monogamy to Harriet Rose. Bid them all goodbye, those women, throngs galore. Wake to me alone, when I show you why."

He was in a deep sleep. So deep, that he was "gone" till morning. Harriet was sitting up in the same bed. She faced a crucial night, and must stay awake. She had all these nocturnal hours in front of her, to figure out—which for weeks and weeks she wasn't able to—what to tell or show Tom that would convince him to shut out all other women from his women-thronged life, and spend his remaining years in lasting fidelity (a complete reversal of character, a radical transformation, an unrecognizable departure), true loyalty, pure love, for, to, with, herself. "I must be as essential to him as air and food. What have I got, within me, to make him turn his back on a gay, roving bachelor life? He has a good job in business, and enough money for his freespending needs. He wouldn't need me for my wealth—some of his girlfriends have much more money than I do. And I only have a modest sum. Some of his girlfriends are much more beautiful than I am. And I'm no great beauty. I have no way of pleasing him sexually better than a great many of his girlfriends presumably do. I have no special talent or aptitude for extraordinary cooking for him or singing to him or making him laugh. What can he possibly want, above all other things, in a woman, sufficient to make him abandon all the other women? Well, the answer is, that he must have a blazing, permanent, fatal love for this woman. There's no love potion to slip into his ear or mouth or under his eyelids, to effect this chemically, or alchemically, by a fabulous stroke of magic. This is not a legend. This is ordinary modern times. I'm only Harriet Rose.

"But he's Tom Gervasi. Every woman wants him. He has a magical effect, on women.

"I'm no exception. That's it—I'm unexceptional. I've admitted it! I've lost. I'm resigned. I renounce my fantastic claim. It was a monstrous dream. I'm no-one special. Even my name is bland. I abdicate my pretense—it was grandiose. I'll confess, when he wakes. It was all fraudulent, on my part. *No-one* deserves him: so *all* do."

LXVI. TOM GERVASI IS LOVED BY ROSE AND IRIS, ALSO BY LILA, WHOM HE PREFERS, BUT NOT ENOUGH TO DISCOURAGE THE OTHER TWO. HE RECEIVES LOVE FROM THREE SIDES. HE SOAKS IT IN. BUT GIVES NONE BACK.

Rose and Iris were positively flowery in garlanding Tom Gervasi in festoons and wreaths and bulging bouquets of love and adoration. "I wish they'd stop," he proclaimed. "I prefer Lila to them. She'd be a Li*lac*, except that she lies in lack of the final letter. Lila is about fifteen percent prettier than Rose, and ten percent prettier than Iris. But why *measure* those intangibles? Love is not in percentages and statistics, by a numerical scale. Love is feeling, pure and simple. Rose, Iris, and Lila all love me. With that abundance of love coming my way, I'm sort of drowned in it, or overwhelmed. I'm too smothered and inundated by it, to have enough loose air of distance to feel love for anyone else. I'm its recipient, not giver. That's bad for the ones who give. Unrequited love is a form of suffering. I'm its cause. In three cases.

"I alternate the three of them, giving on the average two nights a week to each, but Lila remains my favorite, while Rose puts pressure on me to be more demonstratively affectionate, and Iris does too. Shuttled among the three of them, I'm succumbing to sexual exhaustion, to worn-out genitals, to heavy fatigue in the groin. I can barely keep it up any longer. I'm sagging down badly, in the erotic division.

"I could economize by dropping Rose and Iris, and limiting my amorous life to Lila. But then Lila would get too possessive. As it is, since each of the three knows I'm going with two others in addition to her, they're more in awe of my privacy, take nothing for granted, and endeavor always to please. They sort of 'give way,' to me, like Harem members to their master Sultan. I want control. I don't want to *be* controlled. I retain the advantage over each girlfriend by having two others. But this is all so tiring! I'm bored with the whole business. Women, breasts and buttocks! O, for a long holiday, from the arduous life of keeping three women at bay by tempering their love for me with the discipline of maintaining them in a suspenseful limbo of rivalry. And how their love comes pouring in!—with restraint. As though it stops short, at the window pane. While I sit inside, quite dry."

All alone, Lila was thinking, "Tom Gervasi prefers me to either Rose or Iris. Yet he continues to see them just about as often as that fickle brute sees me. I want to clutch him *always*. I remember when as a little girl I had a doll, other girls wanted to play with my doll, but I didn't want to share it with them. Well, Tom Gervasi is that doll today. I want him for my very own. But Rose and Iris take equal lumps of his time, while I pine at home. O Tom Gervasi, please stop regarding it necessary to have two other girlfriends. By the time it's time to be with me again, those hussies, those vixen have drained you of your precious sperm, pumped your old well dry, and you arrive with nothing left for me, while I've been waiting so eagerly, with nervous patience and tense ardor. I feel like exploding. Marry me and be faithful. I'm prettier than Rose and Iris. Their love for you maybe equals mine. But whose love do you *value* most? O dear Tom Gervasi, please decide. In my favor. Have me always. I'll be your darling slave. Rid your life of both Rose and Iris. *Please*, dear Tom . . . Oh, I'm talking to myself alone. He's out of hearing. I'm alone in my apartment. He's out with Rose or Iris. I weep for him. For me. How deprived I am! I know what I'm deprived *of*. Of the best of men. Who spreads himself thin. On inferior rivals. While all alone, I weep at home. O Tom Gervasi. *Please* tire of them. But of me, never. Try me solid and steady, go with me alone, and see how better it'll be for you than playing a stud with a three-mare stable. Monogamy is a decent human invention. It's civilized practice. Try it. I'll make it work, for you."

Lila's meditation became fervent prayer, convulsive sob. Tom Gervasi is her religion. So is he, as well, for Rose and Iris. Here's Rose, in solitary reverie:

"Tom Gervasi, you like Iris as well as me, and Lila better than both, while still falling short of *loving* her. I'm desperate for you. But I brood, in pessimism. You'll *never* love me, I'm afraid. Oh, that horrid word—'never'!"

And Iris, alone, cogitates: "Tom Gervasi, you care for Rose and me a bit, and for Lila somewhat more. That's all you give us, a little trickle, by comparison to which, we bombard you with three lifetimes of immortal love. O foul ratio! If only both my rivals could drop dead! But that's an evil wish. But only that way, could I ever get you, for myself. For all my own."

Tom Gervasi is squeezed of sex, he's gone dry. He sees a doctor, who examines him somberly with some dead-looking instruments in the private parts where male love flowers. The verdict is indeed dismal:

"Tom Gervasi, I have a sad diagnosis to report. You've become impotent, and will remain so for about five years, during which span of time your sexual activity will not even exceed that of a gelded eunuch with a high little girl's voice, called a castrato for lovely madrigals. But this is no music lesson, I'm afraid. You're a neuter now, Tom Gervasi. For five years. Here's my bill. Pay soon. Goodbye."

When Tom Gervasi left the doctor's office, he felt strangely relieved, even exuberant. He raised a wild song of exhilaration. "Thank you, God. Now Rose, Iris, and Lila will recede somewhat,

246

and keep their arms and legs off my own body. My body is my own!

"However, they'll continue to go on loving me. They'll wait for my five-year abstinence to end, my fortunate celibacy. It won't discourage them. Their love for me is fatal—for them, not for me. I do prefer Lila. But not enough to drop the other two. Platonically, I'll go on seeing all three. Even sleep with them, one at a time. But *chastely* sleep. Ah, a long rest. From riots, of the flesh."

Lila accepted this condition, as also did Rose and Iris, in their three-pronged, dogged, unqualified love, on an unconditional basis, for their temporarily monk-like Tom Gervasi. He feels so rested! So quiet! His lusty waters are stilled. He falls back, and dreams of love. Not *from* him, but for.

For him, from dear Lila, and sweet Rose and Iris. He has their love, and can keep it, too. It's all for him. In its "pure" state, as of now: that is, nonphysical. It's for his soul, alone. For *him*, in pure essence. The essential Tom Gervasi. He has Lila's preferred love, reinforced by Rose's, by Iris'es. It bombards him. In soft feathers. In light rain. In weak sunshine. In mild, easy-to-take doses. He sleeps on a soft, downy bed of soft, cloudy love. It's trained on him, with filter. He's regulated it. Like the lighting manager for a theater play, who has light filter down from three nice directions onto a stage basking in it. Nice rays of love. From sweet Lila. From somewhat lesser Rose and Iris. It lights him up, softly. He gleams, with soft highlights. In muted tones. Golden Rembrandt, yellow Vermeer. Subdued. But lit.

LXVII. ANN, AND TOM GERVASI. A MUTUALLY UNFORTUNATE MEETING.

When Ann met Tom Gervasi, it was too late to undo the meeting, for she contracted a fatal passion for him, which he reluctantly failed to requite. Her life was ebbing away. She grew mortally weaker every hour. Her physician, in alarm, summoned Tom Gervasi, and warned him, "If you can't conjure up some artificial love for her, if you can't contrive to manufacture a saving passion for her, Ann is doomed to die of grief, if her present rate of deterioration should go unchecked. I know love can't be *forced*. But her life is at stake. Have you the means to take mercy upon it? Sorry to thrust this burden upon you. Your guilt must be overwhelming, and your conscience all lumped up in agony. Ann can be saved by your love alone. My diagnosis prescribes that relief, and no other."

Ann died. Tom Gervasi tried, with all his might. But his heart wasn't in it. There was no pretending. Ann could tell. She knew only *too* well. That was her final knowledge. Tom Gervasi regrets having ever met her. It cost a human life. The life that was called Ann.

And her death goes by the same name. The name that will forever "accuse" Tom Gervasi. Living continues to be his burden. His guilt is innocent. He hears a miserable misfortune. Called Ann. She's his early death. His own will include it. Meanwhile, he lives sadly. Her sadness passed on. It's brittle, it's his. Ann mourns, inside.

LXVIII. JOAN IS DEAD. WHY?

When Joan heard of Tom Gervasi, she quit her job and prayed: "Dear God, Please don't let me meet that man. For if I do, I'm lost." Either God didn't hear, or there was no God, or God heard and didn't heed her. For she *did* meet Tom Gervasi. All was lost. She fell violently in love with him. But she didn't appeal to him. He tried to be gentle, but not being loved by him was agonizing torture for her.

Having quit her job, she used up her money and then took a new job. Her life was a prolonged misery. "*Why* can't he love me? Oh, why?"

It was no use. She became ill. Her life was ebbing away. She was drained of blood. It was ghastly. Tom Gervasi felt sympathy, but little else.

What can console Joan, at all? Her friends rallied round, assured her of their support, but it was really no use at all. She needed an immediate injection of specifically Tom Gervasi love. That, and that alone, could possibly save her.

He felt pity, but no love. At last, Joan died. Tom felt guilty. But it wasn't his fault. No man can *force* himself to love a woman. Either the love is there, or it's not. Poor Joan. Too bad she ever met him. She had a grim prophecy of it. And grimly, she lived it through.

She's dead. Tom Gervasi lives. He's sorry. That's all he *can* be. It was all so unfortunate. It was all—too unbearable.

He has it on his conscience. It troubles him. She didn't *mean* to have this revenge on him. But it turns out that way. His guilt hurts. "I killed her. She was a real, live human being, like myself. Here I am, still alive. But I didn't love her. My lack of love gave her mortality an outlet. Oh Joan. I'm sorry."

Yes, he's sorry. Within the ongoing of his life. Within further pleasures, ahead.

LXIX. VERONICA, TOM GERVASI, AND THE RECK-LESS PLUNGE.

For the life of her, Veronica just can't arrest her consuming love, her all-consuming love, that saps her strength away, that drains her vital reserves, in a continuous ebbing. The object of this fatal passion? The unwitting, helpless object, terrified at his unintentional power? Tom Gervasi, gentle but powerless, standing by, moaning with mercy; while Veronica sinks, and darkly passes through life into the total void. Tom Gervasi is left to grieve. He groans with innocent guilt. Veronica loved him. What a risky thing to do!

LXX. LOUISE, TOM GERVASI, AND LOVE'S VUL-TURE.

Louise had heard about Tom Gervasi. People warned her. But she was reckless. She flung caution away. She dared to be fearless.

She's paying the full cost. They met, and it's become fatal for her. The doctors can't arrest the longing for him that gnaws at her vitals like the utmost vulture of cruelty.

Her misery will soon be over. Hanging his head, sobbing with guilt, Tom Gervasi moans at her bedside. But it can't save her. His love alone can bring her back to health. But poor Louise, even now, can't inspire it in him. Love is unforced, it can't be willed. Louise dies. Tom Gervasi is the grim witness. His self-accusation is forced, too. How sadly innocent he is! How unjust his guilt! Louise is lost. Tom Gervasi didn't kill her. But he feels he did. His remorse goes deep. Louise packs away: an interior vulture, groaning, "I love you, Tom Gervasi. I love you, till we *both* die."

LXXI. DESPITE HER FRIENDS' WARNING, RE-BECCA MET, TO HER ULTIMATE COST, TOM GER-VASI.

All her friends (the well-meaning ones) begged Rebecca to de-sist in her rash plan, all foolishly arranged with headstrong will-fulness, of meeting Tom Gervasi. They felt she wouldn't long survive it. They were all proved right. Rebecca plunged straight to death, of unrequited love. Tom Gervasi was gentle, but he couldn't prevent it. He stood by, with helpless guilt, as Rebecca ebbed her life out, in the dark tides of love.

Goodbye, Rebecca. You were warned. The risk proved mor-tal. How noble, to love Tom Gervasi! How bold! It was heroic, but your final act. At the dearest cost.

It wasn't Tom Gervasi's fault. He inspired her with the fatal passion, much against his will. It wasn't her friends' fault. They had all soundly advised her: "No."

But she defied them, and met him. And how!, she met him. She met her own end. Her love plunged straight through. Her friends can't tell where.

LXXII. DEBORAH, HER HUSBAND, AND TOM GERVASI.

Deborah had *heard* about Tom Gervasi. It was enough to make her, via mutual contacts, arrange a "casual," "accidental" meeting between them. It was all to appear quite artless. But she had poured in such care toward it, that she distrusted her pose of feigned indifference about the whole matter. Her social circles whispered hushingly. The mill of gossip churned out endless surmisals. The official, well-kept secret was precisely what Deborah had tried to give the opposite impression of: that Tom Gervasi had quite turned her head, by the violent force of his reputation, even before Deborah had ever seen him. This was admittedly true—to herself. But she kept up a contrary appearance. She compulsively told "everyone" how she loved her husband more and more. They saw through that smoke screen. They conspired to keep from her how well it was apparent that Tom Gervasi had fully conquered her heart before they even met! Deborah concealed this disgrace, in bold, pathetic fumbling. She was the joke of the whole social world. Even her husband got wind of it. His pride sank. He brooded on divorce.

Tom Gervasi was indeed fascinating. His conquests of beautiful women, famous women, rich women, were already legendary. Deborah had everything: glamour, the highest social status, grace, elegance, breeding, "aristocratic" pedigree, achievement, money from both her own and her husband's sides, and that certain indefinable "something" that defied description but inspired favorable comments even from those who were bitterly envious. She was in the prime of her beauty, enhanced by the onslaught of her maturity. Rakes and swains the whole social world over had vainly tried their seductive wiles on her. She was, till now, the exemplary wife.

Her husband was really a force to be reckoned with! He wore his respectability with the assurance that all the fear, awe, and respect he inspired in others had deeply implanted in his "nature." Deborah had been his highest acquisition. His wife had been impeccably faithful. Was he to be made a fool of, now, by this grand little man, Tom Gervasi, who had invisibly, from afar, put silly notions in his wife's noble head? The husband was angry—at her or him? His dignity required a prompt settlement of this nasty little disorder. He decided to meet Tom Gervasi before Deborah did: to "have it out" with him. Then, to speak some wisdom to Deborah, along with an ultimatum. He would *control* her heart: and not leave it lightly hanging around, for the amusement of some spunky upstart! He'll put his foot down!— and trample on what he'd prevent. Or, he'll get Tom Gervasi in trouble. Such subtle means as he commanded, could ruin Tom Gervasi's career, and reputation, at a stroke. How dare he tamper with Deborah!—however unintentionally, however her doing. He *can't* be innocent! Not with *that* worldly a name! He'll be treated as an intruder, and humbled accordingly. Public punishment lowers anyone's name. Even that of such a swell who unvirtues women by subtle radiance. Deborah must be saved *in spite of*; her fickle weakness from afar. A divorce is demoralizing. Better the unwitting intruder be brought low, than Deborah and her proud possessor.

The husband made his interception before Tom Gervasi and Deborah finally met. It was at a social occasion, with Deborah absent. "Are you Tom Gervasi?"

"So I am. What of it?"

"I'm Deborah's husband."

"That doesn't enlighten me. Who's Deborah?"

"My wife."

"It *still* doesn't enlighten me. And how is it my concern?"

"Very much. More than you realize."

"I protest, that I'm innocent. Are you accusing me?"

"Yes, of inspiring in my wife, the love of my life, an illicit passion for you."

"Was it based on my reputation alone?"

"Apparently, since she never met you."

"On my honor, I'm innocent. I won't exploit her silly infatuation. You look too important, and too menacing. I believe you'd make trouble for me, if I interfered with your marriage bond. Let's prevent a mess. Let's conspire together, sir, to prevent my *ever* meeting Deborah. You co-operate, from your end. And *I* vow to do *my* bit. Together, with our allied strength, we'll ward off a domestic disaster, dishonor, and your brutal revenge upon me. Let's shake, and be partners, in this."

They shook hands, the husband and his "rival." It was a pact between gentlemen. It was a sacred bond, between true men.

Deborah was in the dark about this. Feeding on her dreams, her Tom-Gervasi-obsession flamed up like a myth. She mechanically went through her social life with grace and charm, oblivious to the rumors about her. Her *real* life was all inward. "Tom Gervasi" sounded like "Don Giovanni." The latter is a Spanish version of the modern American former. Both are sweet legends. She played "Don Giovanni" on the record player, and was transported into strains of rapture, dizzy flights reminiscent of Madame Bovary's French ecstasies. She and Madame Bovary knew how to dream! The banal world can be shut outside. In time, it will intrude. Well, she's prepared. She'll have her dream, and her Tom Gervasi too.

Her contacts informed her that the elaborately planned, carefully staged long-last meeting with the fabled Tom Gervasi would not come off: "The occasion itself, as scheduled, will go on: But Tom Gervasi can't attend. He gave me his regret. But something came up. He must go somewhere else, instead."

Deborah tried not to look hurt. But it was transparent, to the women there. Her face was a cold study in disappointment. It betrayed a blazing passion. "Well, can you arrange *another* occasion? At his convenience, of course. I quite want to meet him. Just a whim, on my part. Indulge it, please. It's nothing serious. I adore, more and more, my majestically important husband, compared to whom—if comparison will so dishonor itself between them—Tom Gervasi is but a pipsqueak, of no consequence whatever. It amuses me to meet him. I need a silly diversion. It's harmless. I assure you."

The others pretended to understand. But they knew better.

The go-betweens promised Deborah to "pin Tom Gervasi down" to an appointment he'll really keep, with no conflict on his social calendar. It'll be an intimate party, for just a select few, quite exclusive. The hit of the season, of course. Everyone who's anyone will be there. As *well* as Tom Gervasi.

"Deborah, listen to me, I'm your husband."

"Of course you are. Who else is?"

"Rumors have been spreading. About you and Tom Gervasi."

"They're untrue, of course. Why, I assure you, my dear (and I'm not exaggerating), I've never yet laid eyes on him. I've heard all about him—who hasn't? He *does* sound amusing. He could be fun, I think. To see what he's *really* like."

"Deborah, the rumors about you and him are ugly. I don't want to sound like Anna Karenina's husband, talking to you, but

I must warn you, from my official position, as a respectable man of the world, and as your husband, what these rumors report. Deny them if you will. But don't take lightly, dear, our reputation."

"Why, husband: You're genuinely angry! What can have possessed you! Can you be jealous!? Silly dear! Of *course* I adore you. Who *is* Tom Gervasi? Why, a nothing!, so far as I'm concerned."

"I can see through your attempts to reassure me. Stop having fun. I'm as serious as death!"

"Is it *that* bad!? Oh dear!"

"I must warn you. Tom Gervasi has a dangerous reputation, as a wrecker of households, a notorious cuckolding adulterer. He exerts a subtle radiance on married women, from afar. Rumor has it—"

"Oh, confound rumor! I, Deborah, am above suspicion. I stand up, now, to my full height. Jealousy demeans you, dear husband. Stop being like Othello. I have no intention of betraying you, with that sorry excuse for a Casanova legend. Your reputation is safe, when reposed in me."

"You *don't* love him? Rumors said you did."

"Rumors can be malicious, spiteful, in envy's venom. The contrary is true. I love you alone."

"Are you *positive*, about that statement?"

"You can have it in writing, if you'd like. In black and white. On legal stationery."

"We're already sufficiently married, by ordinance of the Church. Don't you *dare* desecrate our vows! Or I'll ruin *you*, and bring *him* low!"

"My husband, stop this. Consider your high position, and your well-known dignity. Such petty jealousy, which you display so comically and without the least foundation I assure you, quite crumbles your stature, and levels your gilded marble to rotted clay. *Confound* Tom Gervasi! Would that I had *never* heard of him! He's wrecking our lives, our social standing, our good names. He's an infernal nuisance. I give you permission, dear, to punish him. Get rid of him—of his infernal non-presence. He mustn't come between us. Some of your employees are mobsters, racketeers. Could you assign a few rougher ones to 'rub out' that menace? Then, we'd be rid of our nemesis, our curse. It'll save our marriage! Please!"

The husband was surprised. Deborah had become hysterical. Earlier, her tone was one of banter, light irony, mild sarcasm, Her hysteria worried him. It seemed too genuine not to cause him grave concern.

He phoned Tom Gervasi to have a confidential talk. They met in a dim, out-of-the-way bar. Tom Gervasi said,

"Well, I've done *my* bit. Deborah had commissioned mutual contacts to arrange a social occasion where I'd accidentally, casually encounter her. But I dropped out of it! I told the go-between that I 'couldn't make it—a pressing engagement had intervened, causing me to be away. My regrets, to you all.' That's what I told them. So you see, I kept up *my* end of the bargain. And you—did you have your showdown, with Deborah your wife, yet?"

"I did, sort of. But it's inconclusive. I can't make her out, really. *Rumor* has it that she's in love with you. The social world is abuzz with it. But she denied it—vehemently at the end, half-comically at the start. I'm a bit perplexed. Can you advise me?"

"Hmm. I *still* think we should ensure that Deborah and I never meet. The rumors may not be idle. They may have a sound basis. Others *before* Deborah have fallen for me, just on hearsay.

She's only a woman, and prone to a cloudy passion. The rumors may be stark true!"

"Tom Gervasi, I must tell you what my sweet little wife begged me to do, concerning the matter of what to do about *you*. To rub you out! Via certain henchmen in my field of business. To do you in! She recommended, in fact, your death!"

"That sounds like a confession. That's really going far! My death is no light matter, I assure you! It would make a mockery of my rights, the killing of me would! It would be altogether too violent!"

"But she's my wife. I have no choice, really. I have a weakness, a fondness, for her moods and whims. If she craves your death, and I have means to do it without drawing suspicion on myself or her (it would be 'an official job,' and thus placed in the public domain, far from personal liability or private culpability), then why *shouldn't* it be done?! Sorry, Tom Gervasi!"

"But you've violated our pact we made before, as gentlemen, in alliance against our common adversary, the woman."

"Well, that's dishonorable of me. Deborah and I have two little children. They have their futures before them. It would be injurious to them socially, should a scandal follow them, concerning their dear mother. 'Their mother was a tart, in high circles,' it would be said. Your death could prevent that. It would spare the reputation of our whole family. Have *you* a family?"

"No."

"Then, be sacrificed. The family comes first. The bachelor is taxed extra."

"This seems *most* unfair."

"Was life *ever* fair!? Really! Where's your philosophy, Tom Gervasi?"

The killing was done, and hushed up. It was unobtrusive. However, Deborah still loves Tom Gervasi: *however* dead he is. That's what rumor reports. So even in death, Tom Gervasi is casting a malicious influence on a married lady's heart. It's a scandal between two worlds: life and death. Those are the dimensions of such a scandal. The husband is *exceedingly* embarrassed. He's contemplating suicide. Or, at least, divorce.

LXXIII.   TOM GERVASI, KNOWLEDGE, AND WOMEN.

Theoretically, the more things you have to pay attention to, the less attention you give to any *one* of those things. Not that women are *things,* but does the principle include women? Tom Gervasi is the one to ask. This excerpt is from a recent newspaper interview:

"Mr. Gervasi, is it true—"

"How should *I* know?"

"—Please let me complete the question: Is it true, Mr. Gervasi, that in general the more women one is having to do with, the less care and attention are given to each one?"

"I guess so."

"But don't you *know*?!"

"No. I'm still learning, you know."

Thus, it's still inconclusive, the answer to this question. But who else can be asked? If *Tom Gervasi* doesn't know, then who possibly could instead?

Well, that's a *new* question. As an authority on women, is Tom Gervasi but one of many? Or one of a few? Or the sole one, today?

We won't ask him. He simply won't know.

What *is* known, anyhow? Don't ask Tom Gervasi: *he* won't know.

What *does* he admit knowing? He's modest about the truth, respecting it so. It's all an ongoing mystery. He lives in new unknowns. But experiences women multiply. One by one. He gathers evidence. First-hand. Of what? No conclusion, yet.

LXXIV. TOM GERVASI'S EMPIRE OF WOMEN. CUTTING THROUGH TIME AND SPACE LIMITATIONS. THE VAST ACQUISITION.

"I'd like to be with all women at the same time. However, time and Space won't let me—those spoilsports, those killjoys! So I have to make do. Confined within my limitations, I creepcrawl at a snail's pace, through one woman at a time. One woman at a place. Ever so finite! Well, I'm bound down to mere possibility's modesty, restricted to the humility of the unmiraculous. Would that I could divinely transcend those paltry habitual dimensions of leaden mortality! But I'm only Tom Gervasi. That falls short of God's stature as a slight *inch* to a *mile's* broadchested grandeur.

"*This* woman, I meet her at *this* time and place. Meanwhile, the rest go begging. Next, *that* woman, at *that* time and place. As slow as a mountain's evolution. At this rate, I'll know just a miniscule fraction of great nature's womandom.

"Sampling here and there, now and then, of the groaning bounteous board of the great female feast! Letting so much go untasted! The vast waste, within my greed's micro-capacity, my minilust that nibbles where it would gorge!

"Maybe I can hire and train armies and armies of me, make a huge male recruitment, mobilise them to my standards, and commission them, as delegates for my rampant lechery! Thus Alexander, Caesar, Charlemagne, Napoleon, expanded from personal ambition into enlarging empires, by the might and force of disciplined masses to do their bidding. By the proxy of my minions, I could seize all desired women, and possess them by representing myself through a million able bodies.

"But *they*'ll feel the pleasure, at the local level, my passionately obedient soldiers; I'd get the *abstract* glory, for so many women conquered; from a hilltop, through binoculars and reports by messengers, as my well-strategied campaigns are launched to plunder women wholesale, unleashing satyrs to carry out, down to the last sensual detail, my well-wrought plans on many fronts along the broad belt of the map.

"I'll be the lauded hero. But all my men will win the many maids. They're my army privates, for their private pleasure. I'm their noble general, taking only the general pleasure.

"Theirs, at local concrete, at definite theaters of action; mine, abstracted, from the board of strategy, from remote supervision, as their mist-covered overlord.

"Why can't I be ubiquitous, omnipresent, myself? Why so plentifully must I delegate? I want pleasure at tip's end: *my* tip, not millions of men's.

"Well, I know my limits. Mere possibility hems me about. I'm only one person. Even as Tom Gervasi, I'm the same number of people as the lowest gravedigger: my one only self.

"But there's time, for lots of women. One by one, it *could* add up. Months and years, behind, ahead. A dribble here, a drop there. Thus beavers build their dam, birds their nest, ants their molehill. So Rome and Chartres were built. Thus Don Giovanni added to Leporello's catalogue of conquests by nationality. Bit by bit. A drop here, a drop there. In the *long* run, it all adds up.

"Not, however, all at once. That's forbidden. God alone has that magic power. And God *towers* over me: as sun to tapeworm. As cloud, to fallen twig.

"Pure and simple, I'm Tom Gervasi. That's all. But it's enough. Enough for plenty of women, anyhow. *More* than enough, for them all. I proudly plow through them. I rake them up, like autumn leaves. I collect them, like the greatest stamp collector.

"I'm the Lord of mathematics—higher division. As applied to women. My method is *not* division, *not* subtraction. It's by multiplying and adding. In sure drops of time. At cautious inches of space.

"Thus, I've accumulated. Am I acquisitive? Is it acquisition, I do? Compiling. Adding, extending. Expanding. Seizing. Hoarding. Enlarging my having. An empire's possessiveness? To 'possess' the women?

"I *had* this woman, I *had* that woman. Having and holding. Extending my hold. My multi-tentacled hold. My holdings. The monetary-woman financier. The capitalist of extensive holdings. The holdings of the havings. Still acquiring. To hold what I have. Have, and hold. Not to let go. Not to turn loose. But to clutch. Tight. Tightly climactic. Orgasmic cataclysms, on a simultaneous breadth of release.

"I'll die after growing old. Survived by a reputation. Tom Giovanni. Don Gervasi. That ancient legend, with a modern face."

Marvin Cohen in the 1970s. Photo by Tom Gervasi

Marvin Cohen is an American essayist, novelist, playwright, poet, humorist, and surrealist. He is the author of nine published books and several plays. His short fiction and essays have appeared in more than 80 publications, including *The New York Times, The Village Voice, The Nation, Harper's Bazaar, Vogue, Fiction, The Hudson Review, Quarterly Review of Literature, Transatlantic Review,* and *New Directions* annuals. His 1980 play *The Don Juan and the Non-Don Juan* was first performed at the New York Shakespeare Festival as part of the Poets at the Public Series. Staged readings of the play have featured actors Richard Dreyfuss, Keith Carradine, Wallace Shawn, Jill Eikenberry, Larry Pine, and Mimi Kennedy. Born in Brooklyn in 1931, Cohen has described himself as one who has "risen from lower-class background to lower-class foreground." He studied art at Cooper Union but left college to focus on writing, supporting himself with a series of odd jobs including mink farmer and merchant seaman. He also taught creative writing at The New School, the City College of New York, C.W. Post of Long Island University, and Adelphi University. Cohen currently lives in New York City with his wife, a retired paperback editor.

www.ingramcontent.com/pod-product-compliance
Lightning Source LLC
Chambersburg PA
CBHW020348030726
47496CB00007B/2047